UNCLAIMED LEGACY

*"Know therefore that the LORD your God is God; he is the faithful
God, keeping his covenant of love to a thousand generations of those
who love him and keep his commandments."*

—Deuternonomy 7:9

UNCLAIMED LEGACY

BOOK 2

DEBORAH HEAL

WRITE BRAIN BOOKS
www.deborahheal.com

This title is also available as an e-book.
Other novels by Deborah Heal
Time and Again (book 1)
Every Hill and Mountain (book 3)

Once Again: an inspirational novel of history, mystery & romance
(Book 1 in the Rewinding Time Series)

ISBN: 978-1478311492
Fiction: Christian: Historical
Fiction: Sci-fi/time travel

DEDICATION

To my mom Barbara Woods who taught me the joy of books.

CHAPTER 1

Abby managed to get her mascara on without smudging it. It was not an easy task, knowing that if she glanced at the other reflection in the mirror she'd see Merri's sorrowful eyes staring back at her. At least she wouldn't have to spend any time on her hair. Whatever she did, it dried in a mass of brown curls.

She smoothed on a bit of lip gloss and then, trying not to feel guilty, smiled encouragingly at the pudgy eleven-year-old beside her. "Come on, Merri, it's just a lunch date. I'll be home before you know it. And while I'm gone you'll get to spend some time with your mom."

Merri sat on the edge of the tub and morosely petted Kit Kat, her chocolate-colored cat. "But this is just the beginning. I'll never see you again now that you're going out with John."

Abby was glad Merri wanted her around. It was a big improvement from her first two weeks at the old house in

Miles Station. Thankfully, the troubled girl had finally begun to accept her help and her friendship.

"I don't know if I'll keep 'going out' with John. It depends. Besides, I'm your tutor; I can't go away. You'll be seeing me all summer."

"What do you mean, 'it depends'?"

"Depends on if he turns out like the last guy I dated."

"The one who wasn't interested in your personality?"

"Yeah, that one. But as for John… well, so far so good. He's already earned a star in that department."

"A star?"

Abby blushed. "Well…see, whenever I meet a guy I'm interested in going out with, I imagine a chart for him labeled *Possible Marriage Material*. Then I give him imaginary stars for things I like about him."

"Like being tall and handsome?"

"He is that. But, I'm looking for character qualities." Abby gathered the last of her things and zipped her toiletry case. "Like I always say, beauty is more than skin deep."

Merri continued to pet Kit Kat thoughtfully and Abby wondered if she should stay and expand on the topic. She had already determined that her service project for Ambassador College included much more than tutoring Merri in academic subjects.

But John would be there any minute. She put her arm around Merri's shoulder and said, "We'll talk more when I get back."

Merri's mother Pat Randall poked her head past the door and said, "He's here. You didn't tell me he had a vintage Mustang."

When Abby got downstairs she saw that John was dressed in khakis and a shirt that made his eyes look even bluer than usual. And then, even before she got close, she picked up the scent of the killer cologne he always wore.

"You clean up nice," he said with a grin.

"Hi." She mentally grimaced, just thinking about the last time he had seen her— wearing cobwebs in her hair and old paint-stained jeans. This time she was dressed better, in tan capris and a white camp shirt, but the circumstances were just as awkward. Merri, still sulking, was watching every move she and John made, and Pat was hovering like she was her mother instead of her employer, which was ironic, of course, since she spent so little time with Merri, her actual daughter.

"So, John Roberts," Pat said, "what are you majoring in?"

"I'm in the pre-law program at the University of Illinois."

"Do you have a summer job?"

"I work at the Tropical Frost in Brighton," he answered.

"That's…nice."

"He forgot to mention that he owns it." Abby glanced at her watch and adjusted the purse straps that were already digging into her shoulder.

Pat seemed to be assessing John's height. "I bet you played basketball in high school."

"No, I'm not much into contact sports. But I did run track for a couple of years."

Abby moved a little closer to the front door. John didn't seem to get the hint. Her stomach growled and she wondered where they were going to eat.

Pat's expression was serious, like it was her responsibility to screen for terrorists, serial killers, or other generally un-American guys. Maybe Pat was practicing for Merri's dating debut. But at age twenty, Abby was out of practice with parental inquisitions. Her own parents hadn't been so intense when she went on her first date in eighth

3

grade with Jimmy Gale. Of course his mom had driven them to the junior high and stayed to chaperone at the annual St. Patrick's Day dance. But still.

"What are your hobbies?" Pat continued relentlessly.

Abby glanced over to see if John was getting annoyed. But he was still smiling as if he enjoyed getting the third degree.

"I love reading—"

"What kind of books?"

"Mostly sci-fi. And I love music." Pat opened her mouth and John quickly added "Classic rock."

"Who's your favorite Beatle?"

"Paul." John blinked and darted a glance at Abby.

She smiled and nodded her head encouragingly. Pat folded her arms over her chest and frowned.

"I also restore vintage cars with my dad," John continued. "Oh, and I like theatre. I'll be in my college's production of *My Fair Lady* this fall."

Pat let her arms fall to her side and Abby wondered if that was a sign John had passed her test. She smiled and mentally assigned a star for *patience* to John's imaginary chart.

"So, where are you taking Abby?"

"We're going to see a few things in Alton and then have lunch at Genevieve's."

"Alton?" Merri looked imploringly at Abby. "I'd sure like to see what Alton looks like in modern times."

Abby put an arm around Merri's shoulder and said, "I'll tell you all about it when I get back."

"And when will that be?" Pat said.

"We should be back by 3:00." John checked his watch. "Make that 3:30 or 4:00." At last, he opened the door and said, "Well, we'll be going now."

Pat's cell phone rang and she flipped it open, holding

up a hand to signal for them to wait. "That's great," she said into the phone. "I'll meet you in about twenty minutes."

Merri's face went from sullen to outraged in .002 seconds. "Mom, you promised we'd do something fun."

"It won't take me long to show my clients the house," Pat said, closing her phone. "You can wait in the office for me, Merrideth."

Abby understood Pat's need to get her fledgling real estate business off the ground, but she also knew Merri needed her mother's attention, especially since her father was so distant—both geographically and emotionally. She wondered again, if she should stay home with her. Maybe it wasn't even ethical to begin a relationship while she was on a tutoring job.

"But, Mom . . ." Merri wailed.

"Why don't you come with us?" John said, darting a look at Abby.

Abby's mouth dropped open and she scrutinized his face. No guy she knew willingly hung around kids, especially not bratty pre-teens, and never on a date. She checked closely for signs of martyrdom, but John was actually looking excited at the prospect.

"Could I?" Merri said.

"If you're sure it's all right," Pat said, looking relieved.

"Sure," John said.

Merri turned to see Abby's reaction. "Another star?" she asked, grinning knowingly.

Abby's eyes grew wide in alarm and she put her arm around Merri and leaned in close. "We won't mention the stars, Brat," she whispered. "Will we?"

But it was true. In her imagination, she added a big star for *kindness to children.*

John was a knowledgeable guide. He had grown up in nearby Brighton, but explained that everyone went to Alton for shopping and entertainment. "I guess it doesn't seem like much to you two since you're used to Chicago."

"Well, it's a lot more interesting than Miles Station," Merri said.

"But you'd have to admit Miles Station *was* pretty interesting in the 1850s," Abby said.

John looked puzzled for a moment, but then they reached College Avenue and he pulled the car over and stopped. "Come on. I want you to meet one of our famous sons." He led them to a bronze statue of a tall, thin man leaning on a cane. "Abby and Merri, meet Mr. Wadlow."

"What's he famous for?" Merri asked.

John stood next to the statue. "Take a guess," he said, stretching as tall as he could.

After reading the plaque beside it, Abby looked up in amazement. "Merri, this statue is life-size. Robert Wadlow was 8 feet 11 inches tall, the tallest man ever recorded."

"They have a lot of stuff about him in the little museum across the street, but I think they're closed right now."

After saying goodbye to the so-called "Gentle Giant," John offered to take them to the mall, but Abby wasn't interested and Merri apparently had enough discretion not to offer suggestions for someone else's date.

"I'd like to see the older parts of town," Abby said. She turned to look at Merri in the back seat, who nodded her head in confirmation that it was time to tell John. "We want to see if it looks familiar," she said carefully.

"That's where we're going," he said. "Genevieve's is downtown and—wait a minute. I thought you were both new to the area."

Abby looked again at Merri. "I know you're going to have a hard time believing this," she began.

"And the computer hasn't been working right so we couldn't show you," Merri explained.

"We were going to wait until it's fixed, but we've been having trouble with customer service."

"And since we're in Alton we can't resist seeing if we recognize . . ."

"You're familiar with Alton?" John inserted into the volley of comments.

"At least, Alton in 1858," Merri said.

John's eyes were darting from Abby beside him to Merri in the backseat. He looked so confused Abby had to swallow a laugh. "There's a stop light, John," Abby said, pointing to the intersection they were about to slide through. "You see, when Merri's dad sent her the new computer—"

"He was just trying to buy me off since he never spends time with me after the divorce."

"And there was this program on it called *Beautiful Houses*." Abby paused to gauge John's expression. "Maybe you'd better pull off and stop somewhere. You seem to be having trouble concentrating."

John ignored the suggestion, so she continued. "And one night when we were fooling around with it, something really weird happened."

"Abby tried to talk to customer support, but they thought she was just kidding with them."

"We could see Merri's house in Miles Station," Abby continued.

"Only instead of being run down and crummy, it was brand new," Merri added.

"And then we met Colonel Miles, well not actually met

of course— "

"He's the man who built the house."

"In 1846."

"Wait a minute, wait a minute," John said. He flipped his right turn signal on, moved across two lanes of traffic, and then pulled into the Quick Trip and parked. "This is a joke, right?"

Merri frowned at Abby. "I told you we should have waited to show him."

"You're saying you went back in time to 1846?" John said.

"No, silly," Merri said. "We weren't there the year the house was built. We found that date from the library."

"Oh," he said. "I thought you were trying to tell me that—"

"We were there in 1858," Abby interrupted. "But I'd have to say it was a virtual trip only. I mean, Charlotte never saw us or knew we were there."

"Who's Charlotte?" John asked desperately.

"Colonel Miles' daughter. We got to know her quite well," Merri said.

"As I was saying—try to concentrate, John—no one knew we were there, and as far as I know we never changed the course of history."

John closed his eyes, put his head on the steering wheel, and began mumbling.

"*Beautiful Houses* is sort of like my brother's architecture software," Abby continued. "We could zoom in and control the view of the Miles' house. We could follow Charlotte, inside or out, and feel and experience what she did, go where she went. Like, for instance, when she got on the train and went to Alton for the Lincoln-Douglas debate."

Abby's voice trailed off when she saw John shaking.

"What's wrong?" She put a comforting hand on his arm.

But then he lifted his head from the steering wheel and she saw he was laughing.

Abby quickly withdrew her hand. "We can prove it," she said indignantly. "Take us down to the old part of town."

John continued to laugh and Abby thought how satisfying it would be to hit him with her purse. Really hard. Her roommate Kate had laughed her head off too when she had tried to explain the program to her. She had continued to believe Abby was trying to play an elaborate practical joke on her. Abby snorted her displeasure and crossed her arms tightly across her chest. She'd have to make a new column on the chart for check marks instead of stars. She'd be adding a big black check mark for *mocking* or *disbelieving* or. . . something.

Still grinning, John restarted the car. "Let's go eat lunch."

As they got closer to the old part of town, the streets began to get narrow and steep. And then Abby saw the river and a tugboat pushing a barge upstream.

"Is that the Mississippi?" Merri said.

"That's right, squirt." When they reached the bottom of the hill, John pointed to a huge grain silo that stood near the river. "Do you see that red line painted up there? That's how high the river rose in the great flood of 1993. Whole houses were washed away."

"You're kidding."

"No. They don't call it the Mighty Mississippi for nothing. Alton has always been an important port on the Mississippi River. St. Louis is just across from us."

John turned left onto Broadway. "Many of the buildings here date from the early 1800s. Most of the businesses have moved out onto the new parkway. Now, downtown is mostly for antique hunters and tourists."

Abby wished she could explore some of the old buildings—better yet, do a little time-surfing in them. Who knew what stories they had to tell? Interspersed with them, other buildings, some plain and some outright ugly and obviously lacking the same character and soul, had been built where previous old buildings had given up the ghost in years past.

John parked the car in front of River Bend Pottery and they got out. "Come on," he said. "Genevieve's is just up ahead."

A man carrying a little walnut table came out of an antique store as they walked past. John and Merri paused to admire the paintings in the window of an art gallery, but Abby's eye was drawn to the restaurant next door called My Just Desserts.

"Oh, look, you guys," she said. "Peanut butter pie. I'm trying not to stare, but I think that man in there's eating peanut butter pie." Abby's stomach rumbled and she felt her face turn red.

John laughed. "Don't worry. You'll eat soon."

Genevieve's was a combination gift shop and tea room swarming with visitors. The hostess took their names and suggested they might enjoy browsing in the gift shop while they waited for a table. Abby looked longingly at a tray of salads and sandwiches that a waitress carried past but obediently followed John and Merri to the gift shop.

It was crowded there too. They eased past three over-dressed women who were oohing and ahhing over a display of peach-scented potpourri.

Merri sneezed three times in quick succession. "Wow," she said, rubbing her eyes. "That's strong stuff."

"Wow is right," Abby said. She wondered if customers ever freaked out from the sensory overload. Vases of silk flowers in every hue sat among calico tea cozies, beaded handbags, miniature Beatrix Potter books, along with innumerable other girly treasures. Overhead, garlands of yellow forsythia, each bud with its own tiny white light, cast a warm glow.

John held up a turquoise T-shirt emblazoned with sequins spelling the words *Grandma's Are Just Antique Little Girls*. "My mom's birthday is in a couple of weeks. Do you think she'd like this?"

Not if she's sane, Abby thought. Or understands the rudiments of punctuation. But she was saved from having to come up with a kind reply when the "Roberts party of three" was summoned over the loudspeaker. Following the hostess, they made their way to the dining room, which unsurprisingly was another estrogen-powered extravaganza. The walls were papered with pink roses and each of the round tables was covered in a different floral print skirt, dripping with cream lace.

Abby had trouble seeing John over the centerpiece—an oversized tea pot filled with pink silk hydrangeas. She studied the menu of salads and sandwiches, all of which seemed to feature raspberries. But it was hard to think in the unrelenting pink of the room. The conversational buzz didn't help. The majority of their fellow diners were women over forty, and the majority of *them* wore dresses in floral prints much like that of the table cloths. They all seemed to be enjoying their fruity salads and sandwiches. Obviously, something was wrong with her, Abby thought, because she had the urge to run into the street screaming for a hamburger.

But then John peeked over the hydrangeas and smiled proudly at her. "I hope you like it. Mom said this would be a good place."

Abby's heart melted and she forgot she was annoyed

with John. Would this star fall under *romantic* or *considerate?*

Of course it couldn't get too romantic with Merri there, even though she was good as gold and didn't say much while they ate and tried to carry on a conversation over the centerpiece. But then Merri's phone warbled and she squealed. "It's a text from Mom. She says Dad is coming down to see me tomorrow!"

The women at the table next to them looked annoyed and Abby mentally cringed. But then she thought, tough luck, ladies. She was just relieved that Merri was so much happier.

"Merri's been wanting to go to Chicago to visit her dad, but her mom hasn't been able to take her," Abby explained. She couldn't tell him with Merri there that Pat had been stalling because she didn't want Merri to be around her father's criminal activities, or that it was the reason she had taken Merri and begun a new life in Miles Station in the first place.

"He wants me to pick out a place to go for lunch and I get to choose something fun to do afterwards. What should I say?"

"Well," John said. "There's the Brown Cow. They have really good burgers and steaks."

Abby nodded her head in wholehearted agreement. "That sounds good. I bet he'd like that."

Merri's thumbs were a blur as she texted her mom. "Okay, but what should we do after lunch?"

"Let's go." John tucked cash into the leather check folder the waitress had laid on the table. Then he stood and pulled Abby's chair out. "We'll think of something."

When they stepped outside, Abby pointed to an old

brick three-story building across the street. "Isn't that City Hall?"

"I think that's it." Merri started to cross the street, but John held her arm just before she would have stepped in front of a motorcycle.

"It used to be. Now it's the Alton History Museum," John said. "You'd probably like it since you're so keen on the past."

"Keen? Does anyone use that word anymore?" Abby said, laughing.

"Hey, I like retro words."

A *Closed* sign hung on the door, but Abby and Merri shaded their eyes and blatantly stared through the window. "There's a big picture on the wall," Merri said. "Look, Abby, do you see it?"

"That's it. See, John, there's Abraham Lincoln and Stephen Douglas shaking hands."

"Remember how goofy Lincoln looked, Abby?"

"Yes, but he was passionate about preventing the expansion of slavery, even if his voice was all twangy and weird," Abby said. "We need to come back when the museum is open."

"Do you mean the re-enactment?" John said. "They hold it every October."

"That's right. It was October 16th, 1858. There were chairs set up in front, but most people stood. Hundreds of people were here. They came from miles around."

"It was a really big deal to them," Merri said.

"The band marched along Front Street and then up Henry Street past the hotel where the speakers were staying. Lincoln's son Todd was marching along with the other cadets from the Alton Military Academy."

"Listen," John said. "Enough, already. I'm impressed that you two have studied a lot of history this summer."

Abby sighed when she saw the expression on John's face. "Oh, never mind. Just take us home, John. When we get the computer fixed, I'll show you."

John walked Abby to the front door, which although it was polite, was not very romantic since Merri was also there and didn't seem to be in any hurry to leave.

"Don't the trellises look nice?" Merri said. John had helped install them on the sides of the porch, and the honeysuckle their neighbor Mrs. Arnold had contributed was already starting to bloom. Indeed, the porch was looking good, the perfect place to say goodbye.

"Merri, your mom will be wondering why we're late," Abby hinted.

"Maybe John can help us fix the computer."

"Not this time," he said.

Then Merri suddenly seemed to realize that it was time for her to go. "Oh, right. See you," she said and tripped over the threshold in her haste to get inside the door.

And then finally, Abby was alone with John and it started to seem like a real date.

"Thanks, I had a good time."

John smiled and her stomach fluttered. "Me too, Abby."

She felt herself blushing and knew there was not one thing she could do but wait it out. What? Was she fifteen again? She was startled to find she couldn't maintain eye contact with him either. But when she glanced away she saw his hands, and that was almost as nerve-wracking as looking into his blue eyes. She remembered how strong and capable his hands had been when he helped her with the trellis last week—and how gentle with Merri's little friend Michael when the bullies teased him.

Then he leaned in closer, and his cologne, an

intoxicating blend of something citrus and spicy, went right to her brain and she actually felt faint. He was going to kiss her, and she was going to faint right there on Pat and Merri's front porch. She took a breath and closed her eyes.

Nothing.

Abby opened her eyes and saw that he was looking at his watch. And frowning. "Well," he said, "it's 4:00. I've got to go."

"Oh. Of course." Abby felt stupid. How could she have gotten it so wrong?

"Well, you know when you own your own business you've got to keep early hours."

"Oh."

"See you tomorrow at church?"

"Okay."

She watched as he hurried back to his blue Mustang and continued watching as he drove away down Miles Station Road toward Brighton. She waved, but he didn't look back.

Abby sat down on the porch step and wondered where it had started to go wrong. After a while, she took her phone out of her purse and smiled when she saw there were five missed calls from her roommate Kate. Had it been anyone else, she would have been concerned that there was some dire emergency, but since it was Kate, she knew it was just impatience to hear all the nitty-gritty details of her date.

"Okay, give," Kate said right off.

"Hi, to you too, Kate."

"Oh well, hi, then. You know I'm dying to know how it went, so don't think you're going to torture me with this."

"It was nice. He took me to a fancy-schmancy tea room for lunch."

"That's so romantic."

"Yeah, well, I'm still hungry. Merri, too. She almost asked him to pull through McDonald's on the way home, but I wouldn't—."

"Wait a minute, wait a minute. Back up there, girlfriend. Are you telling me the chubster—I mean youngster—went with you? On your date with tall, dark, and handsome?"

"Hey, don't call her that. Her name's Merri."

"Well, excuse me. You called her that. Chubster, brat, slug, couch potato."

"Yeah…well…I shouldn't have. She's got issues, but she's working through them."

"Okay, *Merri*, then. I guess it wasn't much of a date with her along. No wonder you sound all frowny."

"I'm not frowny! Well, all right, I am now, but that's because you're being so annoying."

"Tell Auntie Kate all about it. What's wrong?"

"It's just that I thought John had such potential. He already has ten stars, and counting. But it got all weird and he rushed off. Right when I actually thought he was going to kiss me."

"Did you ever think it might be because Merri was there?" Kate's laughter made her even more annoyed.

"Don't be an idiot, Kate. Merri went in the house and there was plenty of opportunity, but he left like I had a contagious disease or something."

"But isn't that a nice change from the last guy who couldn't keep his paws off you long enough to carry on a simple conversation? And maybe next time, when Merri isn't tagging along…"

"Yes, but…well…if you must know, I think the real reason is…John thinks I'm crazy."

"Don't be ridiculous. You're the sanest person I—wait

a minute. You didn't tell him about all that time travel hocus pocus, did you? You did, didn't you?"

"It's not hocus pocus. I tried to tell you, we really—"

"Okay, a joke, then. But, Abby, some people just aren't going to think it's funny when you keep on like that."

"Oh, never mind," Abby sighed. "When I get the computer fixed, I'll show you. You and John both. You are still coming down for a visit, aren't you?"

"I will as soon as I can get untangled from some things here. I can't wait to meet John—and the new improved Merri."

"Good. Maybe you can help me get a read on him," Abby said, and then muttered after she hung up, "And I'll introduce you to Charlotte and Abraham Lincoln too."

Merri was waiting for her when she opened the front door and Abby wondered if she had been spying out the window.

"Did he kiss you?" Merri demanded.

"Merri!" Pat said.

"Let's just say you won't have to worry about not seeing much of me this summer, Merri," Abby said and then described John's odd departure.

"What's the matter with that boy?" Pat said. "Why, any red-blooded guy would want to kiss you . . ." Pat's eyes widened. "He did say he likes theatre. I bet that's it. He's . . ." She nodded toward Merri and lowered her voice. "You know... of another persuasion."

"Mom, you don't have to talk in code," Merri said. "I'm not stupid."

"Why would he take me on a date if he's gay?"

"Some gay guys like to use a girlfriend as cover," Pat said. "I saw it on TV. And he's too nice. I mean, what guy wants to take a kid along on a date?"

"I'm sure that's not true, Pat." But then picture of John sitting so at ease among the crowd of women in the flowery tea room popped unbidden into her head.

So, either she was crazy or he was gay—or, hey, maybe both.

CHAPTER 2

Abby stumbled out of the bathroom at 6:43 the next morning on her way back to bed for another sweet hour of oblivion before it was time to get up. Merri stopped her just outside the door. Abby yawned and rubbed her eyes, hoping she was only dreaming. She blinked, but Merri was still there—annoyingly wide awake and fully dressed for church.

"How do I look?" Merri said.

"Awesome, kiddo," she said, stifling another yawn. "I love that look you're going for."

"Thanks. Would you do my hair in a French braid again? We'd better hurry. I don't want to be late."

She smiled sleepily at Merri. Abby knew that Merri wasn't thinking about church so much as she was about her lunch date with her dad afterwards, but still it was good to see her so eager. "I think we're okay for time," she said drily. "Wait here. I'm going to make coffee and try to jolt myself out of this walking coma I'm in."

When Abby had offered to take Merri to the restaurant to meet her dad, Pat had been grateful, saying she didn't have the stomach to sit through a meal with her ex-husband Brad after all the trouble he had caused. She had grudgingly admitted he did love Merrideth—in his own selfish way—and that she couldn't keep them separated from each other forever—no matter how much she wanted to.

Abby just hoped Merri would be able to sit through church without exploding with excitement.

Abby was a little late getting to the young adult Sunday school class, so she had to sit in the last available seat— in the front row. John, near the back with a group of guys, smiled at her when she passed him and she felt relieved. Maybe he didn't think she was crazy after all. Or then again, maybe he was just smiling at her because he was trying to be nice to a crazy person. It was a good thing there were no open seats next to him, because it would have looked like she was chasing him, which she definitely wasn't. He obviously wanted to keep it a casual friendship. And that's what she wanted too. Really.

Mr. Luckert led the class in a good discussion on Abraham's faith. John made several comments that showed he had studied the Scripture passage. Abby was impressed. Maybe she could casually stop him after class and they could discuss it further. But after class, Mr. Luckert stopped *her* to ask how she was getting along and if she were making any friends. He meant well, but she might have had a better chance of doing so if he hadn't delayed her.

Then, when she got to the sanctuary, even if she had wanted to sit next to John, which she didn't, she wouldn't have been able to because he was in the back, managing the audio and recording systems. He didn't look up when she entered the room, so she and Merri sat next to the friendly couple she had met before. Her last thought before turning her concentration to the service was that there would be plenty of guys, with imaginary charts and stars of their own, when she got back to Ambassador College in the fall.

Abby smiled as Merri nearly skipped up the sidewalk to the front door of the Brown Cow. Its rustic decor was totally different from Genevieve's, but it was every bit as crowded with its own variety of enthusiasts. Abby checked in with the hostess, who told her there would be at least a fifteen-minute wait.

Merri stood on her toes to look over the people waiting in front of them. "I don't see him."

"Well, we're a little early."

This time, there was no girly gift shop to kill time in, so Abby took a menu from the wooden rack on the wall to read while they waited. It was certainly geared toward carnivores. Raspberries weren't mentioned anywhere on the menu.

The hostess called the party of twelve in front of them and she and Merri had a clearer view of the dining room.

"What time is it?" Merri asked, studying the crowded room.

Over the buzz of conversation and clink of cutlery Abby heard a faint warbling. "Hey, isn't that your phone?"

Merri pulled her phone out and opened it. "I'm getting a text." The smile drained from her face. Snapping her phone closed, she turned toward the door without a word and elbowed her way through the people waiting in line.

"Wait, Merri! What is it?" Abby followed her out onto the sidewalk, mumbling apologies to the people Merri had trampled, all the while knowing the answer to her own question.

"I *know* it's hard." Abby sat down on the front porch step next to Merri. She looked up at the sky, hazy with humidity and heat, and thought about what to say. "The Bible says we *have* to forgive."

"But he was so mean to me."

"I'm not saying you don't have a right to be angry. What your dad did was wrong."

"He's done it to me over and over again. I can't keep forgiving him."

"One guy thought he was being generous to forgive seven times. But Jesus told him to keep on forgiving, even seventy *times* seven."

"Well, I'm on about 489 and a half by now."

"Let's go in where it's cooler."

"Look," Merri said pointing to the road. She wiped her eyes with her sleeve and grinned. "Your new *boyfriend's* coming to see you."

John's blue Mustang, closely followed by a battered and rusty panel van, turned off Miles Station Road onto their so-called street and stopped.

"What do you know," Abby said softly, "He came back." She resisted the impulse to do a happy dance and run down to the car to meet him.

John gracefully unfolded his tall frame from the Mustang and waited for the guy in the van to wrestle his dented door open. After a struggle, he got out of the van, tugging a backpack with him, and followed John up the sidewalk.

"Hi." Abby stood and brushed dust off the seat of her shorts. John smiled and as usual, her stomach did weird things.

"Hi. Abby, Merri. This is my friend Tim Skyzyptek. He's a computer wizard." He looked the part, with his horn-rimmed glasses and dinosaur-green T-shirt that read: Pterodactyls are Pterrific.

"He might be able to fix your computer."

"Hi, Tim Sk…something…tech," Abby said. "Thanks for coming."

Tim grinned. "No sweat. And just call me Tim."

"Hey, squirt, how did your lunch—?"

Abby elbowed John in his side and smiled brightly at Tim. "Come on in out of the heat." She opened the front door and they went in, John frowning at her in puzzlement. Tim pushed his glasses back into place on his nose and looked around the room with interest.

"When he gets your computer fixed, you can show me your weird program." John said it with a faintly patronizing smile, but that was all right. She'd enjoy the look on his face when he finally went time-surfing with them.

"So, does this mean you believe me now?"

"I didn't say *that*. But if we don't save the program, I'll never know, will I?"

"It's upstairs," Merri said. "Follow me."

Abby started up the stairs after her, but when she heard the guys' clomping along behind her she stopped. John bumped into her.

"Sorry," he said.

Tim grinned. "Maybe you should watch your feet instead of—".

"Shut up, Tim." John's face was as pink as the hydrangeas at Genevieve's.

Abby felt her own cheeks heat. Well, she thought happily, Pat was wrong about his sexual orientation. "We'll have to be quiet. Merri's mom is napping."

"Oh, sure," Tim whispered back.

"What's with Merri?" John said quietly. "She looks like she's been crying."

"Her dad didn't show at the Brown Cow. At the last second he texted her to say something had come up. Didn't even have the guts to call. Says he'll come next weekend for sure."

"Sounds like a swell guy."

"You have no idea how swell. If you guys can get the program going again that would really cheer her up."

Merri stood at the door to the computer room. "There it is."

Setting his backpack on the floor beside the chair, Tim sat down and began to check out the computer. Merri sat in the straight-back chair beside him and Abby and John stood behind them looking over their shoulders.

"You've got 1.5 terabytes," Tim said. "Definitely a flaming sweet beast."

"It is?" Merri said.

"What Timmy Tech means is it's a top-of-the line computer with lots of memory," John said.

"So did your proggie barf on you or did you get the screen of death?" Tim said.

"I'm not sure what you mean," Abby said.

"You know, the blue bomb."

"Tim, you're such a Dilbert," John said.

"Why thanks, Johnny Boy. You're no larva yourself. Sorry, Abby, for brain dumping on you. I mean did your program send error codes, or did everything crash to a blue screen?"

"Here, let me show you," Merri said. She took the mouse and clicked on the *Beautiful Houses* program icon. After the welcome screen came on, this time featuring Frank Lloyd Wright's famous Chicago home, a slide show of houses began to scroll across the screen as usual.

"We thought it was pretty cool to be able to take virtual tours of some really neat houses all over the world," Abby said. "But then one day, *bam*! There was *this* old house looking just like the drawing in the history book we saw, surrounded by shops, a train depot, Colonel Miles' steam mill—the whole village of Miles Station just like it was over a hundred and sixty years ago."

"Man, that sounds off the hook!" Tim said.

"Yeah, it was awesome." Abby pointed at the house that had just come up onscreen. "See. That one."

"That's cool. It looks like this house—only new," John said. "How did they—?"

"That *is* this house," Merri insisted. "Only when the power came back on after the storm last week it was all messed up. Watch what happens when I click on it."

The screen image rolled dizzily and then settled into a long error message.

"Might as well be Greek," Abby said.

"Did you call customer support?" Tim said.

"Of course, but the technicians kept passing us on to other technicians, and nobody was able to fix the problem."

"You probably had a power surge during the storm and it corrupted some of the program files," Tim said. "Did you try reinstalling?"

Abby shook her head. "No software disks. Since it's still under warranty, I've been thinking about just sending it all back to the company and letting them take care of it."

"There's only one problem with that."

"What?"

"They'll format the hard drive and everything will be gone," Tim said. "I wouldn't bet on getting the program back the way it was. But don't worry. I think I can phrack in through the backdoor and clean up the files for you.

That is, assuming they're not totally nuked. Then I have a little app I wrote that will make your proggie pretty much bulletproof."

"Okay. Thanks. I think." Abby looked up for John's reaction.

"Yeah, thanks, Tim."

They watched as Tim's hands flew over the keyboard and he happily chattered away in geek speak, which they mostly ignored. After about thirty minutes he said, "There. Good as new. No more nasty frags floating around. You're all set to go."

"This is going to be so cool," Merri said. "Wait until you see it, John."

"I'm watching."

"And you won't think I'm mental now." Abby clicked on the house, and this time no error message popped up— but then neither did the enhanced program features. "They're gone," Abby said. "The control buttons are all gone."

"What did you do to the program?" Merri glared at Tim.

"Sorry, ladies," Tim said. "That's the best I can do."

"That's it?" Merri said. "No more Charlotte? How will we know what happened to her?"

Merri bolted from the room, and then down the hall her door shut—almost loud enough to be categorized a slam.

"Sorry about that. She's had a really bad day. Thanks for trying, guys," Abby said. It was difficult to be polite when she was fighting the ridiculous urge to cry.

John touched her hand and when she looked up at him, he seemed sincerely distressed. "I'm sorry it didn't work, Abby."

"At least the error messages are gone."

Tim pulled a cable from his backpack and used it to connect Merri's computer to John's laptop. "I'm going to beam the program over to Johnny Boy's laptop so you all can go native," he said, seeming totally clueless about the emotional vibes in the room.

"That's good," Abby lied, because of course it was pointless now that they wouldn't be able to time-surf any more.

"There. That should do it. I've got to take off now," Tim said. "I promised my grandma I'd stop by. Sounds like she's cooked her email program again." He chuckled. "The four gazillion emails she forwards on a daily basis might have something to do with it."

Abby and John followed Tim downstairs. Waving as he drove off, they sat down on the front porch steps.

"If only you could have seen how Miles Station looked back in the day," she said, gesturing toward the west where now only cornfields grew. "I could show you pictures—the history books at the library have a lot of stuff—but there's nothing like seeing it for yourself."

Picking up the laptop beside him on the step, John stood. "I've got to go now, but why don't we go to the library and you can show me? Maybe tomorrow."

It was sweet of him to try to fix the computer. And the suggestion about going to the library obviously meant he still wanted some kind of relationship. But what kind of relationship could she ever hope for if he didn't believe her? Which called into question his status as possible marriage material, no matter how many stars on his chart. Which probably meant she should stop thinking about kissing him.

She sighed and said, "I'll walk you to your car."

When she rose from her seat on the porch step, she saw Merri's raggedy five-year-old neighbor, shuffling down the dusty road toward them, carefully carrying something covered in aluminum foil. "Wait, John. You can't leave yet. Looks like Michael's bringing us something."

Abby had felt a sense of protectiveness from the first moment she saw the little boy playing on the train tracks in front of their house. Because his mother was deaf, Michael had not been exposed to clear speech and so he had several odd speech problems. Abby and Merri had been unable to understand him at first. Some of the neighborhood kids teased and bullied him. At least they had before John set the little thugs straight. His rescue had, unbeknownst to him, earned him a star for *heroism.*

Michael's sweet smile was bigger than ever. "Mrs. Arnold made you cookies." He handed the plate to John. What he had actually said was more like, "Mi-uh Ahnow may oo coo-ees," but they were used to his speech patterns and understood perfectly well what he was saying. He pulled back the foil to reveal a pink glass plate of sugar cookies shaped like flags and iced in red, white, and blue.

"Thanks, buddy," John said, juggling the plate and his laptop. "That reminds me, Abby. I talked with my cousin Lucy about Michael. She's a speech therapist. Works out of her house in Alton, one of those old Victorians near where we were yesterday. Anyway, I called her last night. She's willing to work with him if it's all right with his parents."

"That would be wonderful!" Abby moved closer to John and lowered her voice. "But I don't think Michael's mom can afford to pay a speech therapist."

"Not a problem," he mumbled around the cookie he had stuffed in his mouth. "She'll take the case pro bono. She wants to see him Tuesday morning."

After John and Michael left, Abby sat there wondering how she could cheer Merri up. Her first thought was to take her the plate of cookies, but she knew Merri was really trying not to eat junk food. Besides, using food as a reward was a really bad idea. If Pat hadn't been doing it Merri's whole life, maybe she wouldn't have gotten so heavy. The kindest thing she could do was to remove the temptation, and so she ate two of the cookies while she tried to think of something to do with Merri. After her third cookie, she gave up and called Kate.

"He came back. I thought he was giving me the brush off at church this morning, but, apparently not."

"Really? Did he take you some place romantic again?"

"No, better. He brought his friend Tim and they tried to fix the computer. It didn't work, but still."

"Definitely not romantic."

"Yes, but sweet—in a guy sort of way. Blast it! Now I have to give him another star, which is pointless because he's not really marriage material."

"Why not? He sounds nice."

"Yeah, well, what about trust?"

"Trust? What are you talking about?" Kate said.

There was no way around it. John either thought a) she was crazy, b) she was a liar, c) she's was so stupid she didn't understand what she had seen on the computer, or d) she was joking past all point of being funny, which, of course, was just another way of saying she was stupid. She would have to take him out of the marriage possibility category and put him in the friend category. But what kind of friend was he if he didn't trust her? Then it occurred to her that what was true for John was also true for Kate.

"Abby, are you there?"

"Yeah, I'm here." She sighed. "But I've got to go think of some way to cheer up Merri." And herself. "I'll call you later."

"Okay. Have fun."

When Abby picked up the pink plate to take it to the

kitchen, she discovered it was empty.

Wow, she thought, stress eating was really a bad idea too.

CHAPTER 3

Lucy's waiting room was a carefully restored Victorian parlor with antique furniture. Abby sat in a walnut chair near the front window, hoping she'd get the chance to see the rest of the house. She had fallen in love with Lucy's house the minute they had arrived. It was a three-story Victorian painted a pale, buttery yellow with a gray slate roof and white gingerbread trim dripping from the eaves and front porch. When she saw the house's twin next door, alike in every detail except it was painted a dusty blue, she was doubly charmed.

The carvings in the back of her chair were poking into her spine, which probably wouldn't happen if she sat up as straight as the Victorian ladies had back in the day. She could almost hear her mother telling her not to slouch.

"Merri," Abby said, "while we wait for Michael, let's talk some more about your essay."

"I already started on it last night."

"Way to go, squirt," John said, looking up from the *Classic Cars* magazine he was reading. He was definitely slouching on an antique gold velvet settee that made his modern shorts and T-shirt look strange. "But if you don't learn to procrastinate, your college professors won't know what to think of you."

"I'm here to make sure she doesn't pick up that particular bad habit," Abby said. "I'm proud of you, Merri. So how much did you get done?"

"Well, I did like you said. You know… brainstormed. But…well…"

"So you didn't actually write anything."

"I can't think of anything good to write about."

"How about the history of the Ford Mustang?" John said, indicating his magazine. "Now there's a fascinating topic."

"I really don't think—"

"He's kidding," Abby said. "You should write about something *you* like. So what *do* you like?"

Merri studied the beaded lampshade on the table next to her. "I don't know."

"Why don't you pick a historical topic? You're really good with that." Abby went to stand in front of John. "Move over. Let me see if this is any more comfortable."

John swung his long legs to the floor and absently patted the seat next to him. "See, here's what I'm talking about," he said and held the magazine out to her. "She's a 1967 Mustang just like mine, but. . ."

Apparently the settee had shrunk, because she was way too close to be safe from the effects of John's cologne. It was like a tractor beam dragging her into his field of gravity. Abby wondered if he was doing it on purpose. She had the urge to lean in and sniff his neck. Dang it! She felt another blush begin to bloom.

John blinked at her and seemed to completely forget what he was talking about.

"That's nice," she said at last. "*She* looks good."

"She sure does." He was not looking at the car.

"What are you wearing," she demanded.

"You can't tell this is a Cardinals T-shirt?"

"Your cologne? What is it?"

"I don't remember."

"Well...don't wear it anymore. It makes me..."

"Grouchy?"

Abby jumped up from the settee—she could only hold her breath so long—and went back to the spine-poking chair.

A minute later they heard the sound of running feet and then Michael was there, smiling and chattering.

"Slow down, big guy." John squatted down until he was eye level with the little boy. Michael was dressed in his usual ragged but clean jeans and T-shirt. "Can't understand what you're saying."

Abby smiled and put her hand on Michael's thin shoulder. "What's this about Dr. Bob?"

"Lucy said I can come see Dr. Bob anytime I want to." His eyes gleamed with excitement.

Abby looked at John in confusion. "I didn't know Lucy worked with. . ."

Then Lucy came through the doorway, smiling. "Oh, haven't you met my colleague? Michael, why don't you go back and get Dr. Bob?"

"How did it go?" John asked.

"He's got several conditions—there's a whole slew of technical names, if you want them. It's all consistent with being raised in a household where the primary caregiver, in his case the only caregiver, has speech deficiencies. Michael's mom will, unfortunately, always have speech problems because she's been deaf since birth. But Michael's a very bright boy and has the potential for overcoming his speech difficulties, if his mom is willing to get him here."

"Then maybe the stupid bullies will leave him alone," Merri said.

"Thanks for being willing to help him, Lucy," Abby said.

"My pleasure. He's a sweet little guy."

Michael came back carrying a squirming dog. Wearing a little red bowtie, the dog was white with a brown face and a large brown spot on his side. His rump was also brown, and the white tip of his docked tail gave it the appearance of a bull's eye target, one wagging so fast not even a marksman could hit. Dog and boy wore similar excited expressions. Michael hugged the dog and set it down.

"May I present Dr. Bob," Lucy said. "He helps the children who come for therapy."

Dr. Bob stretched his front legs before him and laid his head upon them as if he were bowing. Then he jumped up and with a canine grin extended his right paw.

Merri kneeled before him and shook hands. "He's so cute! I wish I could have a dog like him."

"You should come along sometime when Michael comes for therapy," Lucy said. "I'd like to get started with Michael right away so we can get as much work done as possible before school this fall. But, unfortunately, it will have to be after I get back from my conference."

"I can get him here any time you say," John said.

"What about your Tropical Frost stand?"

"I can be pretty flexible now that Elsie started working for me."

"If you're such a man of leisure these days, how about housesitting for me while I'm gone?

"When do you need me?"

"I leave next Monday and will be gone a week."

"Sure. I'm going to be in Alton a lot for the next few weeks anyway. We're starting a Habitat for Humanity rehab in a few days."

Lucy laughed. "Oh, no, you don't understand, John. You wouldn't have time to do everything I need around here." Then, her face brightened. "How about you, Abby? And Merri too, of course."

"I'd love to stay in such a beautiful house. What do you think, Merri?" Abby said. "Of course you'd have to continue your school work."

Frowning, Merri sat down on the floor next to Michael and coaxed Dr. Bob into her lap. "I don't think I'd better." Dr. Bob licked her nose and she smiled sadly.

"I pay well," Lucy said. "And you could play with Dr. Bob any time you wanted."

"That would be nice, but…" Merri trailed off.

Abby knelt next to her and asked softly, "What's wrong, kiddo?"

"I'd like to, but when…*if*…Dad comes I'd have to leave."

"Don't worry. We'll work that out. Of course we'll have to ask your mom."

Merri hugged Dr. Bob. "She won't care."

"Then it's settled," Lucy said.

"And I can be here after work," John said.

Lucy looked uncertain. "John, I don't think…"

His face turned red and he answered quickly. "Oh, I don't mean *sleep* here. Tim lives here in town. I'm sure he'd let me bunk with him."

Abby grinned. This time *he* was blushing.

CHAPTER 4

Abby turned into the alley that ran behind Lucy's house. The early morning sun slanted through the windshield, and Merri covered her eyes.

"Lucy's email said to park by the yellow garage," Abby said. "And she wrote *be very quiet* in all capitals."

"Why all the secrecy?" Merri said. "This is crazy."

"I don't know." Abby said. "Maybe they have really strict zoning rules here."

Two identical unattached garages opened onto the alley, one belonging to Lucy's house, and one to its twin house next door. Abby passed by the blue garage and pulled her car up to the yellow one. They got out, shutting their doors quietly, and went to the trunk to unload their assortment of bags.

When Merri started to open the white picket gate, Abby stopped her. "Be careful. Lucy said it squeaks." Merri eased the gate open with only a faint screech, and Abby said, "Remember, no talking until we get inside the house." They made their way quietly up a stone path that led through a well-tended lawn, in the middle of which stood a small gazebo surrounded by a bed of salvia, daisies, and marigolds. Just past the gazebo, the stone path forked, one branch leading to Lucy's house, the other to its twin next door.

When they got to Lucy's back porch they set their bags down. Abby was about to knock on the door, when she saw a sudden movement through the glass pane. Merri burst out laughing when she saw Dr. Bob's little brown and white face begin to pop into view and then disappear, as if he were bouncing on a trampoline just inside the door. He was wearing his red bowtie and barking a happy greeting.

"Shhhh!" Abby whispered. Then Lucy was there, pushing the dog aside to open the door. "Quick, inside," she said.

Looking past them, Lucy said, "Too late."

"Yoo, hoo! We made coffee cake." The voices came in unison from two elderly white-haired ladies coming down the path from the blue house next door. "It's bundt cake, the kind you like."

"It's the Old Dears. I love them to pieces," Lucy said with a sigh, "but now I'll never get away on time."

Abby and Merri stared in astonishment. The women were identical, from their wavy white hair to their sensible tan lace-up shoes. They even stepped in unison, as they slowly and carefully made their way along the path.

"Hello...I'm Eulah," the lady on the left said between breaths. "Welcome to the neighborhood."

"And...I'm...Beulah," the lady on the right said. "We're twins," she added cheerfully. Abby figured no one could help but notice that, especially since they were wearing identical lavender dresses.

"You were sort of vague about when they'd arrive, Lucy," Eulah said.

"But we saw them," Beulah said with satisfaction.

There was nothing for Lucy to do but invite everyone into her kitchen, a comfortable blend of modern appliances and authentic Victorian touches.

"Hey, I've got a new joke," Beulah said. "Knock, knock."

"Who's there?" Lucy said, taking the cake from her. Abby admired the patience in her voice.

"Orange."

"Orange who?" Lucy said, smiling as if her favorite thing in the world were knock-knock jokes.

"Orange you glad we're here?" Beulah cackled at her joke.

"Please don't start with the jokes." Eulah was wearing a sour expression. It was the only difference between the two that Abby could see.

"Don't mind Eulah," Beulah said. "She's wearing her grumpy suit this morning."

Eulah rolled her eyes and explained to Lucy. "She put salt in the sugar bowl again this morning."

"Beulah!" Lucy said, putting the coffee cake down on her counter. "You've got to stop playing jokes on your sister."

"Last time it was fake dog poo on my bed," Eulah said, glaring at Beulah. "And for our birthday she made me a sponge cake. Literally—a sponge cake. I tried to slice it but…"

"I'm just trying to get her to lighten up."

"Well, I've got to be leaving now," Lucy said cheerfully.

"You've got to have some breakfast before you go,"

Beulah said.

"To keep up your strength," Eulah said.

"Okay, then. Let's have some of that delicious looking coffee cake." Lucy looked at her watch. "Real quick."

The twin ladies moved freely about Lucy's kitchen, chattering the whole time about Lovely Lucy and her pretty kitchen. One twin, Abby wasn't sure which, went to a drawer and took out a knife. "Hasn't she done a fine job of remodeling this kitchen?" she said as she sliced the coffee cake.

"If you want to see what it looked like before, come over to our kitchen." The other twin went to a cupboard and took out blue speckled plates and cups, and Abby helped her set them around Lucy's antique oak pedestal table.

One of the ladies handed Merri a stack of napkins, and she set one by each plate. Although she continued to smile and talk, Lucy looked surreptitiously at her watch.

When they were all seated, the twin next to Abby— she kept losing track of which was which—took her hand and asked the blessing. Then one twin began to serve the coffee cake. When Abby and Merri declined coffee and milk, Lucy said anxiously, "Are you sure?"

Abby took a bite of the coffee cake. She chewed for a long time. At last she swallowed. Mostly. "Maybe I will take that glass of milk," she said.

Merri's eyes widened as she desperately attempted to swallow. "Me, too," she managed to choke out.

"I'll get it." One of the twins pushed herself to her feet and went to get the milk.

Lucy was draining her coffee cup at an alarming rate. Abby wondered how she kept from burning her lips off.

"Well, then," Lucy began after she had stifled a cough with her napkin. "Dr. Bob's really easy to take care of.

He'll tell you when he needs to go outside. Make sure the outer gate is kept closed at all times, but we keep the gate between our yards open so Dr. Bob can go visit the Old D—I mean Beulah and Eulah and so he can play Round About."

Abby wondered what that was, but Lucy hurried on with her instructions.

"Keep his water bowl filled and give him only a half a cup of dry kibble twice a day, even if he begs for more. He's such a little piglet."

Merri was looking unaccountably guilty, and then Abby noticed her hand carefully lowering beneath the table. In it was a large portion of her coffee cake. Dr. Bob wolfed it down and then licked her fingers clean.

Lucy stood and began carrying dishes to the sink. "And no matter what he tells you," she continued, "I don't let him sleep on my bed. He had the last sitter completely conned. Just give him his blanket and he'll be fine. John said he'd mow the grass. Please don't worry about cleaning. I have a service that takes care of all that. As a matter of fact, they'll be here pretty soon. There's plenty of food in the freezer. I've got two bedrooms ready for you. You'll see—the lavender one and the green one. I posted my phone number on the fridge. Call me if you need me."

"Okay," Abby said. "But you haven't really given us much to do—not that I'm complaining."

Lucy's smile was mysterious. "Oh, I'm sure you'll keep busy. Okay, I'll be off, then."

"Oh, but Lucy dear, we wanted to show you the progress we've made on our little project," Beulah said. "We forgot to bring it, Eulah."

"*You* forgot to bring it. I brought the coffee cake."

"I'll just go right back over there quick as a rabbit and get it," Beulah said.

When Abby started to offer to help, Lucy waved her hands furiously behind the twins' backs.

"Or not," she said and sat down again.

"I'd love to see it, ladies. But I have to leave or I'll never make it in time for the opening lecture. When I get back next Monday I'll help you with it."

"Monday? That's such a long time from now." Beulah and Eulah looked at each other with matching sad eyes.

"Maybe we could help," Abby said. "How about we come over tomorrow and take a look at it?"

Lucy looked relieved and grateful, and Beulah said, "That would be splendid!"

"And maybe you could show me how to make a sponge cake," Merri said slyly.

Eulah glowered at her twin, but Beulah laughed excitedly. "I'll show you, Merri. It's really easy."

Everyone followed Lucy as she rolled her suitcase, with briefcase and purse snugly attached, to the front door. "Abby, could you help me with this?" Lucy detached her briefcase and handed it to her. "And Merri, could you carry my...my...." She looked around quickly. "Purse," she said, thrusting it into Merri's arms.

As they made their way down the sidewalk, Eulah and Beulah waved cheerfully and called out from the front porch, "Goodbye, dear. Have a good trip."

Smiling, Lucy waved back and then whispered out of the corner of her mouth, "Okay, guys, here's the deal about the Old Dears. Beulah's the cheery one. Eulah's a crab some times, but don't take it personally. If—*when*—they bring you food, eat it at your own risk. You can hide it in the trash. Do *not* give it to Dr. Bob!"

Merri interrupted to say, "Yeah, what was wrong with that coffee cake, anyway?"

Lucy said, "I think they used too much baking

powder. Did you know baking powder has aluminum in it? Which is bad because—but I digress. I usually time my morning run so I can find their newspaper—wherever the paperboy hid it—and put in on their porch. Thursday's trash pick-up day, so please take the garbage bags off their back porch and put them with yours in the trash cans by the alley."

Abby nodded her head. "Okay. Got it. But doesn't the city—?"

"I know it doesn't make sense, but they're convinced they're saving money on trash pick-up if they use my cans. And water their flower pots on the porch from time to time. They always forget and get so sad when their petunias die. Whatever you do, don't let them drive! They'll want to go to church on Sunday morning and maybe to Walmart. Oh, and here's a heads up: They'll invite you for Sunday dinner. If you think about it ahead of time I'm sure you can think of some place you need to be. Okay, I think that's all."

Lucy shut the trunk of her car and got behind the wheel. "Any questions?"

"Two," Abby said. "How old are Beulah and Eulah and are you related to them?"

"Eighty-five and no," Lucy said grinning. "I'm just trying to take that 'Love thy neighbor' bit seriously. Good luck! Remember, I pay well," she called as she drove away.

"Wow," Merri said. "I thought we'd be living the easy life here."

When Abby and Merri turned back to the house Eulah and Beulah were carefully descending the porch steps.

"Sorry, but we've got to hurry off too," Beulah said.

"Yes, we're going to bake you one of our famous rhubarb pies. You're going to just love it. Everyone does."

"We can't wait," Abby said.

"Yes we can," Merri said under her breath.

Abby opened the front door and said, "Okay, Merri, let's get started."

"With what? Torturing me with long division?" Merri rolled her eyes. "Or will it be gerunds and participles this time?"

"We'll get to that, kiddo, but first...let's go exploring."

Dr. Bob was their eager tour guide, his toenails clicking like castanets on the gleaming hardwood floor. Abby oohed and ahhed her way through the first floor rooms, afraid she'd break her neck staring at all the details. Tall ceilings, carved woodwork, and sumptuous oriental rugs gave each room the charm of a long past era. And in each room, Lucy's decorating skill was evident in the coordinating upholstery and polished wood pieces.

"How old do you think this house is?" Merri said.

"I wish I'd thought to ask Lucy. I don't think it's as old as your house."

The first room they came to on the second floor was obviously Lucy's bedroom. The bed was covered with a lush crazy quilt in rich chocolate brown and shades of tan, green, and red. Across the hall, the lavender and green rooms Lucy had prepared for them were just as lavishly decorated.

Between the two bedrooms was a tiny sitting room. "This will be our schoolroom away from home," Abby declared with a satisfied smile.

"Let's call this house our resort away from home and take a vacation from school work."

Abby laughed. "I'll go easy on you this week."

A thumping noise came from the stairs and a voice called, "Man on floor! Man on floor!"

"Come on up. We're decent," Abby said.

John arrived carrying every one of their suitcases and

bags. "Where do you want these?"

"Thank you. Just put them down anywhere." Abby said.

"That sure was thoughtful, John," Merri said, grinning at Abby. She mouthed the word *star* when he wasn't looking.

Abby gave Merri a little shove and smiled brightly at John. "Come on. You can join our house tour."

They looked briefly into the bathroom, which was huge and had an authentic claw-foot tub, and then Abby opened the door of the last room. "I think we've reached the frontier of Lucy's remodeling." Faded wallpaper hung in loose strips, the woodwork hadn't been painted in about a million years, and the wood floor was scarred and dull.

"She must be planning to do this room soon," John said, indicating the ladder, paint cans, and other supplies that stood waiting on a drop cloth. He went to look at a walnut cabinet that was built into one wall. The double doors had stained glass panes and little brass knobs in the shape of peacocks.

"What a cute thing," Abby said. "I've never seen a cabinet like this before."

The hinges screeched painfully when John opened the doors. "The whole thing's loose and hanging off kilter."

John took out a small stack of old newspapers and rags that Lucy had temporarily stored there and set them on the floor. Then he stuck his head into the cabinet and said, "The bottom is falling out of it too. I'll bring some tools over and fix it before Lucy gets back."

When they got to the third floor they saw that it was more of a garret. No doubt, servants had once slept in the dim, low-ceilinged rooms. Lucy was using it as a catch-all for boxes of Christmas ornaments, a few pieces of ugly furniture, and some plastic bags labeled "Goodwill."

Everything was in shades of dingy gray until they came to what looked like a hall closet. Its door was glossy white with a shiny new doorknob that just begged to be opened. Abby obliged, and morning light streamed down from above, gilding a steep staircase that rose to meet it.

"It goes to the widow's walk, I bet," Abby said. "I've always wanted to see one."

"Let me go first and make sure it's safe," John said.

"Don't be ridiculous," Abby said. Then she thought of John behind her watching her rear end and said, "On second thought, be my guest."

John nimbly climbed the steep stairs and disappeared from view. "It's good," he called down. "Come on up."

Abby climbed the steps with Merri gamely following. "Are you all right, Merri?"

"Hey, it's better than the barn. At least this has a rail to hold onto."

John held the little door at the top open and Abby stepped out onto a walkway that circled the house's main chimney, the whole thing enclosed by a chest-high iron fence.

"Oh, wow! Merri, come look. You can see the Mississippi from here."

"Sometimes we watch fireworks here on the Fourth of July," John said.

He helped Merri out onto the ledge and they stood at the rail, the wind in their hair and the sun on their faces, gazing at the world that lay before them.

Abby lay on the bed in the green room letting Kate give her more long-distance advice on her love life.

"It's about time you got a real boyfriend," Kate said,

"instead of that Neanderthal you dated last time."

"John and I are just friends."

"Right."

"I'm telling you, he doesn't qualify."

"How many stars does the poor guy have to get? Try harder. I'm hoping for a double wedding."

"I hate to be the one to point this out, Kate, but Ryan hasn't proposed to you."

"It's only a matter of time. By the way, did I tell you I'm giving *him* another star? He was so brave when he—"

"You may have mentioned it a few times," Abby said.

Merri appeared at the door, holding the grammar worksheets Abby had given her to do. Abby waved her in. "Hey, Kate," she said. "I've got to go. It's tutor time."

"Have fun. But, Abby?"

"Yes?"

"Don't get carried away playing house with John, you know?"

"Don't worry. Merri's a great chaperone." Abby grinned at Merri, and she grinned back. "And besides, I'm telling you, John doesn't think of me that way."

Abby flipped her phone shut and rose from the bed. "That was fast, kiddo. Let's see how you did."

Abby checked Merri's work and found she had completed everything accurately. "That's great. Now let's see how you're coming along with your multiplication and division."

"Hey, I know them backwards and forwards now."

"Hah! Well, we'll just see, won't we?" Abby said in her best heartless tutor voice. But when she drilled her with math flash cards she found that Merri really had learned them. And she was faster and more accurate than ever on long division, too. But then, stress and emotional trauma had been the cause of Merri's school problems and dropping grades—not a lack of intelligence. Merri was the smartest 11-year-old Abby had ever known.

"Math may soon be your new favorite subject," Abby said.

Merri grimaced. "I don't care how good I get at it, math will never be my favorite subject. Can we take a break now?"

"Yes, it's time. Let's go fix lunch before John dies of starvation."

Even though July was fast approaching, Lucy's backyard was still lush and appealing, and the adorable gazebo she'd tucked in among purple salvia and Shasta daisies was the perfect place for a picnic. John was already sitting in its shade, his back to her, when she and Merri arrived with a tray of sandwiches and drinks. "John, I come bearing food." Abby set the tray on the cedar table and then reached over and pulled the plugs from his ears.

He jumped in alarm and let out a shout. "Oh, Abby, you scared the crap out of me!"

"I thought he was going to fall out of his chair," Merri said, giggling.

Abby laughed unrepentantly. She heard faint strains of something loud and obnoxious until he turned off his iPod. "Well, aren't you the lazy one, sitting here in the shade listening to tunes."

"Hey, I've been working. I got the mower blades sharpened, and then I had to go down to the station to get gas for it. I was just resting here because I was too weak from hunger to do anything more." He grabbed a sandwich from the tray. "This looks great."

Abby poured lemonade into plastic cups. "Two

women in Merry Maids uniforms have taken over the house and are cleaning like crazy in there. We figured it was a good day for a picnic anyway."

"It's a nice house and all," John said around a bite of sandwich, "but I wouldn't want one I'd have to have a cleaning service for."

"Hey, maybe you'll have a wife who happens to love polishing tons of Victorian doo-dads." Her stomach flipped over in a funny way when she looked at John sitting across the table from her. It did feel a little like they were playing house together. There was something so domestic—so intimate—about preparing a meal for a man, even sandwiches, that she blushed and looked away from his laughing blue eyes.

But then Merri spoke and the moment passed.

"Look, John, I just reached level six!" Merri said from the plush camel-back sofa in Lucy's family room.

Abby looked up from her game of solitaire. She was sitting at an antique desk in the bay window using Lucy's computer. The lamps cast a warm glow over the vintage wallpaper and antique furniture. If it weren't for the computer and Merri's phone (on which she was playing *Angry Birds*) Abby could imagine they had somehow been transported to the 1800s.

"Oh, and now I'm getting a text from Mom."

"What did she say?"

"She said Dad's *for sure* coming to see me this weekend. Like that's going to happen."

John sat on the floor next to the sofa scratching Dr. Bob's ears. "I bet he'll come this time."

Abby made a face. "John, what is that nasty thing in

his mouth?"

"A hedgehog, obviously." John pulled the tattered toy from the dog's mouth and held it up for her to see. "Everyone knows dogs love hedgehogs." John threw it up into the air and the dog, yipping joyfully, bounced up to catch it. "Good job, Dr. Bob. Here, boy, let's try a new trick." John stretched out on the floor next to the dog. "Now watch closely," he said, rolling across the rug. "See, it's easy." The dog, still clutching the hedgehog in his mouth, cocked his head in puzzlement.

Merri laughed. "Maybe instead of a lawyer, you could become a dog whisperer."

The dog dropped his toy and licked John's nose. Laughing, John turned his face away. "Thanks, Dr. Bob. I like you too. Only don't expect me to lick your nose in return. And no offense, buddy, but *Bob* is such a dorky name. If I had a dog like you, I'd pick a better one. How about Frank? Or maybe Norman?"

"And that's not dorky?" Abby said.

"Hey, Norman is a distinguished name."

"Why don't dogs have last names?" Merri said.

"Who says they don't?" John said. "Well, Norman, give it up. What's your last name? Smith? Jones? No, I know!" He barked out a laugh. "*Conquest.* Norman Conquest."

"What's so funny about that?" Merri asked.

Abby chuckled. "Hmm. He doesn't look like the kind of dog that would have a French accent."

"Then how about Warren Peace?" John said.

"Or Sarah Bellum," Abby said.

"He *is* very smart. But that's a girl's name, silly."

"For Pete's sake. You're both—"

John and Abby laughed. "Good one, Merri," he said.

"What did I say?"

"Pete…Sake," Abby said. "Pete Sake. Get it? And *War and Peace*—it's a famous Russian novel and—"

"Oh," she said, grinning. "I get it."

"Hey, Abby," John said. "Aren't you getting tired of solitaire?" He went to stand behind her and pointed to the screen. "Black six on the red seven."

"That is so annoying. I was just getting ready to—"

"And red queen on black king. Could you please hurry? I want to check *Facebook*."

"Hey, I'm busy here."

"All right. Be that way. If you're going to hog Lucy's computer I'll just have to go get my laptop."

"You're leaving?"

"I'll be right back. It's out in my car."

Merri followed him to the front door. "Hey, John, I've got a new one. What if Dr. Bob was Chinese?"

Abby didn't hear what John said. But then Merri giggled and said, "Rick Shaw."

When John got back to the family room, he took his phone out of his pocket. "I've got one. What if Dr. Bob was Irish?"

"Hmmm."

"You think about it while I call Lucy. I've got to get her wireless password."

John didn't talk long, but whatever Lucy said made him laugh. When he closed his phone he said, "Do you give up, Merri?"

"Yeah. Tell me," she demanded.

"Angie O'Plasty."

"I don't get that one."

"It's a medical procedure," Abby said absently.

"Okay, still Irish, but try *Patty*, instead."

"That's a girl's name," Merri said.

"Could be for Patrick." He waited. "Give up?"

"No, no, wait! Patty O'Furniture!" Merri fell back laughing and Dr. Bob celebrated by covering her face in dog kisses.

"Now," John said. "If I can get past all these houses."

"What do you mean?" Merri said.

"Your *Beautiful Houses* program. It popped up on the screen as soon as I booted up. Maybe it has a virus…maybe it *is* a virus. And what's with the weird blue light?"

Abby spun her chair around to stare first at John's glowing laptop and then at Merri.

"It's doing it again. Like it wants us to…" Merri said.

"It? What it?" John said.

"What if it wants to work here?" Merri continued, ignoring John. "I mean, surely this old house has soul, doesn't it?"

Merri pushed John's hands away from the keyboard and clicked on the screen. "Oh, wow! Abby, come see!"

CHAPTER 5

A classic Victorian house filled the screen. The three-story home was painted a soft buttery yellow and dripped with white gingerbread trim.

"Now, John, you'll see what we were trying to tell you," Abby said.

"But that's not your Miles Station house," John said.

"No, it's *this* one."

"It looks like this house, amazingly like this house, actually," he said staring at the screen. "But there must be a lot of old Victorian houses—"

"It's amazing, John," Abby said, "because it *is* this house. For some reason the program is working here, even though it no longer works in Merri's house."

"What are the odds that this house would show up on the Internet? Lucy never said a word—"

"No, that's what I thought at first about the Miles Station house—maybe an online magazine or even a movie set, something like that. But it wasn't any of those things.

And this isn't either."

She pointed to the screen. "See? We're not in the present time." At the left corner of the screen the rear wheel of a vehicle showed. It was definitely not that of a car or truck. "Here, watch," she said. She clicked on the button that allowed her to zoom out. The wheel was attached to a black buggy which was hitched to a pair of roan horses. Abby activated the sound feature and they could hear them blowing and snorting, their iron-shod hooves clattering on the brick-paved street as they shifted in their harnesses.

Abby showed him how the various control features of the program were activated, and John's face lit up like a boy with a new toy. Abby rotated the house on its axis, and they saw the back of the house and its flower-filled garden. Then Abby clicked on *Interior View*, and they entered the house and began touring the rooms. Although the furniture was different, John admitted it matched Lucy's house, room for room.

When they entered the parlor, a young woman in a bell-shaped blue skirt stood humming at the window. She was very beautiful, her blond hair a glowing halo of curls that framed her heart-shaped face. She went to a settee similar to Lucy's and sat and began to thumb through a book.

John gasped. "It's so realistic. I can hear the pages turning."

"With Charlotte, we thought maybe we had tapped into some strange reality show."

"You thought that," Merri said smugly. "I always knew it was Charlotte."

"It's just a computer program," John said.

Abby and Merri just smiled.

"I wonder what year this is supposed to be?" John

asked.

Abby pointed to the indicator at the top of the screen. "It's 1897."

Abby adjusted the perspective until they were in the kitchen and they watched for a while as a plump older woman in a shapeless dress and apron peeled apples at a chopping block in the center of the room. They followed her as she took a stack of plates to the dining room.

"Let's fast forward," Abby said.

"You can do that?" John said.

"Sure. We're running at real time, but we can speed up."

She clicked on the time control on the menu bar and the plump woman began to race back and forth and then was suddenly gone, replaced by other people coming and going. The windows filled with light, then darkness, then light again in dizzying repetition. Abby increased the speed until the images and sounds were an incomprehensible blur as the years raced by.

"Sweet. It's like multimedia modern art," John said.

After a while, Abby slowed the action to real time and they saw people at a table set with china, crystal goblets and serving dishes heaped with food. Men wearing wool suits with wide ties and women in calf-length dresses were laughing and talking all at once. A smiling young woman came through the kitchen doorway carrying yet another huge dish. Someone cleared a spot for her so she could set it on the table.

"We all know how much you like mashed potatoes, Carl," the woman said.

A young man wearing a crew cut and Air Force fatigues smiled widely. "That ought to be enough to last me a while. Thanks, Boo, this is all swell."

She went back to the kitchen and returned carrying a

china tureen. "And gravy to go with it." She removed her apron of pink and blue flowers and, draping it neatly over the back of her chair, sat down with a contented sigh.

An elderly man at the head of the table smiled gravely. "It will be the best food you've had in a year, I'll wager."

And then the smiling woman came out of the kitchen again, this time carrying a platter piled high with fried chicken. "You don't want to know how many ration coupons this took!" She took off her apron and sat down at the young man's right side.

He leaned over and kissed her cheek. "It's good to be home, Yoo."

She blushed and turned away with an embarrassed smile. "Father, will you say grace?"

"Wait a minute. Stop," John said. "What just happened here?"

Abby quickly paused the action. "What do you mean?"

He pointed to the frozen scene on the monitor. "It's the same woman. She came out with the gravy and sat down. Then she came out with the chicken and sat by that military guy. There must be a glitch in the program. Maybe we still have file corruption."

Abby frowned and looked closely at the screen. "Oh, it's not a glitch," she said. "Look, it's the Old Dears."

Merri leaned forward and studied the monitor, and then laughing, said, "It is."

Frowning, John looked closely at the monitor. "That's crazy. This is just a computer program. It can't be them."

"See the resemblance? Just project forward fifty to sixty years," Abby said. "That's definitely Beulah and Eulah."

"Boo and Yoo," Merri said. "Get it?"

"That's insane! No one could make a program that could—"

"We don't know what this is or where it came from. All I know is that it's awesome," Abby said. "And we really are seeing Beulah and Eulah back in the forties—you got the bit about food rationing, didn't you? And if you think that's wild, just wait until you see what happens when we lock onto one of them and go virtual mode."

"Virtual mode? Show me."

Abby smiled smugly and turned back to the controls. "Okay, John. Hold onto your hat."

First, there was a confusing blur of color and whirring sounds and then…

Beulah walked unerringly through her sister's dark music room and sat down at the baby grand piano that had belonged to their grandmother. When she switched on the lamp, she and the keyboard became an island of light in the dimness, and she imagined, with a brief smile, that she was on the stage at Carnegie Hall, wearing, instead of her pleated skirt, an elegant black dress. She decided to play *Fur Elise* because her hands knew all the moves so well that she could dream for a while.

Her twin Eulah had inherited the piano, along with the other furnishings and the yellow house itself, but she always told her to come over anytime she wanted to play it. She loved Eulah dearly and didn't begrudge her her husband, house, or piano. After all, she herself would someday inherit the blue house. Twin houses for twin girls. And Eulah was lonely too, what with her husband Carl away fighting. He had written in his last letter that he wouldn't get leave to come home again until January.

She didn't linger long on the fanciful idea of playing onstage, moving instead on to her favorite daydream, one that should have been much more attainable. In this dream, she played the piano in her own house, and her own husband was just in the next room. He would be reading the newspaper or perhaps listening to the radio for news of the war. It was easier to sustain the dream when she had the house all to herself, as she did tonight. Eulah was out with some of their friends attending a lecture by members of the Madison County Garden Club on how to plant a Victory Garden. Eulah was sure to come home all fired up about putting her backyard to patriotic use. She, however, would go back to their parents' house next door where she had no say-so over the backyard or anything else.

Of course, she loved her parents, and got along with them just fine too. But when she thought about having to live with them forever she got a little panicky feeling in her stomach. Everyone had assumed she would marry too and there *had* been boys, after her father had decided she and Eulah were old enough to receive callers. But none of them worked out, for one reason or another. Now, almost all the men of marrying age were gone, off fighting in the War. All gone and she was twenty and had never been kissed.

She heard the front door shut, and then her sister's husband was standing motionless in the dimness, holding his duffel bag.

"You look so beautiful in the light," he said almost reverently. "Don't stop playing."

"Carl, you're home. We thought—"

"I only found out two days ago. I wanted to surprise you." He dropped the duffel where he stood, and taking off his cap, started eagerly toward her. That was when Beulah realized his mistake. She stood quickly, shoving the piano bench away. There would have been enough time while he walked from the doorway to the piano for her to say "Welcome home, Carl. Eulah will be here soon," but the words somehow didn't come out. She could have stayed in the light so that he could see her more clearly, but somehow she found herself walking toward him into the darkness. In three steps it was forever too late to correct the error, because then she had allowed him to take her into his arms and rain kisses over her brow and cheeks. She closed her eyes and inhaled his scent, savored the feel of having a masculine body crushed to hers. And pretended. A part of her brain knew that there would be a steep penalty to pay when he realized his error, but another louder voice said, take the kiss while you can.

Abby paused the lives unfolding on the computer monitor and said, "I think we had better stop there." She turned to gauge the others' reactions.

"Dang!" John said. His cheeks were stained red. "That was beyond realistic—whatever it was we just did."

"We call it time-surfing. Cool, huh?" Abby said, grinning. She felt a bit virtuous for not blurting out *I told you so*.

"I've got to tell Lucy," John said. "She'll love this."

"I wouldn't count on it," Abby said drily. "Everyone we tried to tell thought we had gone bonkers, including you, if I remember correctly."

"I'm sorry I didn't believe you, Abby. Wow! That was crazy. I was in Beulah's head. I knew everything she was thinking and feeling."

"It's like being there," Abby said, "except she can't see or hear us." She pushed back from the laptop and stood. "But that was just wrong—on so many levels."

"Yeah," John said, "Who knew that the sweet little

ladies next door had a threesome going on?"

"There's that, but I'm talking about us," Abby said. "I feel like a nasty peeping tom. Maybe we shouldn't be time-surfing."

"Oh, no you don't," John said. "You've been talking my ear off about how cool it is, and now that the program's finally working, I want to try it out."

"Just because we can, doesn't mean we should," Abby said. "Eulah and Beulah—no matter what happened sixty years ago— deserve their privacy."

"It was different with Charlotte," Merri added. "We didn't *know* her, at least at first."

"But just think of the educational value," John said. "We could find out what it was really like in the olden days. Think of the details you could give to your students, Abby. You could make history really come alive for them instead of the boring drivel most history teachers dole out."

"Of course, I'd love all that," Abby said. "But I keep thinking about Beulah. I'm sure she would have been horrified to know people were watching what she did."

"I hadn't thought of that," John said. "Can you imagine what would happen if the wrong person got a hold of this software? No one would ever have privacy."

Nobody said anything for a full minute. And then Merri broke the silence. "But it's like it wants us to do it…to find out stuff."

Abby thought about the persistent blue light that for a while had awakened her every night at Merri's house. Not that a program was capable of thinking, but still it was weird.

"We could set rules," John said. "Number one is we don't tell anyone about this. We can't let this get out."

"Well, all right," Abby said hesitantly, "Maybe we could time-surf, but not in this house."

"Okay," John said. "I can live with that. There will be plenty of other places we can explore."

"And we have to agree not to go in bedrooms or bathrooms," Abby said.

"And I think another rule should be no surfing unless we're all together," Merri said.

"I agree," John said. "That will be a good way to see that we stay on the straight and narrow. Anything else?"

"Obviously," Abby said, "we don't mention to the Old Dears what we saw."

"Agreed," John said.

Abby grinned. "I feel like we should put our swords together and say *all for one and one for all.*" When she saw the question on Merri's face she added, "You know...the Three Musketeers."

They heard a muffled bark. Dr. Bob stood in the doorway, holding the corner of his green blanket in his mouth. He dropped the blanket and barked again.

John laughed. "Do you think he's hinting? It is getting late and I've got to be going. We start that rehab at six."

"A.M.?" Merri said in horror.

"A.M." John said grimly as he closed down his laptop.

Abby followed him out onto the front porch. Merri, thankfully, did not tag along this time.

But John didn't stop, as she had hoped he would, just rushed on down the steps to the sidewalk. He paused to look up at her. "Thanks, Abby," he said softly. "I'll come by after work tomorrow, if that's okay." Before she could answer, he turned away and hurried to his car.

Abby mentally scratched her head. "You'd think he was Cinderella and the clock was striking midnight."

Abby lay on her bed staring up at the dark ceiling.

"Abby," Merri called from the next room. "Are you asleep?"

"No. Are you?"

Merri giggled. "What are you thinking about?"

"I was just wishing Kate were here." Merri didn't say anything and Abby quickly added, "Not that we need any more Musketeers around here."

Merri giggled again.

"But she's good at figuring out guys. What are you thinking about?"

"Charlotte. I wish we could have really gone back in time and met her."

"I know. But maybe it's a good thing it doesn't work that way. Can you imagine how weirded out we'd be if someone from the future dropped in on us?"

"What if someone is watching us right now?"

"Actually, Someone is watching over us right now, so go to sleep, kiddo."

Merri mumbled something and then Abby heard her soft snores.

CHAPTER 6

Abby could hear the doorbell echoing far into the house. "Remember, we're not going to mention what we saw last night. We're here to help with their project, whatever it is, not to pry into their lives. Maybe we should wait for John to get here."

"Hey, we only agreed not to time-surf without him," Merri said. "No reason we can't ask a few questions."

"Well, maybe, if we're subtle about it."

Merri pressed her nose to Beulah and Eulah's front door window.

"Stop that, Merri. It's rude."

Merri had been so anxious to start grilling the old ladies that Abby had been hard pressed to get her to eat her breakfast—much less work on her report.

Merri still hadn't picked a topic. Abby suggested the Civil War, Abraham Lincoln, or the Underground Railroad, because Merri was so interested in what had happened in Miles Station.

"I can't think about that right now. I want to research the Old Dears. Sorry. You'll have to forgive me, right? Remember seventy times seven?" Abby had laughed and totally given up on getting Merri to sit still long enough for any lessons.

Merri raised her hand to ring the doorbell again.

"Wait. I think I hear someone coming." Abby wasn't sure which twin opened the door until she smiled and then it was quite obvious. For a moment, in spite of the white hair and faded complexion, the softly sagging flesh, she could see in her twinkling brown eyes the twenty-year-old Beulah who had kissed her sister's husband. But then the 85-year-old Beulah was back, wearing peach-colored pants and a matching top decorated with beaded purple flowers, and it was difficult to imagine her as a femme fatale.

"Oh, goody," Beulah said. "You've come to help us."

"Did Miss Eulah used to live in Lucy's house?" Merri said.

That was *so* not Abby's idea of subtle. She put a hand on Merri's shoulder and said, "Let's say *hi* first, kiddo."

"Oh, sorry. Hi."

"Good morning. You're very merry, Miss Merri."

Smiling, Abby handed Beulah her newspaper. "It was under the porch."

Beulah pulled the door open and stepped back to allow them to enter. "Thank you, Abby. That was so sweet of you to get it for us. Come in and let's get comfy. Eulah's in the dining room." She smiled at Merri and said, "Yes, dear. Eulah and Carl lived in the yellow house after they got married. Then when he passed on she sold it to Lovely Lucy and moved in with me."

Merri flashed a grin at Abby and mouthed, "We were right."

"That's cool," Abby said. "Twin houses for twin

ladies."

"Oh, they're much older even than us. Father said his grandfather built the houses— the blue one for himself and the yellow one for his widowed mother."

"And were you nicknamed Boo and Yoo?" Merri said.

"Well, Carl called us that, but Eulah didn't like it." Beulah grinned. "When I call her that she gets so mad."

Abby tried to think of what she would say when Beulah asked her how they had acquired that information. But Beulah didn't ask. She just began a slow shuffle down the hall, and they adjusted their stride and followed her. Abby didn't mind. It gave her time to gawk at the rooms they passed. The blue house was indeed a twin to the yellow one, in structure anyway. Unlike Lucy's, however, it had not been renovated, at least not since the 1940s. The wallpaper, curtains, and furniture appeared nearly identical to those they had seen when time-surfing in the yellow house the night before.

"I'm so glad you're here," Beulah said. "We've got a problem with our apples. Well, not with the Smith apples. We've got plenty of them, all shiny and red."

"I thought that kind was green," Merri said.

Beulah continued down the hall, her sturdy beige lace-ups squeaking with each step. "Although Eulah says everyone has some rotten apples." She turned to look back at them apologetically. "Of course I'm sure neither of you have rotten apples."

Abby looked at Merri and saw mirrored on her face the same confusion she felt. "No, they look pretty good," Abby said uncertainly. "I'm sure Lucy wouldn't mind if you wanted to borrow some. Are you going to make another pie?"

They heard a cackle of laughter from the dining room ahead of them. "Beulah, they don't understand what you're yammering about."

Beulah pulled an embroidered hanky from her pocket and held it to her mouth to muffle a laugh. "Oh no, honey," she said kindly to Abby. "Not that kind of apples."

By then they had reached the dining room, where Eulah, wearing an outfit identical to Beulah's, was sitting at a large mahogany table. Its surface, protected with old newspapers, was cluttered with oddly shaped wooden pieces, a glue gun, paint brushes, and bottles of craft paints.

"It's our project. Come see."

In front of Eulah was a large framed mosaic of wooden shapes arranged to form a tree design on a background of blue sky and green grass. Little round wooden pieces painted red to look like apples were attached to the branches on the right side of the tree. Other apples lay in an organized fashion beside the frame.

"Lucy ordered this kit for us on the World Wide Web," Beulah said.

"Have you ever been on it? The World Wide Web?" Eulah asked.

"Why, yes, Miss Eulah, we have," Abby said sincerely.

"Is it a puzzle?" Merri asked.

"In a way it is," Beulah said. "That's where we're hoping you can help."

"It's a family tree, isn't it?" Abby said. "See where they've written names on the little apples."

"We got the tree, the apples, and the background finished," Eulah said. "It was easy—just paint by number."

"And we got lots of Smith apples already on the tree," Beulah said. "We know quite a bit about our mother's side."

Eulah pointed to an apple on the tree labeled in silver script, *Ella Mae Smith*. "That's our mother, born in 1900.

And there? That's her parents and their parents."

"It's cute," Merri said.

"Well, it won't be so cute if only the right side has apples," Eulah said. "I keep telling Beulah there's no sense starting on the project since we don't have the names for the Edwards side of the family."

"Yes," Beulah said sadly. "For the Edwards, all we've got is Father—that's him there, Henry Edwards—and his mother Martha Jones Edwards. I'm afraid our family tree will be really lopsided. Father never talked much about his family. Actually, he never talked about much of anything except work. He was an accountant for the Owen's Glassworks here in town."

"But Grandmother Edwards sure talked about *her* family, the Joneses." Eulah smiled at her twin. "Remember how she and Mother used to joke about the Joneses and the Smiths?"

Beulah grinned. "She said they were the *common* people of the family, not so high in the instep as the Edwards. But I've never understood. If the Edwardses were so lofty, why don't we know anything about them?"

"I have memories of Grandmother Edwards, but we never knew our grandfather," Eulah said. "He died before we were born. Grandmother lived in the yellow house until she died. She was a tiny thing, and always cheerful. We used to go to her house every chance we got because she'd give us ice cream cones."

"She liked to tell us about when she ate her first ice cream cone in 1904 at the St. Louis World's Fair."

"Gee, it must have been nice to have grandparents right next door," Merri said wistfully. "Mine are in North Carolina."

"Oh, you poor girl." Beulah put an arm around Merri and held her close. "Well, while you're staying in the yellow house *we'll* be your grandmothers."

Merri smiled. "Thanks, I'd love to have pretend grandmothers close by."

Eulah shook her head. "Beulah, you realize we couldn't both be her grandmother."

Beulah sniffed. "We're only pretending."

Eulah cupped Merri's chin and grinned. "She's had imaginary grandchildren for years. A real pretend one will be much more fun."

"Would you like an ice cream cone, dear?" Beulah said.

"No thanks, Grandma Beulah," Merri said. "Not before lunch anyway."

Abby noticed a picture in an oval walnut frame on the wall behind Eulah. It was a sepia-toned portrait of a mustachioed young man wearing a dark three-piece suit and a young woman in a pale 1920s flapper dress and hat.

"Are those your parents?" Abby said.

"Yes. Weren't they stylish?" Beulah said.

"They were a beautiful couple," Abby said. "I love her dress. Look at all the tucks and stitching on it."

"I still have it," Eulah said. "I wore it when I married Carl."

Abby wasn't like some of her friends who had been obsessing over wedding plans their whole lives—before they even had serious boyfriends. But still, she wondered what style of dress she would choose when the time came and whether her descendants would someday study it in all its antique glory. She smiled at Eulah who was still gazing fondly at the portrait.

"And we still have Father's watch too. You can just make it out in the picture, there in his left hand. He was so proud of that watch."

Beulah went to a built-in walnut display cabinet,

opened its beveled glass door, and took out a pocket watch on its fob. "The fob gets tarnished so quickly. I'll have to get the silver polish and have a go at it."

Merri took the watch from Beulah's outstretched hand and studied it closely.

Beulah went back to the table and lowered herself carefully to her chair. "Anyway, we don't know how to get more Edwards apples for our project.

"Why don't you ask your relatives?" Abby said.

"There's only one—Priscilla Edwards. She's a cousin of sorts," Eulah said. "But we've never been close."

Abby tried to keep the shock she felt off her face. It was difficult to imagine a family so different from her own large extended one. How lonely Christmases and Thanksgivings must be for the twins. "Why don't you go visit Priscilla? Surely she could tell you more about the family."

"I'm not going over to Prissy's house," Beulah said. "She's mean—and she pinches."

"I think it's safe to assume she doesn't pinch any longer," Eulah said. "She was five the last time, as I recall."

"Well, maybe," Beulah said uncertainly. Then she straightened in her chair and said, "I'd be willing to risk it for the cause."

"When Lucy gets back we can ask her to take us."

"There's no need to bother Lovely Lucy," Beulah said. "She'll be so busy when she gets back from her conference. I'm sure we can manage just this one time," she said confidently.

"You know as well as I do we're as blind as bats," Eulah said.

"We can take you," Abby said quickly, suppressing a shudder at the thought of the Old Dears in Alton traffic.

Beulah smiled broadly. "Oh, that would be grand!"

"When do you want to go?" Abby said.

"I'll get the keys," Eulah said. "You can drive our car."

"Shouldn't we call first?" Abby said.

"No," Eulah said firmly. "If we call, she may tell us we can't come over. Priscilla always was an uppity thing."

"This way she'll have to let us in," Beulah said happily.

"Do you remember the address?" Abby said.

"Oh, we'd never forget that," Eulah said. "They named the street in her subdivision after her."

"And the number is 666," Beulah said. "You know—the mark of the beast." The twins looked at each other and giggled and Abby imagined them as mischievous little girls.

The Old Dears' car was an ancient turquoise and white Lincoln Park Avenue in mint condition. It roared to life right away so Abby assumed Lucy must look after it along with all the other things she did for them. It barely fit in their little garage, built for buggies, not cars as big as boats. But she managed to back out without scratching the paint, and then Merri closed and latched the garage doors and climbed into the passenger seat. Abby parked the Lincoln in front, and Eulah and Beulah, with much fussing and two trips back to the house for forgotten handkerchiefs and plastic rain bonnets, because "you can never be too careful," finally settled into the back seat.

"Okay. Where to?" Abby said.

"Go straight," Eulah said. "I'll tell you when to turn."

Feeling child-sized behind the wheel, Abby checked her mirrors and carefully piloted the Lincoln into the street.

On the way, the twins described their experiences with Priscilla's branch of the Edwards family. They had only visited a few times, the last when they were twelve, and only at the instigation of their mother who was trying to be friendly to her husband's relatives. Priscilla wouldn't let them touch her dolls, much less play with them. Priscilla's mother Deloris wouldn't even let them touch the floor. She had commanded the twins to stay on the sofa, so as not to make tracks in the freshly vacuumed rugs.

"As if we were little heathens who planned to run amok in her home," Eulah said with disgust.

Deloris never offered them refreshments and there were never any hugs exchanged at their departure. After the shabby way they were treated, the twins' mother never brought them back, except for Deloris's funeral a few years later, and even then, they didn't stay long.

The family tree project must be very important to them, Abby thought, if they were willing to risk further abuse. She felt a sense of protectiveness welling within herself. If Priscilla insulted Eulah and Beulah today, she'd have to answer to her. Abby hoped she'd be able to think of some really good snappy comebacks to put her in her place.

After their description, she had expected 666 Priscilla Avenue to be an expensive house in an expensive part of town. But what had seemed like an enviable house to Eulah and Beulah when they were twelve was now an aging house in a declining neighborhood.

A pretty and plump young woman in bright pink scrubs answered the door and let them in with only minimal explanations.

"Your timing is perfect," she said with a faint southern drawl. "Miss Edwards is having a good day and she's awake. She doesn't get much company, so I'm sure she'll be so happy to see y'all." The young woman took off energetically and they followed as fast as the twins could manage down a hall and toward what had once been the living room.

"Yes," Eulah said drily, "I'm sure she'll be just thrilled."

"She has a maid! How about that?" Beulah said. "Of course she's very old now—eighty-seven."

"Wow!" Merri said. "That's *really* old." Abby frowned a warning to her.

"That's only two years older than you, Beulah Mae."

"And you, too, Eulah Mae."

Abby didn't get the chance to explain to Beulah that the woman was no maid. She had read her name tag, which indicated her name was Annie and that she was from Angels Hospice Care. Prissy was more than old. She was dying.

The sofa the twins had been confined to had been replaced with a commercial hospital bed to which Priscilla Edwards was now confined.

"Miss Edwards," Annie said cheerfully. "You have company."

Priscilla Edwards didn't answer, although she was awake and her dark eyes in her pale, shrunken face darted to look at each of them. Her mouth began to work like a fish out of water, but no words came out.

"Miss Edwards has been unable to speak since her last stroke," Annie said.

When she lifted her claw-like hand a few inches from the bed, Beulah drew cautiously closer and after a momentary hesitation took it into her own. Eulah drew a little closer too. "Do you know who we are, Priscilla?"

"Ow!" Beulah said and pulled away. "Yes, I think she does. She just pinched me!"

Abby was frustrated that she couldn't think of a single snappy come back. And even if she could, how could you yell at a pitiful old bag of bones like that?

"I guess we waited too long," Eulah said sadly.

Other than the roar of the car's engine, the ride home was quiet. Beside her, Merri stared out the side window, lost in thought. Abby glanced into the rear view mirror and saw that the twins looked uncommonly serious. They had to be thinking about their own mortality after seeing Priscilla's condition. She didn't know what to say. Her own life seemed to stretch out for years in front of her. But theirs had to be closing in on them.

"Was it upsetting, seeing your cousin so sick?" Abby hoped she wasn't making things worse. "With hospice there and all?"

The Old Dears snapped out of their twin reverie. "What? Oh, you mean because she's dying?" Eulah said.

"Well…yes," Abby said cautiously.

"You're a sweet girl, Abby," Beulah said. "We're not afraid of dying, are we, Yoo?"

"Don't call me Yoo. No, we're ready to go whenever the Good Lord wants to take us."

"It's a better world we're going to, that's sure," Beulah added. "But I *would* like to get our project done first."

"Don't be ridiculous, Beulah. You won't be caring about our little project once you're in Heaven."

"It's just that it would be so nice to have the tree done. Maybe have something for people to remember us by."

Merri turned around in her seat and looked at the Old Dears. "I'll remember you, Grandma…er…Grandma*s*, I promise."

It was amazing that Merri had formed such a strong attachment so soon. It was probably because she had so little family. But then that must not be it, because Abby found herself wiping at a tear that was making it difficult to see where she was driving. "Me too," she said.

CHAPTER 7

"I know, Merri, but we all agreed we wouldn't time surf here." Abby turned the key and opened Lucy's front door. A blast of blessed cool air greeted her, beckoning her to enter, but she politely stepped aside and let Merri go first.

"But it would be so easy to find out the Old Dears' Edwards relatives. All we'd have to do is keep going back."

"First of all, I'm not sure it would even work. Remember, this house was built for Mr. Edwards' widowed mother. The Edwards family per se never lived here."

"We could try to—"

Abby held up two fingers. "Second, I for one don't want to be a peeping tom like that nasty creep that was after Charlotte. How would we explain to the Old Dears that we spied on their private lives? Sure, for a good cause—but still." When Merri started to speak, Abby held up a third finger. "And third, TMI. I don't want to ever know that much personal stuff about people I know again. It'll be hard enough every time I see Beulah not to remember—"

"Abby, wait—"

"Merri, I just explained—"

Merri put her finger to her lips and whispered, "No, listen! Do you hear that?"

Abby put her hand down, closed her mouth, and listened. There was a scraping sound coming from upstairs. She grabbed Merri's arm and pulled her back. She tried to think. With an intruder, the first thing to do was call 911. She opened her purse and rummaged for her phone. No wait. What was she thinking? The first thing was to get out of the house. She grabbed for the door knob but it wouldn't turn. She must have locked it. Of course, that was the safe thing to do. But not if an intruder was in your bedroom and might come back downstairs at any minute to see who was making all the noise. She turned the dead bolt, opened the door, and shoved Merri onto the porch. She eased the door closed behind them.

Just before it clicked, she heard a loud thump from upstairs and a familiar voice say, "Oh, crap!"

She threw the door open again and marched in, yelling, "John? Is that you?"

"Yeah." His voice was muffled and he sounded annoyed. "Could you come help me? Please?"

Abby started up the stairs with Merri right behind her. Dr. Bob stood on the landing, grinning at all the excitement. "John, what on earth are you doing? I thought you had to work."

"We got delayed. Some kind of building permit thing. Could you hurry? Please?"

They glanced in Merri's room and then hers. No John. "Where are you?"

"The last frontier."

John was trying to remove the broken cabinet. It was

hanging at a weird angle, half in and half out of the wall.

"I need you to help hold it level while I pull it out of the wall. Hopefully, without breaking the glass doors." He muttered the last under his breath.

Abby lifted the front edge of the cabinet and John pulled. It moved a fraction of an inch.

"Wait," Merri said, peering through the glass doors. "Something's stuck in there."

John shifted his hold on the cabinet so he could look where Merri was pointing. "It looks like a book has fallen down where the back is loose on the cabinet. It must be stuck on a nail or something. Merri, your hand is small. Can you reach in there?"

"I'll try." Merri carefully opened the glass door while Abby and John continued to awkwardly hold the cabinet level.

"Hurry. It's getting heavy." Abby heard a scraping sound, amplified by the walls of the wooden cabinet.

"I've got it!" Merri said.

"Okay, now let's try again." John pulled the cabinet while Abby held it steady, and it slid out into his arms. Then, staggering a little, he set it on the floor and squatted to look at it.

"Can you fix it?" Abby said.

"Sure. It should be easy enough to nail it back together. Maybe a little wood glue too."

"Abby." Merri's voice was odd. "Look at this."

Abby stood and wiped her hands on her shorts. "What is it?"

Merri handed the book to her. "It's a Bible."

Its leather cover was scuffed and worn. There was a deep gouge where it must have been stuck on the nail in the wall. Abby felt a little sick thinking about the disrespectful treatment to which they had unknowingly subjected it.

"Open it," Merri said and then impatiently reached over to do it for her. "There. See?"

John came up behind Abby and read over her shoulder, "Cool!"

"But here's the good part," Merri said, turning the page. "Look."

Abby stared in disbelief. "And just think," she said, darting a look at Merri. "If you hadn't grabbed it when you did, it would have fallen down in the wall and we never would have found it. We've got to go show the Old Dears."

"You two go on. I'm going to stay and work on the cabinet," John said.

With her frail, veiny hands, Eulah reverently opened the Bible. Beulah, her hand an exact match, reached over and, pointing to the beautiful flowing script at the top of the page, read,

This Bible is the treasured possession of Frances Anne Edwards. 'Thy Word giveth light; it giveth understanding unto the simple. Psalm 119:130.'

Eulah licked a finger and then turned the page. The twins gasped in unison. "It's the Edwards family tree!" Beulah said. "Oh, just think of all the apples we'll have now!"

"My lands! I never expected to get this far back. Look at that one—Alexander James Edwards, born 1786 in Virginia. His wife was Charity Anne Wempleton, born

1788."

"Isn't that awesome?" Abby said. "Goes all the way down to Frances Anne Edwards, born 1851."

"The only problem is," Eulah said, looking up from the Bible, "I have no earthly idea who Frances Anne Edwards is. She may not even be from our branch of the family."

"But since this was in the yellow house, doesn't she have to be?" Abby said.

"You're probably right," Beulah said hesitantly. "But how do I know where to put their apples on the family tree?"

Beulah pointed to the page before her. "You can see she married. But, the name in the space where a husband would go has been scratched out."

Merri looked closely at the scratching. "I can see some writing under there, but I can't make it out."

"So it ends with Frances," Eulah said.

"Maybe not. You have a library here in town, right?" Abby said.

"Yes. How many years has it been since we went, Eulah?"

"Most libraries have genealogy departments," Abby said. "We could go do some research and see what we find out about this Frances Anne Edwards. Would you like me to take you there?"

"You bet!" the twins said in unison.

"Do you want to rest before we go?"

"Shoot," Eulah said. "We'll have plenty of time to rest when we're dead."

Abby decided she didn't much like the assistant

librarian in the genealogy department. The discovery came only two minutes after they had entered her domain on the second floor of the Alton Public Library. The first minute had been spent showing her the Old Dears' Bible and explaining the missing links they were looking for, during which time the librarian's gimlet eyes bored into theirs as if they were bothersome bugs she was thinking about stepping on. Then with a deep sigh, and addressing Abby as if Beulah and Eulah weren't there, she had pointed vaguely toward the genealogy department's two computer stations and in a bored voice rattled off a complicated procedure for using them.

When she turned away Merri and Eulah looked at each other and rolled their eyes.

"Oh dear," Beulah said.

"Could you please repeat that?" Abby said.

"Well, if that's too complicated for you, I'll demonstrate. But we'll have to make this quick." The librarian—her name tag said Susan P., Asst. Libr.—sat down at the computer and quickly clicked her way through a series of windows. Then, holding her hands expectantly over the keyboard, she said, "Grandfather's full name and place of birth, please."

"Beulah and Eulah don't know their grandfather's name. As I explained, we're here to find—"

"Then start with their father's name. I presume they know who their father was?"

"Henry Albert Edwards," Eulah said in a clipped voice.

Now even Beulah was frowning daggers at the back of the librarian's head. Abby patted her arm reassuringly. "He was born here in Alton on July 20, 1900."

A genealogical web site popped up. "There, that should keep you busy for a while. I'd start with deeds first, assuming their father was a property owner. Now I really must go. I'm giving a lecture to the Alton chapter of the D.A.R."

"What's a D.A.R.? Merri asked.

"Daughters of the American Revolution, obviously. My great, great, great grandfather fought with Washington at Valley Forge."

Abby worked up a half-hearted smile. "That must be so nice for you."

The librarian blinked in surprise. "Yes it is. I guess that's why I've always had an interest in genealogy."

"Oh, Sue?" Abby said. The librarian frowned and looked down at her brass name badge. "Would your last name be Perior, by any chance?"

"No. It's Paulson. Why?"

"Just wondering."

"Yes, well I've got to go." The expression on her face as she left was possibly supposed to be a smile, but looked more like a painful grimace.

When the librarian was out of sight Merri pulled her sleeve. "What was that all about?"

"Sue. Perior. Superior. Get it?"

Merri giggled. "It would fit her, all right. If only your Bible went back a little further I bet you could be in the D.A.R...whatever it is," she said fiercely to Beulah. She shot a glance at Abby, which she interpreted to mean, "It would be easy enough to time-surf and find this out."

"I don't think I could have taken much more of that dragon lady," Eulah said.

"She sure has a bee in her bonnet," Beulah said. "I was wishing Prissy was here to pinch her."

"Merri, we're going to be a while with this," Abby said. "Why don't you go talk to that nice librarian downstairs? You know, the human one? Maybe she can help you decide on an essay topic."

"Good idea."

Eulah beamed at Abby. "Isn't that World Wide Web amazing?"

Beulah wiped her eyes with her hanky. "I can't believe you found him."

Merri came around the corner carrying a stack of books. "Found who?"

"Albert William Edwards," Eulah said. "Our grandfather at long last."

"We found the transfer of deed," Abby said. "Henry inherited the blue house from his father Albert William Edwards. Now if we can just find a connection to Frances Anne Edwards."

Merri dropped the pile of books on the table next to them.

"Shh," Abby said. "I'd hate to see Dragon Lady when she's mad."

"The library lady downstairs got all excited when I told her you were looking for stuff on the Edwards family. She thinks I should write my essay about them. She said we should find something in these books."

Abby picked up the top one and read the title aloud, "*First Family of Illinois.*"

Merri pulled out a chair and plopped onto it. "It's about Ninian Edwards—personally, I would have changed my name—anyway, he was the first governor of Illinois. Edwardsville, the county seat, was named—"

"Wait a minute," Abby said. "I thought Shadrach Bond was the first governor."

"Where did they come up with these names?" Merri

shook her head in bewilderment. "I don't know. That's what the librarian lady told me. She said the Edwardses were a pretty big deal in Illinois back in the day."

"I'm sure our family is not nearly so illustrious," Eulah said.

"But you never know," Beulah said. "Show us what you've got."

They divided up the books Merri had brought and waded through decades of Illinois history. After a while Merri said, "I'm confused. One book said Ninian Edwards was born in 1775, but this one says 1809." Abby looked up from the book she had been skimming and chuckled. "Apparently Ninian thought his name was so cool he named his son Ninian too. By the way, I was right. Shadrack Bond was the first governor of the *state*. Ninian, Sr. was the governor for the *territory* of Illinois."

Squinting identically, Eulah and Beulah were sharing a thick book. Eulah pointed at the page and turned to her sister. "Did you know that? I didn't know that."

"I sure didn't." Beulah turned the book around for Abby to see.

"I didn't know that either," Abby said.

"What? What?" Merri said. "Show me."

"Another bit of Lincoln trivia, Merri. Ninian Edwards, Jr. was Abraham Lincoln's brother-in-law. Ninian's wife was Mary Todd's sister."

Eulah smiled at Merri. "Maybe you *should* write about ole Ninny."

Stifling a yawn, Abby stood and stretched. "This is interesting, but it's not getting us anywhere with *your* project."

"Well," Beulah said, "we don't know anything more about our particular Edwards family, but it's always good to learn new things."

"Maybe you'd better have a go at this last book, Abby," Eulah said. "The print is too small and too faded for my old eyes."

The book was titled simply *Edwards*. It didn't really qualify as an actual published book, being comprised of old-fashioned purple mimeographed sheets unprofessionally bound with a plastic spiral.

"It looks like some kid's high school project." Abby thumbed through it, but stopped and said, "Well, what do we have here!" She turned the page so the others could see.

"Oh, oh! It's a family tree," Beulah said.

"For Ninian Edwards' whole family," Abby said.

The genealogy chart continued over the last four pages of the book, which made it difficult to follow the various lines of the family. Abby poured over the faded purple ink, running her finger over each name. "See, there's Ninian, Jr. and his wife Elizabeth Todd. And her sister Mary with her husband Abraham Lincoln. Cool."

"Oh, oh!" Merri reached over her shoulder. "There she is. *Frances Anne Edwards*."

"Well how about that?" Abby grinned at Beulah and Eulah. "It won't get you into the D.A.R., but I bet the Dragon Lady will be jealous. You're related to the illustrious Ninian Edwards, first governor of Illinois."

"Are you sure it's the same Frances we know?" Eulah asked.

"Look at the birth date— May 20, 1851—just the same as in your Bible," Merri said.

"And her parents and grandparents are the same," Abby said.

"But what's that written in the margin?" Merri said.

Abby looked closer at the page. "Someone wrote in light pencil *Buchanan* right after the *Edwards*, and then *died in childbirth 1871 Shake Rag Corner*."

"How sad," Beulah said.

"Yes, but just think, *Buchanan* has to be her husband's name," Eulah said. "Now if we can just find out how she fits into the family."

"Why didn't they include *him* in the family tree?" Abby said. "As detailed as this report is, it's hard to believe they didn't know his name."

"And why did Frances scratch it out of her Bible?" Eulah said.

"Curious," Beulah said. "Curious *and* confusing."

"Where's *Shake Rag Corner*?" Abby said.

"I'm not sure," Beulah said.

"It sounds vaguely familiar," Eulah added.

The librarian, the friendly one at the main desk, explained that Shake Rag Corner was once a settlement just south of Alton. "There's nothing left of it now," she said. "But the state built a museum about Lewis and Clark down there because the expedition embarked on their journey near there." She looked eagerly at Merri. "That would be another good topic for your report. The museum has some nice exhibits there." She turned back to Beulah and Eulah. "I don't know that you'd find anything about your Frances Edwards, but if you like history it would be worth a trip out there to see the museum."

Abby turned to the twins. "Are you getting tired?"

"Oh, no. We're having a great adventure," Beulah said. "I feel so footloose and fancy free."

"I love museums," Eulah said. "Only let's get lunch before we go. I'll treat."

"Oh, I'm so sorry," Abby said. "I bet you're starving. It's after 2:00."

"Can we drive through the golden arches?" Beulah said. "And get French fries?"

"Sure we can," Abby said with a smile.

"You realize we won't actually drive through any arches—golden or any other color—don't you?" Eulah said.

"Of course I do." Beulah sniffed. "Don't be such an old grouch. I was speaking metaphorically."

The Lewis & Clark Historic Site was a modern building of concrete and glass, which the brass plaque in front indicated was built in 2005. Abby and her fellow adventurers walked into the museum in time to join a family of vacationers that planned to spend the summer retracing Lewis and Clark's journey to the Pacific Ocean. A short stocky man with white blond hair whose name tag said *Charles Rohst, Director* was explaining that the Corps of Discovery began the journey where the museum now stood.

Abby nudged Merri and leaned over and whispered, "Do you suppose his friends call him Chuck?"

Merri's forehead wrinkled for a minute and then she snorted and covered her mouth. "Chuck Roast," she whispered back.

When Abby could get her mind back on what Mr. Rohst was saying, she learned that during the winter of 1803, they had built Camp Dubois, where Captain Clark had interviewed, enlisted, and trained the men who would travel up the Missouri River and on to the Pacific Ocean at the behest of President Jefferson. Mr. Rohst led them to the observation deck on the upper floor of the museum so they could see the Mississippi River and the convergence of the Missouri River three miles to the north.

"The explorers entered the mouth of the Missouri on May 14, 1804," Mr. Rohst said, "and they labored against its current until they reached the Continental Divide in April of 1805. From that point, they floated down the current on to the Pacific Ocean, which they reached November 16th. They spent the winter there and arrived back at Camp Dubois on September 23, 1806, after a journey of two and a half years and over eight thousand miles."

After they had all marveled at the view for a while and Mr. Rohst had answered numerous questions from the family of tourists, he led them to the lower floor and to the museum's pride and joy: a life-size replica of the explorers' keelboat.

"If there are no further questions," Mr. Rohst said, "please feel free to examine the artifact displays until the film begins in the auditorium. After the film, you will be directed to the exit that will take you to our replica of Camp Dubois behind the building. Our costumed re-enactors will be happy to tell you about the explorers and answer any questions you have. Thank you for your attention."

After thanking Mr. Rohst, the parents herded their five children away from the keelboat to a chorus of "I gotta go pee," and "let's go get a Coke," and "I want to go to the souvenir shop," and "I'm hungry," and one plaintive "can we leave now?"

"Wasn't that fascinating?" Beulah said.

"Maybe I *will* write about Lewis and Clark," Merri said.

Abby and the twins approached the museum director while Merri drifted away to examine the museum's displays.

"Hello. Thanks for joining us." Mr. Rohst smiled

warmly. "Is there anything I can help you ladies with?"

"Oh, I hope so," Beulah said. "It's about our apple tree. You see—"

He looked confused. "I'm not sure. . ."

"Don't mind my silly sister," Eulah said. "It's about Frances Ann."

He looked from one sister to the other. "What exactly...?"

"We're doing research on the ladies' family tree," Abby explained. "And we were told there was a settlement called Shake Rag Corner near here."

Mr. Rohst's face brightened. "Oh, yes, that's right. But I'm afraid I don't know much about it." He removed his glasses and began to polish them with a handkerchief he had pulled from the pocket of his navy suit. "My studies have been focused almost entirely on the Lewis and Clark Expedition. That is, their time spent in the Illinois country."

"Anything you could tell us would be helpful," Abby said. "We found a clue in the library just now that said a relative of the ladies named Frances Ann Edwards apparently lived—well, died at least—in Shake Rag Corner in 1871."

"Do you mean the village or the inn?"

"I don't understand," Abby said.

"Well, you see, the whole area came to be known as Shake Rag Corner, but the name originally belonged to a house that served as a stage coach stop here. No doubt you saw the old derelict building across the street when you drove into our parking lot."

"Yes," Eulah said. "We noticed that when we got out of the car." She stopped and frowned at her sister. "What on earth are you looking for, Beulah?"

Beulah was rummaging in her pocketbook but then

smiled triumphantly as she pulled out a roll of Lifesavers and politely offered them to the others.

"Thanks," Abby said.

"You got a lucky green one," Beulah said.

"No, thank you, ma'am," Mr. Rohst said. "Anyway, as I was saying, it's nothing but an eyesore now, but at one time Shake Rag Corner was a lovely stage coach inn. If a customer wanted to board the stagecoach, someone in the house would lean out a window and shake a bright rag so the driver would know to stop to pick them up."

"I've always wished I could see what life was like in the olden days," Eulah said. "Not that I'd want to actually live back then."

"Well, if you ladies will step right this way, I can show you a picture of the house in its heyday." Mr. Rohst led them to his office. The wall behind his desk was nearly covered with framed photographs. Some were contemporary photos chronicling the construction of the museum. But others were faded old photos of buildings and people. "That one," he said, "is the old house that used to stand on this site." Beside it was a picture of bulldozers at work. "They just shoved all the rubble into the basement and built the museum on top. But here's the one you're interested in." He took down a faded sepia photograph of a two-story house. On the porch, which extended the whole front, wooden barrels overflowed with flowers and a pair of rockers flanked the door. A stagecoach and team were parked to the left. People with luggage waited on the porch, presumably to get on the coach.

"How charming," Beulah said.

"Do you know the date of the photo?" Abby said.

"Not precisely. But I would estimate it to be from the late 1860s—after photography became popular, but before the railroads replaced stage coaches in the early 1870s."

"The time would be right for our Frances Anne," Eulah said. "It's a beautiful house."

"Yes, too bad she's so decrepit now," he said.

Abby thought at first he was referring to Frances Edwards, but then smiled inwardly when she realized Mr. Rohst was talking about the house. Thinking of it as a living person rather than a building didn't seem all that strange after their experiences with Colonel Miles' house.

He removed the photo from the frame. "Wait right here."

He was soon back with a photocopy of Shake Rag Corner, which he handed to Eulah and Beulah.

"You're so kind." Their words came out in unison and made him chuckle.

When they returned to the museum display area he said, "Sorry I can't help you more."

"That's all right, Mr. Rohst." Abby gestured toward Merri who was peering at an enlargement of one of Lewis' botanical drawings. "Besides genealogical research, I'm also helping another friend doing historical research for a report. Looks like she may have found a good topic."

Abby and the twins joined Merri and they spent nearly an hour viewing the exhibits. Eulah suggested Merri write about the plants and animals Lewis and Clark discovered on the trip.

"Maybe," Merri said.

"Or how about the Indians?" Beulah said. "I never realized how many different tribes there were."

"Maybe."

They all marveled at the dedication and perseverance it took for the men to successfully complete the mission President Jefferson had set for them. Finally, the twins admitted they were getting tired. Mr. Rohst himself held the door for them as they stepped out onto the sidewalk.

He pointed across the parking lot and said, "It's such a shame you have to see that on your way out of the museum."

What had once been the charming Shake Rag Corner stagecoach stop was now only a sad sagging house, its roof caving in and its windows broken out in past run-ins with either vandals or bad weather.

"If only the walls could talk, think of the history of such an old house," Mr. Rohst said.

"Yes, I know what you mean." Abby turned and caught Merri's secretive smile. "Too bad no one has kept it up. It's so ugly."

"Well, nothing like the picture anyway," Beulah said.

He took his glasses off and began polishing them again. "Imagine it with a larger porch and without the nasty beige siding. Someone put that on in the '80s. It totally destroyed the vintage character of the house."

"You would think they'd either do something with the property or tear it down," Eulah said.

"The city's been trying for three years to acquire the property, but got nowhere. Mr. Buchanan is one stubborn Scot."

They all turned to stare at him. "You mean a Buchanan owns that house?" Abby said. "How can we get in touch with him?"

"I have no idea," he said. "Of course he obviously doesn't live there now."

Abby glanced in the rearview mirror. The Old Dears were arguing about one of Clark's journal entries.

"It said *bars*," Beulah insisted.

"They didn't spell the way we do today. I'm sure they didn't eat *bars*."

"You can think what you want." Beulah let out a loud huff. "And I'll think what I want."

"I think somebody needs a nap," Abby whispered to Merri. "This is probably more than they've done in years."

"Let's call John," Merri said. "He could bring his laptop and we could time-surf in Shake Rag Corner. I bet we could find out more about Frances."

"I was just thinking the same thing. But even if the program works here, and we don't know that it will—"

"Why not? It worked in Lucy's house."

"But Shake Rag Corner is abandoned. There's no electricity, much less Internet connection there. Besides, we can't just walk into somebody's house—even if they don't live there anymore."

"So that's it then?" Merri said. "We can't find Frances?"

The silence stretched out inside the Lincoln until they were almost home. Then Abby said, "I think I have an idea."

CHAPTER 8

Is Mr. Rohst still out there?" Abby whispered.

John took another quick look around the display of 19th century weaponry they were standing behind. "Coast is clear. Ol' Chuck just went into his office."

"Why don't we just ask him?" Merri said.

"Some people get all cranky about letting you hitch a ride on their Internet service," John said.

"Come on. Let's go." Abby led John down the hall to the museum's theatre. "In here. The sign said the next showing for their documentary film is tomorrow morning, so we should be okay."

John sat down and turned on his laptop. "This is a long shot, you know."

Abby sat down next to him and watched the program boot up. "I know, John, but think about it. We may still be able to get vibes from the old house that once stood here, because the basement of the house is still here, below the museum. Mr. Rohst said they bulldozed everything into it and built the museum over it."

"So assuming the house was here in 1871…" John began.

"Then we can use the controls to see across the street to Shake Rag Corner and find Frances," Merri said.

"That is, if Frances actually lived there," John said. "Like I said, it's a long shot."

"Well it won't hurt to try," Abby said.

The *Beautiful Houses* logo flashed on the screen and then disappeared followed by a confusing blur of images and sounds zipping by so fast Abby's brain had no time to interpret them.

"Wasn't that a fort?" John said.

"Oh, that must be the Lewis and Clark Camp Doo-whatever that Mr. Rohst talked about!" Merri said.

"Camp Dubois," Abby said. "Look! There's a log cabin. For some reason, we're flipping back and forth through time—and way too fast."

Merri put her hands over her eyes and turned away from the screen. "I feel really dizzy."

"I don't know what I feel…sad… worried…happy," Abby said.

"Mostly I feel scared," Merri said. "But I don't know why."

"Just think of all the history in this spot," John said.

"I think we're picking up vibes from several buildings—and the feelings of all the people who lived in them," Abby said. "I'm feeling like I might be sick. Maybe you should turn it off, John."

"Hold on, I've got an idea." He stood and carried the laptop toward the front of the room. "This theatre we're in T's out from the rest of the museum, right?"

"Oh," Abby said, following him. "I get it. We're not exactly over the old basement."

John held his laptop against the door leading into the museum and the blurring images, sounds—and the emotions they engendered—came to a sudden stop. And then the screen blacked out.

"That stinks," John said. "I've lost it."

But then the screen filled with a beautiful kaleidoscope of colors, which after a few seconds settled into an image of a white house set in a lush green countryside.

"You were right, Abby!" Merri said. "It worked."

"It looks newer, of course," Abby said, "but I think that's the house Mr. Rohst showed us."

John held the laptop and Abby used the *zoom* tool to see up close. The house was plain and unadorned. In spite of its beautiful backdrop, the house had a dismal, unloved look, as if no one lived there. But then she thought she saw a movement at one of the windows and wondered if someone was behind the curtain. When she zoomed out, they could see a man with a team of horses plowing a field behind the house, the black earth turning over as he went along.

Merri stood on her tiptoes to see, and John moved the laptop lower for her. "Look at the tiny horses," she said. "They're so cute."

Abby clicked on the rotate button and they saw the back of the house and then, maneuvering the view further, a barn, an outhouse with a half-moon door, and white chickens scratching industriously in the dirt.

"Okay, cross your fingers," Abby said. "I'm going to try to get us across the road to Frances' house." She zoomed out and there was Shake Rag Corner, smoke rising from its chimney, on the other side of the road.

"That's it!" Abby said. "Just like the picture—only in beautiful living color."

The house was two stories covered in white

clapboards with a tin roof and cheerful blue shutters at each window. A deep porch ran along the whole front. On it were two rocking chairs and barrels of red flowers.

"It's hard to believe it's the same ugly old house out there right now," John said.

"Look!" Abby said. "Here comes the stagecoach."

Six horses pulling a shiny lacquered black and red coach came into view, slowing as they approached the house. The dust churned up was so thick they couldn't make out anything of the passengers, but they saw the driver turn to look at the house. And then a young woman hurried out onto the porch, waving a piece of blue and yellow calico.

"Maybe that's Frances," Merri said.

The driver pulled on the reins and the team came to a stop in front of the house. After a short while, a boy of about eight or ten and a man carrying a suitcase came out onto the porch. The man handed the case up to the driver, who secured it to the roof, while the boy climbed into the coach. Then the team heaved to and, gathering speed, they drove out of sight beyond the trees. The woman holding the calico rag stood on the porch and seemed to be staring right through their computer screen at them. She used one hand to shade her eyes and raised the other to wave.

"She's waving at us!" Merri said.

"It sure looks like it, but of course she can't see us." Abby said.

"But I still feel like I should wave back at her," Merri said with a giggle.

"I wonder who she is waving at," John said.

"Whoever is hiding behind the curtains in the house across the road," Abby said. "You know, the house that once stood where we are right now."

"Can you lock onto her?" John said. "Hurry, she's

going back inside."

"I'm trying, but it's not working," Abby said.

"There's something else coming down the road," Merri said.

"Surely it's too soon for another stagecoach," John said.

A black buggy pulled by a spotted horse came rattling down the road in a cloud of dust. "It's turning in here," Abby said. And then…

Bertram White slowed his buggy and turned into the lane, eventually coming to a stop in front of the barn. He lumbered down from the buggy and unhitched his lathered mare. Slapping her rump, he turned her out into a pasture that lay beyond the board fence that ran behind the out buildings. He took off his gray felt hat and wiped his face with his handkerchief. His face was red, his mouth set in angry lines, a vein prominent on his nearly bald head.

Kicking at a chicken that was in his path, he stormed across the yard and up the steps onto the porch, the boards creaking under his weight. The screen door wailed softly before banging shut behind him. He walked into the dim kitchen and looked around in disbelief. Supper not even started. He swore in disgust and started down the dim hallway, his boots falling like sledge hammers on the wooden floor. When he reached the parlor at the front of the house, his footsteps were hushed by the Oriental rug, but still an aura of violence followed him into the quiet room. He saw that his wife sat staring out the tall front window, its mullions casting a cross-hatched shadow on her face.

He flipped open his pocket watch and she jerked out

of her reverie and turned to him. Her face drained of color and she stood, stumbling against the chair leg in her haste.

"It's getting on to six o'clock," he said, snapping the watch case shut. "But for some strange reason I don't smell supper cooking." His voice was like angry hornets looking for the farmer that had stirred up their nest.

"I was watching for the stagecoach." She made her lips turn up in a smile, because sometimes she could jolly him out of a bad mood. "Only two riders today, Bertram. We'll miss seeing the stage coaches go by, won't we?" A little breeze pushed its way into the stuffy room, shushing the burgundy damask drapes and playing with a few strands of dark hair that had escaped from her chignon. She lifted a pale, thin hand and nervously smoothed it away from her face.

"Well, I for one, am happy to see the railroad come, but that's neither here nor there. I warned you about having my supper ready on time."

"I'm sorry, Bertram. I'll get right in the kitchen and I'll—"

"It's too late for your excuses now." He took off his jacket, laid it neatly over the arm of the settee, and unbuttoned his top shirt button. Even that didn't take away the angry redness from his face.

"You have to obey me! The preacher said so, 'Wives, submit to your husbands.' Ephesians 5:22."

"I will. I promise I will."

He whipped his leather belt through the loops on his pants. The snapping sound caused her to flinch.

"You make me do this," he said, grabbing her arm.

John snapped the laptop shut and stalked off. "That's

enough," he said, exhaling loudly.

In the gloom of the museum theatre Abby could barely see him, but she heard his breath coming in a sort of wheezy pant. Then she realized she was wheezing too. "I wish there was a way to call the cops on him."

"*I* wish there was a way I could get my hands on that sanctimonious toad for just one minute," John said.

Abby sank onto a seat in the front row. "He's so full of hate. Guess he forgot that next verse about men loving their wives. I feel a little sick to my stomach."

Merri sat down next to her. "And I thought my parents' marriage was bad. Please don't ever make me go inside that guy's head again. And why did we, anyway? One minute we're watching that woman waving at us and the next—"

"I was trying to lock onto her, but we're too far away from Shake Rag Corner. So it locked onto that Bertram White guy when he drove up."

John came and sat on Abby's other side. "I wish we could get closer," he said.

Abby blinked. But then she realized John meant get closer to Shake Rag Corner. She wished he would put his arm around her and hold her for about an hour. She was sure if he did, the hate and violence of the scene they had just witnessed would go away.

Abby's phone trilled in the darkness and she nearly fell out of her seat. She stood and dug in her pocket, finally answering it after three rings. "Hi, Kate. You scared me to death. We're in a dark theater and I didn't expect—"

"I love matinees," Kate said. "What's playing?"

"Not that kind of a theater, or trust me, I wouldn't be talking on my phone. No one else is here."

"Except John, I hope."

"And Merri."

"Aren't you carrying that chaperone thing just a little too far? Surely you can control yourself long enough to watch a movie."

She stepped away from John and Merri and lowered her voice. "It's not a date, silly. I got the idea to bring John's laptop to the museum and try it here."

"Museum? I thought you were at the theater."

"We are. Try to concentrate, Kate. So anyway, it worked. You wouldn't believe the creepy wife beater we just saw."

"In a museum? I hope someone called 9-1-1."

"That's what I thought, but unfortunately, you can't do that for something that happened over 140 years ago."

Kate was laughing in her ear when light streamed into the darkened auditorium and Abby saw that Merri had cracked the door and was peeking out. "Hey, you guys, no one's out there."

"What time does the museum close?" John said.

"I don't remember," Merri said.

"I've got to go, Kate," Abby said, "or we're going to be locked in here for the weekend."

"In that case, it's a good thing you brought along your little chaperone. Especially if John's wearing that cologne again."

"I'll call you," Abby said and closed her phone.

"Let's go." John hoisted his backpack and then held the door for the girls.

As they hurried through the exhibits Abby began to mentally take stock of her purse's contents and wondered how long they could survive on breath mints, gum, and one half-eaten granola bar. But when they rounded the keelboat they saw Mr. Rohst, briefcase in hand, at the front door.

"The museum is closed now," he said, looking at his

watch. "I was just leaving." He smiled at them in confusion. "I thought you had left. A long time ago."

"Oh we did," Abby said. "We had to take the Old…Beulah and Eulah home."

"They were very tired," Merri added.

Mr. Rohst looked inquiringly at John, who was carefully shifting the backpack on his left shoulder, and Abby realized Mr. Rohst was waiting for an introduction.

"This is John," she blurted.

"He's her boyfriend," Merri said.

"No, he's—"

"I wanted to see the museum." John's face was red. Abby wondered if he was still angry about Bertram White or embarrassed to be called her boyfriend.

"So, we brought him along," she said.

"Because the museum is so cool," Merri said.

"It's very cool," John repeated.

"Thank you," Mr. Rohst said. "But…"

"And I needed to do some more research," Merri said. "For my paper. About Lewis and Clark." Abby and John nodded their heads in agreement.

"I'm so impressed," Mr. Rohst said, smiling in satisfaction. "So many young people are so busy playing electronic games—"

"Like *Angry Birds*," John said, helpfully.

"Or *Bubble Game 3*," Merri added.

"—that they don't have time to visit museums. And if they do decide to get busy with their school assignments and need to do research," Mr. Rohst continued, "they only want to use the Internet. But as for you…well done. Come again. Anytime," Mr. Rohst said.

"Thank you, Mr. Rohst. I'm sure we'll be back," Abby said.

"Very soon," John said.

CHAPTER 9

It was difficult to think with John so close—difficult to talk for sure—but Abby managed to say, "Isn't that too heavy? I can help you hold it." She was squeezed up next to him holding a carpenter's level against the repaired cabinet so he could see it as he reattached it to the wall. John was being such a guy—holding the whole weight of the cabinet in place with his left hand and his power drill with his right.

"Just hold the level. Oh, and try to keep the glass doors from swinging shut on me. Lucy would kill me if I broke those."

After he had sunk two screws through the cabinet's back into the wall stud he said, "Okay, you can put the level down now."

She stepped out from under his arms to get a breath of John-free air. That was much better, except that then she was forced to see the way his T-shirt stretched over his back as he worked. And then there was that tool belt he was wearing. Get a grip, she thought when she felt her face warming. She tore her eyes away and tried to think about something else. Maybe she'd think about Christmas. When she was little, that had been the sure-fire way to get her mind off bad dreams. Not that John was a *bad* dream.

At last, John stepped back and set the drill down. "Not bad, huh?" he said.

That's for sure, she thought.

He tested the doors and seemed happy when they closed properly. "Now I'll definitely be Lucy's favorite cousin." John gathered up the drill, level, and extraneous screws and started for the door. "Come on. Let's go find something to eat."

"But you just had dinner an hour and a half ago."

"And a fine dinner it was, too. Did I say thanks?" John grinned at her and she thought her brain might short-circuit.

"Yes. Hey, do you think we'll have snow for Christmas?"

"Huh?" John said.

Abby listened for the popcorn to finish popping in the microwave while John thumbed through the telephone directory. "At least a half a page of Buchanans," he said. "Maybe I'll call a few."

"You can if you want to, but even if we knew which one was the owner I don't know if I could bring myself to call him. I mean what kind of guy lets his house go like that? Seriously, did you get a good look at that run down old place?"

John put the directory on the counter and searched in Lucy's cabinets until he found bowls for the popcorn. Abby took out three cold Cokes from the refrigerator and they carried it all out to the family room.

"Hey, Merri Christmas," John said, "time for a break."

"Or not," Abby said after she got a look at the computer monitor. Except for her name at the top of the page, Merri's screen was a blank white canvas.

"I can't think what to write," Merri said. "I've got so much stuff about Lewis and Clark that I don't know where to begin."

"What's your thesis?" Abby handed Merri a bowl of popcorn. Dr. Bob trotted in and stood by her chair looking hopeful.

"My what-sis? Merri asked.

"You know, the main idea for the report."

"Well, duh. Lewis and Clark."

"Well, I know *that*," Abby said. "But you'll have to narrow down the topic, unless you're planning on writing a 500-page book. I'm just saying."

"I don't bother with all that," Merri said, turning back to the computer screen. "I just let my creative genius flow. I always get A's."

"Really?" Abby said doubtfully.

"Why don't you write about the Lewis and Clark journals?" John suggested. "I've always thought they were cool."

"Maybe," Merri said.

"Yes, I saw some reproductions of those at the museum today," Abby said. "I hadn't realized that some of the other men—besides Lewis and Clark—wrote journals too."

"Actually," John said around a mouthful of popcorn, "The display said all the men were encouraged to write. President Jefferson wanted different perspectives of the expedition."

"Writing about writing?" Merri said. "You've got to be

kidding."

"Okay, how about writing about the keelboat? That was my favorite," Abby said.

"Maybe," Merri said.

"Well, while you're pondering those deep questions, we'll be doing some searching for the Buchanans." Wiping his hands on a napkin, John sat on the couch and opened his laptop. "Maybe we can find one that lives—used to live—in Shake Rag Corner."

"Okay," Merri said, scooping up the dog. "Dr. Bob and I are going to take our popcorn outside."

"You really need to think about narrowing your thesis, Merri."

"Come on, Dr. Bob. Let's go think about my what-sis."

Abby and John spent a frustrating hour trying to find information about the Buchanans. "All these websites and we still can't get anywhere," Abby complained. "Just about the time we get close enough to nail down a fact they block access and ask us to pay a subscription fee."

"I'm about ready to pull out my hair," John said.

Abby smiled. His hair stood up at odd angles as if he had already attempted to do so. "Don't do that. I rather like your hair," she said, patting a silky lock back into place.

"Really?" he asked. He seemed to have no idea how handsome he was. She would have to award him a star for *modesty*. But then he bolted to his feet and hurried to the other side of the room.

All right, then. He obviously wanted a distant sort of friendship, one that didn't include touching. Either that, or she was showing early signs of leprosy or maybe bubonic plague. Sighing, Abby lay down on the couch, put her feet up on the arm, and watched John pace the length of the family room. After a while, watching him made her dizzy, so she closed her eyes.

Merri and Dr. Bob came in, both panting happily. "I found out what Round About is."

"And how does one play Round About?" John asked.

Merri knelt and took the smiling dog onto her lap. "Well," she said, scratching behind his ears, "first, you run up on our porch and then down the path and onto the Old Dears' porch. And then you run back to our porch. And then you do it all again—over and over and over. Dr. Bob thinks it's hilarious. Don't you, buddy?"

Dr. Bob didn't answer, just smiled.

Merri looked from Abby to John. "So, what's up?"

"Not much," Abby said. "How about you? Did you decide what you're going to write about?"

"Yep."

"Well?" John said. "Don't keep us in suspense."

"Sorry. It's a secret. So, now can we do some time-surfing again?"

"Not here," Abby said. "We agreed that—"

"Okay. Settle down," Merri said. "I was just asking."

Abby sighed. "I guess I'll go ahead and pay for a subscription to one of those genealogy organizations."

"Why do that?" John said.

"To quote Merri—duh. Because the Old Dears really want the information, that's why. And I, for one, am finding it difficult to disappoint them."

"I know. Me too. But why pay for it when we can just go to Shake Rag Corner and time-surf until we find the information?"

"I hate to repeat myself, but duh, John. There's no Internet in that old dilapidated house."

"I know, but I've been thinking. The museum has wireless Internet for all those computer stations in the main display room, right?"

"You mean you could pick up their signal on your laptop? But isn't the house too far from their wireless router?"

"Yes and yes. I should have listened to Timmy Tech when he tried to tell me to get a laptop with mobile broadband. But I bet he's got something that would help. His phone has more gizmos than a Swiss Army Knife. Come to think of it, I think he has a can opener on that thing. Are you two up for another trip to Shake Rag Corner?"

"At 10:00?" Abby said.

"P.M.?" Merri added.

"Mr. Rohst did say to come back any time we wanted."

"I hope no one thinks we're trying to break in." Abby and the others were huddled under the overhang of the museum's front door. She took a quick look. The parking lot was still as empty as when they first arrived.

"Don't worry," John said. "We're not doing anything illegal. Per se. So what do we do, Tim?"

Tim took out his phone and flipped it open. "Lead me to the computers."

"Down this way," Abby said, pointing to the right.

Tim began slowly walking along the brick wall, staring down at his phone the whole way, the others trooping along after him.

"First, we get as close as we can to the museum's wi-fi router. These days you can pick up a signal almost anywhere. Except, apparently, here." He frowned and walked a few feet farther. "My app will score the museum's wi-fi password. Then you can take John's laptop to Boo

Radley's house over there. You should be able to piggy back off my phone to do whatever it is that you're trying to do."

"But won't the connection be too slow to run our program?" John said. "I mean, it's much more complicated than if we were just checking our email."

"Oh, Johnny, boy. I'm so disappointed in you," Tim said in mock disapproval. "Of course it wouldn't work. I mean my phone's smart, but it's not a genius." He looked at his phone again. "There, I'm getting a signal."

"Oh, good," Abby said. "Merri, you'd better stay with Timmy Tech...I mean Tim."

"That's fine with me. I don't want to go stumbling around in a haunted house in the middle of the night."

"And you're right, John," Tim continued. "For anything other than email, it would be so excruciatingly slow you'd want to scream..."

"So we'll just zip on over to the house—" Abby said.

"...even with state-of-the-art blue-tooth technology to act as a good signal repeater, which is pretty amazing when you think of the..."

"And I'll just wait here," Merri said, rolling her eyes at Tim, who didn't notice. "While you two go ahead and go."

"...which wouldn't even work in this situation because the range is only about thirty feet. And with the Boo Radley House across the parking lot *and* across the street..."

Abby tugged on John's arm. "We'll try to hurry."

"...you're lucky. With this bad boy app I wrote I'll be able to shoot some signals at you. It was easy. First, I calculated the optimum—"

"Tim?" John interrupted. "Thanks."

Tim looked up from his phone. "Sure, man. No sweat."

106

They started across the dark museum parking lot, Abby pointing the way with her flashlight. When they reached the old house's yard they slowed. It was as ill-kempt as the building itself.

Abby shone the flashlight over the tall grass and weeds. "What if there are snakes in there?"

"I'll go first." John waded into the overgrown grass.

"Okay," she said quickly, stepping into the tracks he made. She would begin first thing tomorrow to be a more fearless woman. "Make lots of noise so they'll know you're coming."

"Ready or not, all you snakes, here we come," John sang out. "You better run away home or we'll step on your slithery little heads."

Abby chuckled. "Run, John? Really?"

At last Abby and John reached the sagging porch. She shone the light on the front door. It would be easy enough to get inside the house. It wasn't even closed all the way, much less locked. But a "No Trespassing" sign was tacked to it, clearly readable even without her flashlight. When John put his hand on the door knob, Abby put her hand on his. "Maybe this isn't such a good idea," she said.

"Oh, all right, be a spoil sport. I'll try it from the porch."

They sat on the steps and John opened his laptop and loaded the program. Just as it had been at the museum, there was only a confusing mix of flashing, blurred images, sounds, and emotions. Her head began to pound again.

"Oww," John said, rubbing his temples. "Timmy Tech's app seems to be working. But I don't think we'll be able to get enough clear vibes unless we take this into the house."

"Here, let me try," Abby said.

"Well, hurry. I don't think I can take this much longer."

My head feels like Athena's trying to pop out. But, hey, since she's the goddess of wisdom, we can ask her what to do."

"Well, I bet she'd say it wasn't wise to trespass, but if she breaks open your skull you won't be able to hear her, will you?"

Abby tweaked all the settings, but nothing worked. Groaning in frustration, she looked at John.

"Come on," he said. "That sign is to keep out vandals. It's not like we're going to hurt anything."

"Oh, all right. But let's be quick."

He stood and held out a hand to help her up. "But watch your step. A broken neck would sure ruin our adventure."

Abby held the laptop while John muscled the sagging door open, and then she shone the flashlight into what must have once been a living room. It was empty except for dust and neglect. To the left, a steep stairway rose into the deeper gloom of the upper floor. Across from them, a hall led to other rooms.

When John took the laptop back, Abby swiped a cobweb from her hair and went back to holding her head. "It's not any better," she said. "Let's move farther in."

"Hold on," he said. "Let's make sure—"

"Come on, hurry. We've got to do this and get out of here."

"I'm not letting you break a leg in my adventure."

"*Your* adventure?" Abby sputtered. "So, you're not *letting* me—"

"I mean..." John put a hand to his head as if thinking were really difficult. "Abby," he began again, "I would really be upset if you got hurt during *your* adventure."

"Just bring the laptop and follow me."

"Oh, all right, but don't come crying to me—"

There was a sound of rotten wood breaking and Abby felt the floor give way. Her flashlight pinwheeled out of her hand in a dizzying light show. When it clattered to the floor the room went pitch black.

"Abby! Are you all right?"

"Don't even say it," she said, gasping a little.

"Okay. I won't say that you shouldn't have rushed in there until we knew it was safe. Where are you?"

"Here."

She heard a shuffling sound and then the flashlight came back on and it was John's turn to gasp. Abby, arms outstretched, was lying flat on the floor, except for her lower half, which was dangling somewhere below.

"Hurry," she said. "I think there may be rats down there."

"I'm more worried about you falling through to the cellar and breaking your neck."

"Oh! Then don't come over here or you'll fall in too."

"Don't be a dummy. I'm coming to get you." Training the light across the floor, John moved closer. "I think the rest of the floor is okay. Looks like there's been some water damage where you are."

"I guess I was just lucky to find this spot." She hoped sarcasm would keep her mind off the cellar. Maybe jokes would help, or maybe she could recite that poem Miss Allen made them memorize in sophomore lit class. But her mind was a complete blank. Except for the rats.

Setting the laptop on the floor, John knelt beside her, put his hands under her arms, and began to pull her out. At last she was standing on solid ground again, but their combined weight made the floor creak ominously until John pulled her farther away from the hole and into the shelter of his arms. She put her head on his chest and tried not to cry.

"Are you all right?" he said into her hair. "Do you hurt anywhere?"

"Just my leg. It's scraped, but I don't think anything's broken." Her voice came out muffled by his shirt.

"Let me get you out here before…" He started to pull away, but Abby held on to his shirt. After a pause, he put his arms around her again.

Then she looked up. "John," she said, sniffing, "my head's stopped hurting."

"Yeah, now that you mention it, so has mine."

They both turned toward the laptop on the floor.

"We're in." John picked it up and held it where she could see. The Shake Rag Corner house filled the screen in close-up detail. "Let's set this somewhere," he said, looking around the room.

"There on the stairs," Abby said.

"Good idea." John lowered himself onto the third step, setting the laptop on his knees.

Trying not to think of the probable filth there, Abby sat down next to him. "Switch to *Interior.*"

The image blurred and then resolved into a view of a kitchen. The door stood open allowing sunlight to pour into the room. Steam arose from a pot simmering on a cast iron cook stove that sat against a stone chimney.

"Sweet," John said.

"Not nearly so fancy as the house across the street, but I'd rather live here any day than with that Bertram White guy."

"I can almost smell what's cooking."

"There's no *almost* about it," Abby said. "I smell cinnamon."

Then a young, very pregnant woman in a blue and yellow calico dress waddled over to the cook stove, and using a rag, lifted the lid and stirred the contents.

"Oh! That's got to be Frances," Abby said. "Lock onto her."

"Okay. Let's go virtual...."

Franny smiled, thinking how pleased Rube would be to have cinnamon—his favorite spice in the whole world—in his oatmeal when he came in from chores.

Next she opened a bin and began to measure flour onto the work table. Then, forming an indentation in the mountain of flour, she added salt, yeast, and finally, a dipperful of water. It looked like what she imagined a volcano must. She'd never seen a picture of one but heard a man telling about them at the mercantile one time. Using only her hands, she expertly mixed the ingredients. Then she sprinkled more flour on the work table and began to knead the dough, humming as she worked. A shadow fell over her. She looked up and her face lit with joy.

Rube, so handsome it sometimes made her feel a bit faint, came in through the open door. "Franny, what would I do without you?" he said. Then hanging his hat on a hook on the wall, he came to gather her—belly and all—into his arms.

"Mind my doughy hands," she said, laughing. She picked up a rag to wipe them. "Go sit and I'll get your bowl."

"What smells so good?"

"It's the cinnamon."

Before Rube could move away from her another shadow fell over the room, but this time Franny did not smile. Mr. White, with his busy eyes and sneering mouth, stood at the door. He took his hat off and offered a pleasant greeting, but she knew it was a false civility.

"Morning, Rube. Miz Franny."

Rube moved toward White, instinctively putting himself between his wife and the man in the doorway. "Morning, Bert." He knew the man expected him to call him Mr. White because he owned more land—240 acres to his 40— and because sometimes, when he needed a bit more money than he could make on his forty acres, he accepted jobs from him, but mainly because Rube's ancestry included Kickapoo, and Bertram's was as white as his surname. Rube didn't figure any of that meant he had to put a mister in front of the man's name if he wasn't willing to put one in front of his. If he had a mind to tally up such things—and he didn't—he would have reminded Bertram that his forty acres had been in the family a lot longer than Bertram's had been in his.

But his voice was pleasant. "What can I do for you?"

"I'm needing to get some hedge rows cleared before winter sets in. I figure it'll add another ten acres all told for corn next spring. I'll pay you good money to burn them out for me."

Franny pulled on Rube's shirt sleeve and he turned to look at her. "Rube, we're not needing any money," she said quietly. They both knew it wouldn't be good money anyway—in any sense of the word.

Rube turned back to White and said, "I'll think on it."

"Good. I'll ask you again tomorrow," White put on his hat but then paused and smiled. "I'll give you some free advice, Rube." He gestured toward Franny. "You'd better nip that in the bud or your woman will think she's the one should be wearing the pants. It's a wise man that keeps his woman in her place. Good day, Rube, Miz Franny."

Franny turned earnestly to Rube. "I don't mean—"

"Don't pay any mind to that toad, Franny." He took her into his arms again and she pressed her face into his shoulder.

"But I don't want you working for that man." Her voice was a bit muffled by his shirt.

Rube gently rubbed her belly. "I'll stay close. I know you're getting nervous with your time coming on—"

"That's not why."

"Well, why then, honey?"

"I just don't like you being around that man."

"Well you might not be nervous about the baby coming, but I am. I aim to have a little extra put by in case we need it."

Franny continued to breathe in the smell of Rube's shirt, of his own clean scent.

"Honey?" he said.

"What, Rube?"

"I'm hungry. Can we eat whatever you've got cooking over there?"

John's computer flickered and a low-battery message popped up. "Oh, come on! Why did it have to conk out now?" He closed down the program and shut the laptop. "Man doesn't that White guy make your skin crawl?"

"Yeah, but aren't Franny and Rube sweet?" Abby said.

"Franny is surely a nickname for Frances," John said, "but what kind of name is Rube?" He trained the flashlight around the room and then settled it on an arched doorway. "I bet the kitchen's in there."

Abby shuffled after him, keeping well away from the hole in the floor. The room turned out to be a dining room, but they found the kitchen just through another doorway. She followed the beam of John's flashlight as it glanced off sagging cabinets, a rusted sink, and a filth-encrusted electric stove. "It sure looks different from when

Rube and Franny lived here."

"I don't think this was their kitchen," Abby said.

"What do you mean? Of course it's the kitchen."

"Not when they lived here. Where's the stone chimney? Besides, the door's all wrong."

"Oh, yeah. I guess you're right."

The door stood open and John went to it and shone the flashlight into the next room. "Be careful," he said, pointing the light down at the threshold. "The floor's uneven here."

A stone chimney stood out in the darkness, sparkling in the light from the flashlight. Abby ran a hand over the cool stone. "Franny's iron stove stood right here," she said.

"You can see where the stove pipe went into the chimney," John said.

"And her work table was in front of it," Abby said. "I can still see her making bread on it. It's so sad."

"Homemade bread makes me happy—very happy."

"Sad, because it looked like she didn't have much time left before her baby came."

"Oh. Right. Therefore, not much time before she died." Abby couldn't see John's face clearly in the dim light, but he sounded shocked. "I guess time-surfing has its down side too," he said.

"Yeah. It's something you have to get used to," Abby said.

"We'd better get back. Merri will be worried."

"Hey, I was just about to go get you, ghosts or not," Merri said as Abby came limping up, John at her side. "Are you all right?"

"She nearly fell through the floor," John said.

114

"I'm fine." Abby said. "Just a scrape on my leg."

"Hey, man, did it work?" Tim said.

John looked up at his friend. "Oh. It was awesome, and thanks to you, we found what we were looking for."

"Merri, we found Frances and her husband," Abby said. "His name is Rube and they're going to have…" She stopped. There was no sense reminding Merri that Franny was going to die in childbirth.

"Come on, Abby," John said. "Let's get you home so I can take a look at your leg."

"Yeah, dude, I noticed she has killer legs." Tim whispered it, but not so softly that Abby didn't hear it and smile.

John frowned and shoved Tim toward the car. "She's hurt, you moron. And it's time for you to go home."

Abby was sitting on a wooden chair in Lucy's kitchen, her injured leg propped up on John's thigh where he squatted in front of her. He frowned fiercely at her. "You should have told me how bad it was. I would have taken you home right away."

Merri came in, carrying an assortment of first aid supplies. "Here," she said. "You can clean the blood and dirt away with these wipes. I don't know if any of these bandages will fit."

"Thanks, Merri." John grinned. "You may need to give her a shot of whiskey and a leather belt to bite down on."

"I hope she doesn't kick you," Merri answered.

"Could you please stop talking like I'm unconscious?" Abby said. "It's no big—"

John tentatively touched the medicated wipe to her

calf. "Oww! That hurts."

"Now who's being a baby?"

"I am *not* ...a... baby." Abby took a deep breath and let it out. "And to prove it, I'm going on a quest at the library tomorrow."

John dabbed more disinfectant on Abby's leg. "That doesn't sound like much of a challenge."

"Humph," Merri said. "You obviously haven't met Dragon Lady."

CHAPTER 10

Abby's leg only twinged a little when she sat down at the library's genealogy computer station the next morning. "Maybe we'll get somewhere now that we know Franny's husband's name. We should be able to find them in the census records."

"Yeah, but what kind of name is Rube?" Merri said.

"That's probably a nickname, but it will help—if I can remember how to navigate this site."

"I'm going to go look for stuff about Lewis and Clark," Merri said.

"Good. But try to hurry. If we're lucky we can get out of here before Grendel scents us here in her lair and comes back to crunch our bones."

"Grendel?"

"Well, not Grendel," Abby said absent-mindedly. "More like Grendel's mother."

"Huh?"

"Never mind, Merri. Go read up on Lewis and Clark."

Abby heard a muffled thump and looked up from the computer monitor. Merri had just set a stack of books on the library table. Abby smiled distractedly and turned back to the computer. "Looks like you found plenty of information."

"Yeah. I found some good stuff. How about you?"

"Yes, but I'm so confused. I found Frances and Reuben Buchanan. Rube—get it? They're in the 1870 census for Shake Rag Corner. But by the 1880 census they've disappeared, all three of them. Even if Franny died in childbirth like the booklet says, where's Reuben and their baby? But then I wondered if maybe the baby went to its grandparents. So I searched for Franny's parents, Franklin and Anne Edwards, in the census records. They weren't in Shake Rag Corner, but I found them in Alton. In 1870 the census just lists Franklin and Anne. But in the 1880 census guess who's living with them?"

"Franny's baby?"

"Yep, a boy named Albert William Edwards. Only by then he was nine years old."

Merri frowned in confusion. "But that's the grandfather's name, right?"

"Yes, indeed. He's the link that connects Franny to the Old Dears."

"But I don't get it. If he's Franny and Rube's little boy, how come his last name is Edwards and not Buchanan?"

A shadow over the monitor startled Abby and Merri and they looked up to see the librarian looming over Abby's shoulder, squinting at the computer screen.

"Obviously, he was a bastard."

Merri's eyes widened before changing to a fierce glare.

"Hey, you don't even know him."

Susan P., Asst. Librarian, straightened, adjusted her glasses, and smiled nastily. "He was illegitimate."

Merri turned to Abby. "What does *illegitimate* mean?"

Abby logged off the computer and stood. "Merri," she said sniffing the air, "do you smell sulphur?"

"What?"

"Come on. It's not safe in here."

Sue P., Asst. Librarian, was frowning harder than ever when they left.

Abby reluctantly pushed the Old Dears' door bell. Dr. Bob began to bark and they heard his nails clicking as he ran to the front door. Then there were people footsteps and Beulah opened the door, already smiling. Abby expected to find them tired and frail from their excursions the day before, but Beulah looked happy and energetic.

Abby tried to smile back, but her face felt stiff. Merri's smile didn't seem to be sticking so well either.

"Eulah, it's the grandkids!" she called over her shoulder. "They're just in time for tea." Turning back to Abby and Merri she smiled gleefully and lowered her voice to a conspiratorial whisper. "And just in time for the trick I'm going to play on Eulah!"

"Did you put salt in the sugar bowl again, Grandma Beulah?" Merri said.

"No. Not this time. Just wait until you see!"

When they got to the kitchen, Eulah was taking a pie out of the oven. "We finally got that rhubarb pie made. Like we promised you."

Dr. Bob was following each move she made with an excited grin.

"It looks delicious," Abby said cautiously. She turned away from the twins and whispered to Merri. "But to paraphrase what I've been telling you," she said eying the pie suspiciously, "delicious is more than crust deep."

"I'll get two more cups," Beulah said. "We're using Mother's china."

The kitchen table was set with tea cups and plates a delicate cream color with pink roses around the rims. The table was covered with a pink tablecloth, crisp and spotless, with matching napkins beside the plates. A small bouquet of purple salvia sat in the center. It reminded her of being at her Grandmother Flo's for Thanksgiving.

"Wow," Merri said. "It's so fancy."

Abby smiled, happy that Merri would get to experience a real tea party. Merri's mother rarely cooked and served most of their meals—usually sandwiches or take-out from the deli—on paper plates.

"I picked the flowers this morning," Beulah said. "But don't get too close. They don't smell so good."

"They sure are pretty," Merri said.

"We hoped John would be able to come too," Eulah said.

"He's been very busy working at the Habitat for Humanity house," Abby said.

"He's such a good boy, and so handsome, don't you think?" Beulah said slyly.

Willing herself not to blush, Abby changed the subject. "Can I help with anything?"

"It's all ready. Come on, girls. Let's sit." Beulah went to her chair and eased herself onto it. Apparently it was her turn to pray, for with no consultation with Eulah she began to speak: "Thank you, Lord, for all you give us, especially our granddaughters Abby and Merri. And thank you, Lord, for this pie we are about to eat. You know rhubarb's our favorite. Amen."

"Amen," everyone echoed.

"You pour the tea, Eulah. And I'll go cut the pie." She paused on her way to the counter and winked broadly at Abby and Merri behind Eulah's back.

There was a sudden clatter at the sink and Beulah called out loudly, "Oh no! I seemed to have cut the dickens out of my finger." She turned and staggered toward them, clutching her hand to her chest.

Eulah turned in alarm. "What happened?"

"Look," Beulah said and thrust a small matchbox under her sister's nose. "Open it."

Eulah slid the matchbox open to reveal her sister's severed finger lying on a bed of bloody gauze. "Oh, Beulah, how did you—?"

"Surprise!" Beulah cried with glee and then pulled her perfectly fine finger from the matchbox and waved it along with the other four at Eulah.

"Oh, for crying out loud," Eulah said in disgust. "Will you ever grow up?" She pulled herself to her feet. "I'll get the pie. You sit down and behave."

Abby found herself agreeing with Eulah. Why was it some people failed to grow out of the practical joke phase once they were past junior high?

Beulah laughed and sat down next to Merri. "I'm just trying to liven things up around here."

"How did you do that?" Merri said, giggling in delight.

Beulah handed Merri the matchbox. "It's easy. Just cut a hole in the bottom for your finger. I used red food coloring for the blood."

"That was a good one," Merri said. "I'm going to try it out on my mom when I get home."

Pat would probably not be thrilled with the extracurricular subjects Merri was learning, but she would be pleased to know she was having a good time.

Eulah returned with the pie and began dishing it up.

"Thank you," Abby said when Eulah set a plate in front of her. Merri wore skepticism all over her face and Abby smiled weakly. But Dr. Bob apparently wasn't worried about any unpleasant surprises with the pie. He sat next to her chair, smiling in anticipation.

"Oh, don't worry," Eulah said when she noticed their faces. "Beulah never plays practical jokes on anyone but me."

"Well that's good to know." Abby reached into her tote bag on the floor and pulled out photocopies of the census pages.

"Merri and I found more about your family today." She paused and looked from Beulah to Eulah. "The name that was scratched out of Frances Edwards' Bible," she said carefully, "was Reuben Buchanan."

"*Reuben*," Beulah said in satisfaction. "A good Bible name. Won't that look so nice on his little apple?"

"And," Abby continued, "we found out how Frances is related to you."

"She's your great grandmother," Merri said.

"She and Reuben had a child—a little boy named Albert William, born November 9, 1871."

"But Albert William was our Edwards grandfather..." Eulah said. "That baby would have been..."

"Oh, Abby!" Beulah said. "You young people are so clever."

Eulah picked up the photocopy and studied it. "The baby was illegitimate."

Beulah's eyes widened and she pulled out her hanky and fanned herself with it. "Oh my."

"I shouldn't have said that," Eulah said. "I've always thought that *illegitimate* was a most unfortunate thing to call a child, as if the child were *illegal*. Like the baby committed a crime." She let out a loud huff. "But this Reuben fellow's the one that committed the crime. What a scoundrel, to not marry her."

Beulah looked worriedly at Eulah. "Does that mean we're not really Edwards?"

"It means we should have been Buchanans all along."

"Buchanan." Beulah seemed to be trying the name on. "It's a good name, I guess."

"Hmph!" Eulah said. "Don't be putting an apple on our tree for *him*."

"But they felt so married," Abby said. "And he was so nice."

Merri nudged her arm and when Abby turned she was telegraphing a warning.

"I mean I'm sure there's some reason…" Abby stopped talking and took a bite of pie. Her eyes watered and she swallowed quickly.

"Oh, dear. It is a bit tart, isn't it?" Beulah said.

"I told you it needed more sugar," Eulah said. "Well, at least we'll have shiny Edwards apples, Beulah, even if we don't have any Buchanan apples."

"Yes. Who wants Buchanan apples anyway?" Beulah said sadly. "At least I can put Frances and our grandfather on the tree now."

Merri gently touched Beulah's arm. "Do you want some help with it?"

Beulah wiped her eyes and mustered up a wobbly smile for Merri. "I'd love some help."

Merri extended her arm for Beulah and she rose to her feet and led the way into the dining room where the family tree project still lay on the table.

"I, for one, will be glad to get the mess out of here," Eulah said, following them into the dining room.

Beulah neatly lettered two apples in a beautiful silver script. "There you are, Frances Ann Edwards, and you, Albert William Edwards." Then, after blowing on the apples to hasten the drying ink, she said, "Okay, Merri, you can glue them on. Only be careful of the glue gun. It's really hot."

"That looks better," Eulah said, "It's still unbalanced, but at least now the line is unbroken from Alexander Edwards in 1786 down to us."

"I hate it that Frances doesn't have a husband apple," Beulah said.

After that, Abby helped the twins hang the family tree mosaic on the wall across from the portrait of their father.

"It ends with us then," Eulah said. "No apples for us, Beulah Mae." She smiled sadly at Abby and Merri. "You see, Carl and I were never able to have children."

Beulah rubbed her eyes and sighed.

"Are you all right, dear?" Eulah said.

"Just a little tired, I guess."

Abby had almost forgotten Dr. Bob was there until he came trotting into the dining room with the hedgehog toy in his mouth. He dropped it at Beulah's feet and looked up at her expectantly.

"Oh, Dr. Bob." Beulah lowered herself into her chair again and reached out to pet the dog. "That's so thoughtful of you to bring me your favorite toy. You're trying to cheer me up, aren't you?"

Dr. Bob stretched his front legs before him and bowed, and then bounced up and extended his paw for a shake. Merri took hands with him and then scratched his ears. "He's such a good boy."

"We'll leave so you can rest," Abby said.

"Goodbye, dears. We'd love to babysit Merri again anytime."

"Thanks, Beulah," Abby said, smiling at Merri's expression.

Merri picked up the wiggling dog. "Come on, Dr. Bob, you can babysit me while I work on my essay."

John had warned her not to park too close, and when Abby turned onto Warren Street and saw the Habitat house under renovation she understood why. There were probably nails everywhere just waiting for the tires of unwary drivers. A dumpster overflowing with rotted wood and drywall sat in the front yard only a few feet from the house. A man on the roof, bare-chested and wearing a red bandana on his head, dumped a shovelful of old shingles into the dumpster below and then ascended the slope of the roof and disappeared over the peak to the other side.

Renovation was noisy work. The closer she got to the house, the more she had the urge to cover her ears. She could hear Red Bandana and other workers thumping and pounding up on the roof. From somewhere inside the house, a power tool whined and at least three different hammers pounded out a crazy rhythm. Over it all, a radio blasted Switchfoot's *This Is Home*.

The front door was propped open so Abby invited herself in. The small living room was an obstacle course of tools, drop cloths, and paint cans. A girl about her own age wearing paint-spattered overalls looked down from her ladder and smiled. "Hi. I'm almost finished here. The last bedroom still needs to be painted—but you can't start until Timmy Tech is finished with the wiring."

"Oh. Sorry. I can't help right now. I'm looking for John Roberts."

"You must be Abby." The girl's smile grew wider and

she pointed to the ceiling. "He's on the roof. Go through the kitchen and out the back door. You should be able to see him from there."

"Thanks." Abby stepped carefully around a paint spill and went into the kitchen. Like the living room, it was modest in size. But its walls had recently been painted a warm peachy color and the cabinets a fresh white. It would be a welcome spot for the new owners.

The back door opened onto a tiny porch. An extension ladder blocked her way and she edged past it, reminding herself that what they said about ladders was only a superstition.

When she got out into the yard far enough she saw three men on the roof. Red Bandana was carrying a stack of shingles. Two men kneeled on the roof, one blond guy dealing out shingles like playing cards, and next to him John, pounding them into place with a nail gun.

The roof looked so high, and the pitch so steep, that Abby wondered whether she should call out to them. What if she startled them and they fell off? But then Red Bandana looked down at her and let out a loud wolf whistle, and John and the other man stood and clambered over to the edge of the roof, seemingly unconcerned with their peril. All three, their teeth gleaming white in their sunburned faces, wore tool belts, knee pads, and leather boots.

John pulled the red bandana off his friend's shaved head and threw it over the edge of the roof. "Don't be a jerk. It's Abby." Then frowning down at her, he said, "Hi, Abby. Sorry. I can't come down until we're finished."

"Hi. That's all right. I'll just watch for a while," Abby said.

"That idiot is Jamal. This is James," John said indicating the blond-haired guy on his other side.

"Hi, Abby. We've heard about you," James said. "A lot. Haven't we, Jamal?"

"Yes, we have," Jamal said. "Sorry I whistled. I couldn't help it. I don't suppose you'd give my bandana back?"

Abby picked it up from the grass and climbed the first few steps of the ladder. "It would serve you right if I didn't. That was so not cool, you know."

The back door opened as Abby was handing the bandana up to Jamal. An older man came out and went to the ladder to steady it as Abby descended. She saw that he had been painting. His black face was speckled with white paint, like stars spangling the night sky.

"What are you three hoodlums up to?" he called up to the guys on the roof. "Are you bothering this young lady?"

Abby started to come to their defense before she realized the man was smiling good-naturedly.

Taking a handkerchief out of his pocket, he began to wipe unsuccessfully at the paint on his face. "Come down off there before you broil in the sun."

"Thank you, Master Joe," Jamal, John and James said in near unison.

The man's laugh boomed out. "Don't you 'Master Joe' me." After returning his handkerchief to his pocket he extended a hand to Abby. "Hello. My name is Joe Franklin. Nice to meet a nice young person for a change instead of the riffraff I have to put up with."

"I know what you mean," Abby said seriously. "Good help is so hard to find."

Joe chuckled and then he whispered confidentially to Abby. "If I don't make them stop they'll just keep going until they drop. They're working so hard to get the house done so the Matthews family can move in."

"And here I was feeling bad for interrupting them.

"The house looks great. I'm sure the Matthews will really like it."

"We're all proud of it," Joe said. "If only you could see what they're living in now."

When the guys were down from the roof Joe said, "You three jay-birds get out of here." He consulted his watch. "We'll resume work on the roof at 0500 hours tomorrow. Hopefully, it'll be cooled off by then."

"We'll be here," John said, turning to look at his friend. "Won't we?"

"Yeah, yeah, yeah," Jamal said, obviously faking reluctance.

"Good. See you then." Joe went back into the kitchen, chuckling to himself.

"He seems really nice," Abby said.

"Yeah," John said. "Joe's a retired engineer. Heads up a volunteer crew every summer."

Jamal stuffed his bandana into his pocket and then took his T-shirt from the porch railing and pulled it on over his head.

Abby smiled to herself. Funny how with John in the vicinity she hadn't even noticed how buff Jamal's bare chest was.

"Let's get Timmy Tech and go grab some lunch," James said.

"You guys go on," John said. "I'm going to grab a shower first. Come on, Abby."

"Oooh, la-la," Jamal said.

"I mean…don't pay any attention to those guys," John said.

John made her wait in the lobby of Tim's apartment

building while he went in to shower and change. "Trust me," he said when she protested, "it's not any cooler inside, and it's a lot scarier. It's not fit for a civilized person's eyes."

"Oh, all right," Abby said, plopping down on the stairs. "But hurry. I can't wait to tell you what Merri and I found out."

Sixteen minutes later they were seated at Jack-in-the-Box eating lunch. Abby explained what she had discovered at the library, all the while marveling at the massive quantity of food John was virtually inhaling. He had already leveled a mountain of fries and was on his third cheeseburger.

"It might not be true," he said, slurping down the last of his strawberry milkshake. "Just because the dragon lady said so."

"I'd love to wipe the smirk off her face," she said.

He paused with his cheeseburger halfway up to his mouth. "There are worse things than being illegitimate. Until you found out Reuben was a Buchanan, I wondered if he and Franny were both Edwards. You know—cousins or something. With the kind of wedding where they play banjos."

She laughed in spite of herself. "You're terrible."

"Let's go to the courthouse and check for a marriage certificate—just to be sure."

"You're not too tired?"

"Nah. But there is one thing before we go. Are you going to eat the rest of your onion rings?"

The courthouse clerk smiled sadly from behind her counter. "I'm sorry. I can't find any record of a marriage between a Frances Ann Edwards and a Reuben

Buchanan."

"I just know they were married." Abby turned to John. "Didn't they seem married to you?"

"I thought so. They really loved each other."

The clerk frowned in confusion.

"How about Albert's birth certificate?" Abby said.

"I'm sorry. I didn't find that either."

"Well, it was worth a try," John said.

"Have you tried the newspapers? Sometimes you can pick up information that way."

Abby looked up from the Alton Telegraph's archive microfiche viewer and rubbed her eyes. "This is horrible. My eyes hurt."

"Yeah, too bad the older newspapers haven't been digitized yet. You've been at it for an hour. Let me have a turn," John said.

"I won't argue with that," Abby said.

They had been focusing on the Telegraph's birth and death announcements, a boring and tedious business that had so far yielded exactly zero leads. But even though her eyes were tired, Abby couldn't seem to stop herself from following along as John continued to scroll through the 1871 issues. Then a front page headline caught her eye. "John, Look."

Shake Rag Corner Arsonist to Be Sentenced.

CHAPTER 11

Abby was wishing she could be someplace else. Maybe they should do this later, she thought. But then John reached up and rang the twins' doorbell. "I'd rather walk backwards to St. Louis—make that Los Angeles—than have to tell them this," she said. "They were already so sad."

"Barefoot," John added glumly. "In the snow."

"Or on hot blacktop roads in August."

"Yeah, with fire ants crawling up my legs."

Abby smiled half-heartedly. "And honey dripping from my hair."

"And a snake around your neck."

Abby shivered. "Well, maybe not that."

This time, Merri came to the door, looking pleased with herself. If she was an accurate barometer of feelings, she and the Old Dears must have gotten over their funk. In a way, it would have been better if they were still sad. With the news she and John came bearing now, the fall back into the *Slough of Despond* would be steep.

"Hey. Come see what we're making." Merri opened the door and stood aside to let them in.

John ruffled her hair as he stepped into the front hall. "Hey, Merri Christmas, it smells like cinnamon in here."

John's smile was awful and Abby was surprised Merri believed it. But Merri gave an answering smile and said, "It's the snickerdoodles."

"Oh, I love them," Abby said.

"Wouldn't advise that you actually eat them," John said. "Didn't Lucy warn you?"

"Yeah," Abby said. "But what can you do?"

"The first batch of snickerdoodles was terrible." Merri grimaced in memory. "Turns out it was supposed to be one *teaspoon* of cream of tartar, not one *tablespoon* like Beulah thought. Who knew a little thing like that would make such a difference?"

When they got to the kitchen Eulah, wearing padded mitts, was lifting a cookie sheet out of the oven. "Oh, John. We were wondering when you were going to come see us."

"The secret is snickerdoodles," he said. "I smelled the cinnamon and hurried over."

Abby set her tote bag on the floor and sat down at the table next to Beulah, who was doing something with lime green and purple yarn. "What are you knitting?"

Beulah set aside her work and smiled happily at her. "Not knitting, sweetie. It's crochet. I'm teaching Merri and she's taking to it like a duck to water."

"Let me see, Merri," Abby said.

Merri picked up her own yarn and held it up to show Abby. "It's going to be a hat."

"That's great, Merri. My Grandmother Flo tried to teach me, but I wasn't so good at it."

"Where have you two been?" Eulah said, handing

John a plate of cookies.

"First we went to the courthouse." John took a cautious bite of cookie on his way to sit at the table and then gave a quick grin and thumbs up to Merri. "Awesome snickerdoodles, ladies."

"Why, thank you, John," Eulah said. "Have another."

"Don't mind if I do," he said, snagging three more cookies.

Abby shook her head in amazement. "Back to the courthouse," she said. "We went there, hoping Dragon Lady was wrong and we'd find a marriage certificate."

"Well, at least you tried," Beulah said.

John held up a finger. "Not so fast. Then we went and snooped around in the newspaper archives."

"And she *was* wrong." Abby said. "Frances and Reuben were married."

"Really? Oh, that's marvelous!" Eulah beamed.

Beulah clapped her hands. "Oh, now Frances can have her husband apple!"

"It said so in the newspaper article anyway," Abby said. "I'm sure we'll find the marriage license eventually."

"So…" John looked at Abby as if he were wishing she'd throw him a life preserver. When she shrugged her shoulders, he continued. "Turns out that's not the reason Reuben's name was crossed out of Frances' Bible."

"What do you mean?" Eulah said.

"Come sit down," Abby said. "Please."

Abby opened her tote bag, took out some photocopied sheets, and set them on the table. "We found these."

"Newspaper clippings." Eulah looked from John to her. "What do they say?"

Abby glanced at him and paused. "I'll read them to you."

Shake Rag Corner Arsonist to Be Sentenced.

The Honorable Walter Lee Knight, Judge of the 3rd Judicial Circuit Court, has ordered that the prisoner Reuben Buchanan of Shake Rag Corner, found guilty of murder and arson, be brought before him to be sentenced tomorrow. Regular readers of the Alton Telegraph will recall that Deputy Sheriff George Benton arrested Buchanan, it being alleged Buchanan, on the 14th of October, 1871, set fire to the house of his employer Mr. Bertram White, destroying it and killing Mrs. White.

Beulah and Eulah put their hands to their faces in identical expressions of distress, crying out in unison, "Oh, no." Abby put a comforting hand on each sister. When Eulah said, "Go on, we'll be all right," she began to read again:

Evidence of his guilt accumulated during the course of the two-day trial. Mr. Joseph Nichols, proprietor of Happy's Market, testified that Buchanan purchased two gallons of kerosene from him for the alleged purpose of burning hedgerows. The grief-stricken widower testified, giving as motive Buchanan's jealousy of White's larger acreage and superior dwelling. Mr. White did testify that Buchanan probably believed Mrs. White to be absent from the house at the time he set fire to it. Buchanan admitted setting fire to the hedgerows near Mr. White's property under his direction, but claimed that he did not cause the destruction of the house.

Neighbors testified to ill will between Buchanan and Mr. White, although none offered the reason for their animosity. Buchanan was also charged with assaulting Mr. White earlier on the day of the arson, causing substantial contusions, abrasions, and a broken nose. The defendant refused to say why he had attacked Mr. White.

It is the hope of this reporter that a better, more honest class of citizens will, in the future, inhabit Shake Rag Corner and other villages in Alton's outskirts.

"Everyone has rotten apples in their closets." Beulah wiped her eyes with her hanky. "But I never thought I'd find any murderers in ours."

"You're mixing your metaphors, dear." Eulah patted her sister's arm and then sighed. Holding onto the table for support, she rose shakily to her feet and went to stare out the back storm door.

"What's that other paper that you have there?" Beulah said. "Does it say what his sentence was?"

"No. We'll have to go back and search again." Abby avoided looking at Beulah. She gathered up the papers and began to put them back into her bag.

Beulah put her hand on Abby's. "What is it, dear? Don't beat around the bush."

"There's a bit more in it. But it's not good." John took the paper from Abby's hand and paused.

Eulah turned from contemplating her back yard and made her way back to the table. Sitting down next to her sister, she said, "Go ahead. Read it to us."

"It's a letter to the editor of the Alton Telegraph," he said. "You won't like it." John read:

Our esteemed Representative Andrew King is to be commended for his insistence that our laws be enforced, yes that the laws prohibiting marriage between races be obeyed. One assumes the respected Edwards family wishes it had put its collective foot down in preventing the marriage of their daughter to the "half breed" who has so prominently figured in recent news. It is widely believed that Reuben Buchanan's Indian blood, inflamed by copious amounts of "fire water," led to his savage and cruel crime. As if the disgrace of having a criminal associated with the family were not enough, it was evident to any who, in civic duty, attended the recent trial, that the Edwards daughter will soon deliver evidence of the taint in the family's illustrious blood lines.

"It's such a load of bull," John said, throwing the article to the table. "It makes me madder every time I read it."

"I know! Can you believe the bigotry?" Abby said. "I mean, maybe he was a murderer…"

"Don't forget arsonist," Beulah said.

"But that had nothing to do with his Native American blood," Abby said. "The writer of that letter is a complete racist."

"It must have been so horrible for Albert William to grow up knowing his father was a murderer," Eulah said.

"Maybe he didn't know," Merri said. "After all, he lived with his grandparents and they changed his name to Edwards."

"I have a feeling they're the ones who crossed Reuben's name out of the family Bible," Abby said. "Not Franny."

"Father *was* quite dark," Beulah said. "He was such a handsome man, wasn't he?"

"Yes, he looked a lot like Reuben," Abby said.

The twins looked at her curiously.

"I mean…if we could have seen him…not that we could have, of course…"

"Of course…" John said, forging on. "That wouldn't

be possible. After all, that was a long time ago—over one hundred forty years ago."

"It was bad enough when we thought Reuben Buchanan hadn't married Frances Ann, but this!" Beulah said. "I guess our family tree is going to have to stay lopsided, because I'm not putting an apple on it for a murderer."

Abby cracked the oven door and peeked in. The lasagna was brown and bubbling nicely so she turned off the oven and went back to the salad she was working on. Merri called out something from the family room where she'd been typing away for the past hour, Dr. Bob keeping vigil at her side.

"I didn't hear you," Abby called back. She rinsed two celery stalks in the sink and then began to chop them on Lucy's cutting board.

"I said, how long does it have to be?"

"In inches or pages?" Abby said. "Because if we're doing inches, I'm thinking about twenty-four or five."

"What...?"

"You know, Harry Potter?"

"No thanks. I'm not thirsty," Merri called.

Abby tossed the celery into the salad bowl and laughed. "Just keep writing and I'll be there in a minute."

"I already have three pages," Merri called.

"Okay, okay, I'm coming," Abby hung up the dish towel and hurried to the family room. Reading over Merri's shoulder, she said, "Looks like you're really making progress."

"It's done," Merri said.

"Really? I hate to tell you this, but this is your rough

draft. Now you've got to revise it."

"I already ran Spell Check," Merri said.

"Good, but that's only a minor part of the revision process. We'll read it after dinner. But dinner's ready. Come help me set the table."

Abby's phone rang and she saw that it was Kate.

"Hi, Kate. I can't talk right now. I've got to get dinner on the table for John and Merri."

"That sounds positively unliberated. With all that time travel, you sure you're not stuck in the 1950s? Please tell me you're not wearing an apron."

"Hey, what's wrong with cooking for your friends? Merri's been working on her report, and John's busy researching for the Old Dears, so I'm making dinner."

"You sure I don't need to come down there and do an intervention?"

"I don't have time for an intervention. But I wish you would come visit me." Abby lowered her voice. "I need your guy radar. I still can't figure John out. One minute he's sending out signals all come here and let me kiss you. The next, he's running away like Cinderella when the clock strikes midnight."

"It's called psychological ambivalence," Kate said. "I learned about it in psychology class."

"I'm sure he's perfectly sane and healthy," Abby said drily. "He's just not that into me. He obviously wants a purely platonic relationship."

"Maybe he's fighting his attraction."

Abby poked her head into the dining room. "Dinner is ready."

John didn't answer, but this time it wasn't because of his iPod. For the past hour, he had been zoned out, only periodically looking up from his laptop to blurt out some factoid before turning back to his research.

"So when are you coming?" Abby said to Kate. "Soon, I hope."

"I can't for a while, and it's all your fault."

"What did I do?"

"I was telling Mom about your genealogy project and she gets all wide-eyed and says 'isn't Abby such a sweetheart to help them with that. I sure wish I could do our family tree. If only I knew how to work the computer.' So now we're in the thick of it and she'd murder me if I left now."

"Have fun, Kate. I've got to go now."

"Bye. See you eventually."

Merri, with Dr. Bob following faithfully along behind her, edged past Abby, carrying a stack of dishes.

"Hey, John, move your laptop, will you?" Merri said. When he nudged it over only about half an inch, muttering something about leg irons, she shook her head and set a fork to the left of his laptop and napkin and glass to the right of it.

Only when Abby returned and threatened to set the steaming lasagna on his laptop did he snap out of it. "Oh, sorry, Abby. You should have asked me to carry that in for you."

"Don't be silly. I'm not helpless. Besides, you're cleaning up after dinner."

"Only fair. That looks amazing." John rose and put his laptop and notes on the china hutch.

"Thanks, but Lucy had this in the freezer for us. However, for the record, I do make awesome lasagna myself."

John returned to his seat. "Here, give me your plates and I'll dish it up. I'm trying to be polite here, but hurry. I'm starving and feel a snarl coming on."

"It seems like only a little while ago you were snarfing

down cheeseburgers."

"That was then and this is now. Dear God, thank you for inventing lasagna," John said. "Amen."

"That was the shortest prayer I've ever heard," Merri said and laughed.

"Yes," Abby agreed. "But it sounded so heartfelt. So give, John. What did you find out while I was playing Susie Homemaker?"

"I looked for more information about Reuben's case, but couldn't find anything."

"So we still don't know what his sentence was?" Abby bit down into a piece of crusty garlic toast.

John swallowed a huge bite and wiped his mouth with his napkin. "Not exactly. I found the prison's list of inmates on a genealogy website. He only served two years."

"Wow! I thought back in those days the sentence for murder was more like hanging, not two years in prison," Abby said.

"No, you don't get it," John said. "He died in prison of natural causes. I still haven't found out how long his sentence was."

"I didn't know they even had prisons back in the olden days," Merri said.

"Sure," John said. "There was a prison right here in Alton, built in 1833—the first in the state."

"So that's where he died?" Abby said.

"Yeah, and I think I know where he was buried. After dinner let's go see—"

"Are you trying to get out of kitchen duty?" Abby said.

John grinned. "No, I promise. But if we're going to find Reuben, we've got to go now before it gets dark."

There was a state marker in front of a partial stone wall and crumbling cells, indicating where the first prison in the state of Illinois had once stood just off State Street.

"The cells were so small." Abby stepped off first the length and then the width of one of the cells. "I figure about four feet by six feet. Tall guys wouldn't even be able to stretch out flat."

"I'm getting a little claustrophobic thinking about it." John shuddered in distaste. "The website I found said the prison was designed for solitary confinement. I don't know which would be worse, that or being crammed in a cell with two other guys—which is what happened when this prison was used to house Confederate soldiers during the war." He squinted at the information sign, trying to read the faded print. "It says about 2,200 inmates died of dysentery and smallpox."

"I guess it didn't matter how many years the judge gave you," Abby said. "It was a death sentence when you got sent to Alton Prison."

John gazed down at the Mississippi River rolling by on its way south to the Gulf. "No wonder. We're only about fifty yards away from the river. I bet the cells were damp and nasty. And in the spring when the river rose—well it was a stupid place to build a prison. They closed it down eventually and moved the prisoners to Joliet."

"What's dysentery?" Merri asked.

"Some kind of intestinal infection," John said. "You get diarrhea, I mean *extreme* diarrhea."

"What a horrible way to go," Merri said. "pooping yourself to death."

"Come on," John said. "We'd better hurry. I think the cemetery closes at dusk."

They followed State Street as it climbed the steep hill

away from the riverbank and found Alton Prison Cemetery tucked away in what was currently a quiet residential neighborhood shaded by mature oak trees. A black wrought iron fence enclosed a small green plot. Standing sentinel in the center was a stone obelisk, like a miniature Washington Monument. The cemetery's iron gates were closed and Abby thought at first they had gotten there too late, but they swung open on well-oiled hinges and she stepped inside. The grass grew thick and healthy, as if no one ever walked on it.

"I never knew there was such a thing as a prison cemetery." Something about the quiet beauty of the place had Abby whispering the words.

"I didn't either until I found a website about them," John said quietly. "It said a lot of families don't come to claim the body when a prisoner dies—after an execution or even when it's of natural causes."

"I guess no one wants a murderer buried next to them in the family plot." The obelisk seemed strangely compelling, and Abby started toward it, curious to examine it.

"Even for really bad guys, prisons have some sort of burial service," John said. "Usually a chaplain comes, or at least the warden, and they say a few words."

"So where are the graves?" Merri said, catching up to Abby.

"Well," John said slowly. "Actually, we're walking on them."

Abby stopped and looked down at her feet in alarm. "What?"

"See, when the Confederate soldiers started dying so fast from dysentery—and then the smallpox epidemic—they couldn't keep up with all the burials. They'd just put up a wooden cross to mark the spot and move on to the next grave. And then when Alton Prison was shut down, no one thought to take care of the cemetery. The men's families were far away in the South. The wooden markers eventually rotted out, and now no one knows exactly where the graves are."

"That's terrible," Merri said indignantly.

"Yeah, well, that's why some Southern organization put up that monument," John said, pointing to the obelisk.

When they reached it, Abby saw that dozens of names had been engraved on brass plaques attached to it. "So Reuben's name is on here someplace?"

"Well, no," John said. "This is just for the Confederate prisoners. But I'm hoping he's down there." Beyond the obelisk, the ground sloped gently into a green valley studded with a dozen or so white headstones that hadn't been visible when they entered at the gate.

A dove sang its mournful tune from high in the branches of an oak tree as Abby slowly made her way down the rows, caught up in the stories the headstones told. She almost forgot what she was looking for until she heard Merri shout. "I found it! Over here."

Reuben's marker was near the fence at the bottom of the hill. The words were faint and worn on the slab of sandstone. Kneeling, Abby traced them with her finger: *Reuben Buchanan, #327-320, Died March 23, 1873, aged 22 years.*

"He died so young." Abby pulled a weed that had grown up next to the stone and tossed it away.

"Yeah," John said. "Only one year older than me."

"He may have been a murderer, but Franny loved him so much." Abby stood and went to put an arm around Merri. "Here we are in a sad cemetery again. We shouldn't have brought you."

"I'm all right."

"Even if he was a murderer, it's sad," John said. "Since they scratched his name out of the family Bible and left him for the state to bury in the prison cemetery, I guess it's safe to say Reuben never got a chance to see his son."

"And," Merri said, "they changed his son's name to Edwards."

"And soon," Abby said, "Reuben's name will be completely worn off this sandstone."

John stared off into the trees in the distance. "And you know? I'm just not convinced he's guilty. If they had had a solid case they would have hanged him."

"Maybe it was an accident," Abby said.

"That would make it second degree murder or even involuntary manslaughter. Surely the Old Dears would feel a lot better about having a convicted felon in their family tree if it was an accident—not on purpose."

"Yeah," Merri said. "At least maybe the guy would get an apple with his name on it."

John took Abby's arm and started toward the Mustang. "Let's go back and see what really—"

"I sure don't want to see—"

"Yeah," Merri interrupted. "I think we should add another rule for time-surfing. No watching people burn into crispy critters. Should be an R rating for that kind of violence."

"Well, if you two don't want to watch it, I could go alone. Tim gave me the app for my phone. I could put it on the sidewalk outside the museum and—"

"Oh, no you don't," Abby said. "That's a rule. No one surfs alone. We do it together."

CHAPTER 12

"Watch out for the hole," John said.

"Trust me, I'm watching out for the hole," Abby said. "If we stay on this side of the room we should be okay." She felt her phone vibrate and pulled it out of her pocket. "It's Merri."

"Get out!" Merri said.

"What's wrong?"

"Someone's snooping around in the yard. He's— Get out now!"

Abby pocketed her phone and tugged on John's arm. "Quick! Out the back. Someone's here."

Before they had taken more than a few steps, the front door screeched open and slammed against the wall. A strong light filled the room, blinding them. Abby shaded her eyes with her arm. When she squinted she could see the outlines of a hulking figure behind the light.

The man cursed and started toward them. "What are you doing in here? This is no place for making out," he said, adding a muttered, "Stupid kids."

Abby started to back up and remembered the hole in the floor. "We weren't making out," she squeaked indignantly. Like that was ever going to happen.

"Well, what are you doing then?"

"Could you turn that light somewhere else besides our eyes?" John said.

The man lowered the light a bit but remained a hulk-like figure with a vague but menacing face.

"Research," John said. "We're researching old stage coach stops."

"Well, go *research* somewhere else. This is private property."

"Are you Mr. Buchanan?" Abby said.

"None of your business." He raised the light again to their faces. "You get out right now."

"Okay, okay. We're going." John took Abby's arm and they skirted past the man and out the front door.

Merri met them in the street. "I'm sorry I couldn't warn you sooner. He just showed up. Who is he?"

"I think it's the Incredible Hulk," Abby said, "but I'm not hanging around to find out."

"Wait." John held onto Abby's arm. "I want to see what he's up to."

They ducked behind a tree and Abby worked at catching her breath. The man's light wavered in the front windows and then settled into a steady glow. Then came the unmistakable sound of metal striking stone.

"What's he doing?" Merri said.

"I don't know, but hopefully he'll finish whatever it is and get out of there."

"You're crazy. We're not going back there," Abby said.

"Let's go around to the back. I bet he's parked there."

John took off around the side of the house. Abby followed him into tall grass and weeds. Merri was behind her, muttering about snakes and being arrested for trespassing.

"Shhh." John stopped and Abby ran into his back. "There's his truck."

A light-colored pickup was backed right up to the porch. A dim light shone from the kitchen window, wavered crazily, and then got brighter.

"He's coming." John ducked behind an overgrown shrub and Abby and Merri huddled beside him.

They could hear the man trying to open the back door. It shook and screeched part way open then slammed shut, like some invisible prankster was leaning against the door. He cursed and kicked at it. The door flew open and they saw him, backlit in the doorway. He carried something in his arms, something so heavy he grunted from the exertion. He came down the porch steps and slowly lowered the something to the bed of the pickup. When he pushed it farther into the truck the thing made a harsh grating sound against the metal bed. Wiping his hands on his pants, he stepped onto the porch and went back inside the house.

The light from the open door wavered again and then got steadily dimmer. The sound of metal striking stone started again.

"A rock?" John whispered. "The guy's stealing rocks?"

"First he had acted like he owned the place," Abby said, "but now he's sneaking the stones out like he's afraid of being caught."

"Maybe we should call the police," Merri said.

Abby and John ignored her suggestion.

"Where's he getting them, anyway?" John said.

Abby felt Merri squirming beside her. "What's wrong?"

"I gotta go. Can we go home now?"

"Can't you go over there...or something?" John said, pointing vaguely back to the overgrown shrub.

"No, John, I can't."

Abby laughed into the soft summer night, imagining Merri's eyes rolling in disgust.

John was still wiping the last of the dishwater off his hands onto his jeans when he and Abby stepped out onto Lucy's front porch. Abby propped her elbows on the porch rail and inhaled the scent of four o'clocks and night-blooming nicotiana in the humid air. It was the smell of summer and home and she thought of her father's garden. "At last it's cooled down a little," she said.

John didn't seem to notice. "We've got to get back to Shake Rag—"

"Shhh. Listen," she said. "The Old Dears are on their porch too."

Abby heard the squeak of the twins' porch swing and then their voices drifting on the sweet summer air. She couldn't tell their voices apart.

"Remember how Father used to sit out here and swing and swing?" one twin said.

"We took turns sitting on his lap while the other one sat on the swing next to him," the other twin added.

"Funny, I can't remember him ever saying much. He just smiled at our chattering and hummed."

"*Amazing Grace.*"

"And every day we'd hunt in his shirt pockets to find his Juicy Fruit gum."

"He'd pretend to be so surprised it was there."

"Do you think he knew?"

"Of course he knew. He put it there."

"Not the gum, silly. About his grandfather. That he was a murderer?"

"Maybe. That could be why he never talked about his family. He must have had cousins and such."

"It would have been nice to have cousins."

"Even Prissy."

There was a long pause with only the squeak of the swing accompanying the crickets.

"At least we had each other growing up."

"And for a few more days we've got pretend grandchildren."

The chain on their porch swing rattled and a twin grunted as she struggled to stand. "I'm going in. You coming?"

The second twin grunted and the swing rattled again. The door snicked open. "I just got an idea. Since Sunday's the Fourth of July—" The door closed and the swing's creaking slowed and stopped.

"I feel so bad for the Old Dears," Abby said. "No family—unless you count us."

John pulled away from the column he'd been leaning against and came closer. He grinned and his teeth gleamed white in the darkness. "Hey, don't forget that old pincher Priscilla."

"And now they find out their grandfather was a murderer."

"*Great* grandfather, or maybe not so great. I'd go back tonight and try to find out, but I'm too beat."

"No wonder. Climbing around on roofs by day and then going up against incredible rock-stealing hulks by night." Abby grinned until she saw that John's face was coming closer, so close his lips nearly touched hers, and then she had to concentrate on just breathing.

"Abby...?"

"Yes?"

"Is tomorrow Thursday?"

"Yes."

"Don't forget to set out the trash cans." John stepped away and she fell back. Fortunately the porch column was there. "I'll see you tomorrow." He hurried down the steps, two at a time. "I'll come by after work to mow the grass and then later we can do some time-surfing."

"Oh. All right, then," she said and plopped down on the top step and watched him drive away. Would she ever understand what was going on in his head?

CHAPTER 13

Abby stretched another inch but still couldn't reach the newspaper that had fallen behind the shrubs in front of the twins' porch.

"What in the world are you doing?" Merri said behind her.

"I'm on a quest." Abby dropped to her knees and crawled behind the bushes until she could reach the newspaper in its plastic wrapper. "Would it hurt them to take one more nanosecond to aim a little better?" As she backed out, a sneaky azalea branch latched onto her shirt. When she had disentangled it she stood and looked down at her dirty knees.

"Here," Merri said, "You've got a twig in your hair." She picked it out but then flung it to the ground. "It's alive!" she said, doing what Abby thought of as the Yikes-I-Just-Saw-A-Mouse dance.

"Calm down. It's just a praying mantis."

"Oh." Merri exhaled in relief. "I know about them."

The petunias in the planters hanging from the twins' porch were more brown than pink, the leaves a crispy, grayish green. "These will never make it," Abby said, frowning. "Looks like the Old Dears have been forgetting to water again. And... well...I sort of forgot too."

"Could we buy them more?"

"That's a nice idea," Abby said as she rang the doorbell. "Let's see if the Old Dears want to go shopping."

Abby had never thought of Walmart as a particularly dangerous place. But that was before she had gone shopping with two 85-year-old speed demons driving motorized carts. There was the danger of a cart running over her heels if she walked in front of one of the twins. But she was just as likely to get her toes flattened if she walked in back. The twins favored sudden, unannounced reversals. And when they blocked aisle three with their tandem carts, preventing harried shoppers who wanted to stock up on potato chips from passing in either direction, Abby feared a riot would break out. She finally convinced Beulah to park on the same side of the aisle as Eulah, and the danger was averted.

"I didn't know you had trouble walking, Beulah," Abby said. "You did so well at the museum and library."

Beulah smiled happily. "We just like to ride in the carts."

Eulah turned to smile back at them. "Since we don't get to drive anymore, this is about as exciting as it gets." Abby weighed the two options and decided letting the twins terrorize Walmart shoppers was better than letting them loose on the streets of Alton.

"Let's get the extra cheesy, extra crunchy ones,"

Beulah said, pointing to the top shelf.

Abby took down a bag of cheese puffs and put it into Beulah's cart. It added a nice touch to the weird assortment of items already there. Among pots of replacement petunias there was a tub of yogurt, hearing aid batteries, a cake with red, white, and blue icing, a roll of cellophane tape, toilet paper, tan shoe laces, four ears of corn, and a stuffed penguin dog toy. Her selections together with Eulah's—her cart was even fuller—came from all four corners of the 60,000- square-foot store.

"Is there anything else you need?" Merri was smiling, but Abby could tell her patience was wearing dangerously thin.

"I think that's it," Eulah said.

"Unless you think we need more shampoo," Beulah said.

Abby stifled a groan. The shampoo aisle was at least five miles away at the other end of the store.

"I think we've got plenty left…but I *was* wanting to try that new kind they had on the TV. Gives you extra body."

"Let's wait until next time," Beulah said. "It'll give us something to look forward to."

Abby let out the breath she had been holding and chanced a glance at Merri. She was already in line at the checkout.

Abby turned the hose to low pressure and gently watered the petunias she had just set into the porch planters.

"Oh, that's darling," Beulah said. "They look like red, white, and blue flags. Just in time for the Fourth of July."

"Red, white, and *purple*," Eulah said. "But I guess it's

close enough. Now we'll just have to remember harder to water these."

"Sometimes our rememberers don't work so well these days," Beulah said.

"Is there anything else we can do for you ladies?" Abby said.

"Oh, we wouldn't want to impose," Beulah said.

"But there is one other thing…" Eulah looked like she was forcing herself to say it. "The light bulb over the sink needs changing. Beulah will fall and break her neck trying to do it."

Abby had the alarming image of Beulah on the floor. "Oh, no. Don't you be getting up on a ladder. We'll do it."

After that, the twins remembered the kitchen scraps that needed taking out to the compost bin in back, which made them remember that the beans needed picking, which led to the discovery that the weeds were getting out of control in the garden.

Abby tossed a pile of weeds into the compost bin and then stretched her back. Merri, her face red and sweaty, dumped an armful on top of that and then stood panting in the sun.

Abby rubbed at a scratch on her arm. "Good job, kiddo. I think that's all."

John, in shorts and a sleeveless T-shirt, came around the corner of the house pushing the lawnmower. He turned off the mower and smiled when he saw them. "I'm all done. How about you?"

"I hope so," Abby said, wiping her sweaty face with her sleeve. Her shorts had muddy brown and weedy green stains that probably wouldn't come out. No telling what her hair looked like.

"Can we go home now?" Merri said. "I'm exhausted from loving my neighbor."

"I don't know how Lucy does all this and still has time to see patients," John said, pushing the mower into the garden shed.

"Don't look now, but here they come again," Merri said.

Beulah stood on the back porch waving at them. "Yoo, hoo, we've got a treat for you."

John whispered, "You don't think they were baking again, do you? What is it now? Another chalky coffee cake? Another sugar-free pie?"

"Yum. How about gooseberry? That's extra tart," Abby said.

"How about an Abby pie?" John said, his voice all velvety and low. "That'd be extra sweet." He smiled into her eyes and her heart did something weird in her chest.

Abby realized she was blinking stupidly. She probably looked like a fish. Then she was angry. He wanted to be just friends, but then he had to go and say a thing like that. "Come on," she said, wiping her hands on the seat of her shorts. "They'll just walk all the way out here if we don't go up there." Abby exhaled and headed toward the house.

"What?" John said. "Abby, are you mad at me?"

Abby pretended not to hear and continued up the path to the house.

"What did I do?"

"Beats me," Merri said and followed Abby up the path.

"Ice cream cones," Beulah sang from the kitchen. "Just like *our* grandmother made for *us*."

"Hurry," Eulah said, handing Abby a tall vanilla cone, "before it melts."

"Thanks." Surely there was no way they could mess up ice cream.

"And don't think this is the only thanks you're going to get."

"We're inviting you over for dinner tomorrow night," Beulah said proudly. "We're going to make roast beef."

After wiping her hands, Eulah took down a Walker's Toffee tin from the kitchen hutch and opened it. "And here's a little something, too." She took out some dollar bills and handed them each three.

Merri said, "Gee, thanks, Grandma."

Abby hadn't had an allowance since she was twelve. She opened her mouth to decline, but the twins looked so pleased and dignified that instead she ended up saying, "Thank you."

John looked like he'd just been handed a dead fish instead of legal tender, but he smiled politely, said thanks, and put the money in his pocket.

"It will be a real family dinner," Eulah continued. "Only we'll have to go shopping again."

"They have electric carts at the Shop 'N Save too," Beulah said.

"Sorry," John began. "But I'm going…" He seemed to be thinking furiously.

Merri telegraphed a frantic message to Abby. "I'm afraid we can't make it tomorrow," Abby said. "It's Merri's dad. That's what it is. He's coming for a visit. And we're going out to eat."

"That's wonderful, Merri! Can we meet him?" Eulah said.

"Maybe after we get back from the restaurant, we could come by," Abby said. "What do you think, Merri?"

Merri smiled at the twins. "Sure. I want my dad to meet my new pretend grandmothers." Then her eyes widened and she said, "I know. Why don't you go with us. We're going to go to the Brown Cow."

"Oh, goody," Beulah said.

Eulah put her arm around Merri and hugged her. "We'll all be together—like a family dinner."

"You too, John," Beulah said.

"So I get to be an honorary grandchild too?"

"You sure do," Beulah said.

"Only makes sense." Abby sniffed. "You're just like the older brother we never had, right, Merri?" Except, of course, *she* already had older brothers and really didn't need any more.

Merri grinned. "Hey, big bro."

John pulled Merri's hair. "Okay, Merri Christmas. But you realize this means I get to tease you unmercifully?" And me too, apparently, Abby thought.

When they had said their goodbyes and stepped out onto the back porch, Merri rushed ahead of them down the path. "I'm getting out of here before they *remember* any other jobs for us to do."

"Yes," Abby said. "Their rememberers seem to be working just fine today."

John put a sweaty arm around Abby and pulled her to his side. "There's something I have to clear up before you go."

Something must be seriously wrong with her, because even his sweat smelled good. Then she remembered pheromones were excreted in sweat and tried not to inhale. "What?" she said suspiciously and pulled back a step. She was running out of Christmasy things to think about. It was still six months away and she had already thought of a gift for everyone on her list.

"I'm sorry," he said.

"For what?"

"I don't know. Whatever you're mad about."

"Fine," she said and turned to follow Merri.

"Good. So how soon can you be ready to go back out to Shake Rag Corner?"

She mentally staggered. "Are you kidding?" She meant, there you go again being all ambivalent, but he misunderstood.

"Oh, right. I guess you're too tired," he said.

"That's for sure," Abby said. Sick and tired, she thought, nodding her head sadly.

"Okay, then," John said. "I'll meet you at the restaurant tomorrow. We can go afterwards."

CHAPTER 14

John joined them just as the hostess called them for their table, but Merri's dad still hadn't arrived. Abby reminded her it was only three minutes past six.

"Be sure to tell my dad where we're sitting," Merri said to the hostess. "His name is Brad Randall."

The woman smiled kindly at Merri. "I sure will, honey."

"You all just order anything you like," Eulah said. "I am going to get steak"

"You don't have to pay for ours," John said.

"Nonsense," Eulah said. "You have done so much to help us. It is the least we can do."

"Oh my," Beulah said when she had opened her menu. "It has been a while since we've eaten in a nice restaurant." After a pause she said, "Maybe we *had* better go Dutch, Eulah."

"That would be perfect," Abby said with relief.

Merri took out her phone. "No bars," she said

mournfully. But then she looked up and her face lit with sudden joy. "Dad! Over here." She nearly overturned her chair in her eagerness to get to the man standing in the doorway.

Merri threw her arms around him and he kissed the top of her head and stroked her hair. "You're so skinny, Dad." At last she turned him loose and took him by the hand. "Come see my new friends."

He looked confused. "I thought it was just us, Merri." As they drew closer to the table he seemed to realize he had been rude. "I'm sorry. I'm happy to meet you all. I'm Merri's dad, Brad Randall."

"This is Abby," Merri said. "I told you all about her. And John's her boyfriend. And these are my friends Miss Beulah and Miss Eulah."

"Hello," Eulah said. "We've been having the most delightful time getting to know Merri. You must be very proud of her."

"I am, ma'am." Brad sat in the chair next to Merri.

"She's agreed to be our pretend granddaughter," Beulah said. "It's so nice to have her right next door."

He looked in confusion to Merri. "I didn't know you had new neighbors. What happened to Mrs. Arnold?"

"She lives in Miles Station, Dad. Beulah and Eulah live next door to Lucy."

"Refresh my memory. Who's Lucy?"

"She's the one who's helping Michael. Don't you remember?"

Brad sniffed and rubbed his nose. "Michael? Er...I guess I forgot that part, honey."

"Oh, we have such trouble with our rememberers too, don't we, Eulah?"

Brad picked up the menu and opened it. "Well I'd better have a look at this before the waitress comes."

Stroking his thin beard, he concentrated on the menu, while the others discussed the comparative merits of rib eye and sirloin steaks and the degree of doneness each should be.

After they ordered their steaks, Merri bombarded her dad with questions about home. His answers were vague and she seemed to be getting frustrated with him. Abby glanced at John but he was looking down at something, and she wondered if it was his phone. When her own phone vibrated, she frowned but pulled it discreetly out of her purse. John had texted her: "What's with this Brad? See how his hands shake? Is he on something?"

Abby saw that Brad, his eyes darting around, was tapping his fingers rapidly on the table. Abby gave John a tiny shake of her head. She put her phone back in her purse and a big smile on her face. "Tell your dad what Eulah and Beulah have been teaching you, Merri."

"Oh, yeah. Dad, they're teaching me to crochet and make cookies. Wait until you see what I'm making you."

Eulah beamed at Brad. "You're in for a big surprise."

"Here comes our waitress," Abby said. The waitress set the huge tray on a stand near their table and started handing out plates.

Across the table from her, Eulah and Beulah were looking confused. Maybe the waitress had gotten their orders wrong, Abby thought. But then she turned and saw they were watching two police officers purposefully coming their way.

The older officer wore a white crew cut and sagging jowls. "Bradley Randall," he growled, "you're under arrest for the manufacture and distribution of methamphetamines, possession of cannabis, child endangerment, contributing to the delinquency of a minor." He paused and pointed a thumb at the parking lot out the window, "And parking in a handicap space."

Brad's eyes were huge and he put his hands up, whether to show he was unarmed or to make the nightmare stop, Abby didn't know.

As they all stared in shock, the younger officer hauled Brad to his feet and cuffed his hands behind his back, all the while reciting his Miranda rights. Abby sat there in a daze, but Merri bolted to her dad and threw her arms around his waist.

"Daddy, no. You can't take my daddy."

The officer holding Brad Randall looked like he'd rather be somewhere else. "It'll be all right, honey." He turned to Abby with a helpless look, as if little girls were too much for him to handle. John pushed his chair back and went to pull Merri away from her father. "Come here, Merri," he said, hugging her close.

At last the paralysis left her and Abby hurried to comfort Merri. A part of her brain registered the shocked expressions and exclamations from the other diners.

As the officers took him away, Brad turned and looked in anguish at his daughter. "I'm sorry, baby."

Abby flipped her phone shut and went into the twins' living room. Merri still sobbed on the sofa next to Eulah, who was patting her back and crooning over and over, "It'll be all right."

John was nervously pacing. His head snapped up when he saw her. "Did you reach her?"

"Yes. She's showing a house not far from here." Abby sat down next to Merri and took her hands into hers. "I finally got a hold of your mom, sweetie. She's coming right over."

She handed a tissue to Merri, who wiped her eyes and nose and then held it clenched in her fists. "They're wrong. They're lying. My dad wouldn't ever do what they said."

Abby took a deep breath and exhaled slowly. "Merri, honey...you'll have to talk to your mom when she gets here. She told me that—"

"It's true then?"

Abby paused and looked into Merri's reddened eyes. "That's why she took you away from there, to protect you."

Merri began to cry harder, wailing over and over, "He'll go to jail and I'll never see him again."

Abby looked helplessly at John, who had stopped pacing and come to stand behind the sofa.

Finally, Pat arrived, near tears and out of breath. She kneeled in front of Merri, and, ironically, repeated her ex-husband's last words to their daughter, "Oh, baby, I'm sorry."

To give Merri and her mother privacy, Abby and the others went to the kitchen and sat at the twins' table.

"He was cooking meth right in their back yard," Abby explained. "Merri's mom was afraid the whole place was going to blow sky high."

"Is that against zoning?" Eulah said. "I know the big cities are very strict."

"I'm glad Alton's not so strict," Beulah said. "I'd hate it if we couldn't have weiner roasts anymore."

Abby felt a huge laugh begin in her throat and swallowed hard. John wasn't so polite and belted out a laugh, before covering his mouth and looking guiltily toward the living room door where Merri was still crying softly.

"Merri's dad wasn't arrested for outdoor cooking," Abby explained patiently. "He was making illegal drugs and selling them."

Beulah and Eulah wore identical wide-eyed expressions of horror.

"Oh," Beulah said.

"Well, this is a fine kettle of fish," Eulah said glumly.

John's smile sort of fell off his face and he slouched in his chair. "It would be bad enough to find out your dad was a drug dealer without being there for the arrest."

"As the whole world watched." Abby propped her elbows on the table and put her head in her hands. "It was bound to happen sooner or later. Pat said he just laughed it off when she tried to get him to stop."

"From his nervousness at the restaurant, I'd guess he's been sampling his own product too much, if you know what I mean," John said.

"I wonder how much prison time he'll get."

"He'll get extradited back to Cook County."

"Do they let kids visit in prisons?" Eulah said.

"I think so," Abby said. "But can you imagine how horrible that must be?" After a moment of silence, she continued. "In a way, your grandfather Albert William was lucky."

"What do you mean?" Eulah said.

"At least he never knew his father was a murderer."

"Or arsonist," Beulah added. "I'm going to make us something to eat. We've got to keep our strength up, especially with all this conflaberation going on."

When Eulah saw the tray her sister had prepared, she rolled her eyes. "I don't think Merri's in the mood for cheese puffs and peanut butter sandwiches."

Beulah sniffed. "These are peanut *better* sandwiches— just what she needs to cheer her up."

Beulah looked so crushed that Abby smiled and said, "Well, I'm hungry. And I'm sure John is too."

John looked up with interest. "We did miss dinner."

Eulah pushed herself up from the table. "I'm sorry, Beulah Mae. You're right. Merri needs to eat. Here, I'll take it to her."

John stood quickly. "You ladies go ahead and check on Merri. I'll bring the tray." John watched the swinging kitchen door shut on the twins, then pulled a wad of dollar bills out of his pocket and went furtively to the hutch. "I've been waiting for a chance to do this."

"Here," Abby said, laughing as she took the lid off the Walker's Toffee tin. "Put it back quick."

Abby and John waited on the twins' front porch for Merri to wake up. The creaking of the swing and chirping of the crickets were the only sounds as they sat in the dark. Merri had conked out on the twins' sofa, exhausted from crying. Pat had wanted to take her home. Abby smiled sadly in the darkness thinking of Merri's reaction to that. Even though she was worried sick about her dad, she had insisted she had to stay and finish her housesitting job.

"Did you catch what she was mumbling as she drifted off to sleep?" John said sleepily.

"No. What?"

"Something about her dad dying of prison pooping."

Abby couldn't stop the laugh from slipping out. "It's not funny, I know. We'll have to find a way to reassure her that inmates don't die of dysentery anymore."

John put his arm along the back of the swing and she wished he would put it around her, if only for a short while. She heard firecrackers popping and thought, wow, he wasn't even touching her. No telling what would happen if he kissed her.

"Sounds like people are getting a head start on the Fourth of July," John said.

"Oh," Abby said. "I thought I was imagining things."

The porch light came on and they covered their eyes against the glare. Then the front door opened and Eulah stuck her head out.

"Is Merri okay?" Abby said. The swing jangled loudly as she and John rose from it.

"The poor little thing's all tuckered out, bless her heart," Eulah whispered. "I think she'll sleep through the night. But will you be all right over there alone in the house, Abby? You could spend the night with us too."

"I'll be fine," Abby said.

"Good night, then. Bye, John."

After Eulah shut the door, John pulled Abby close and gave her what could only be described as a brotherly kiss on the forehead. She knew she should be grateful he was even touching her.

"I think that was Eulah's hint for me to go home," he said.

She inhaled his scent and soaked up his warmth while she could. Then he pulled away and said, "Come on. I'll walk you home."

"I thought we were going to go back to Shake Rag Corner."

"I'm dying to go to Shake Rag Corner. But I know you must be tired, and besides, what if Merri needs you?"

"You heard Eulah. She'll sleep through the night. Come on. Let's go see if we can find out more about Reuben."

CHAPTER 15

"What do you think, Miss Franny? Will Lucinda like it?"

"She's going to love it, Jemmy. Won't she, Reuben?"

Reuben chewed his last bit of bacon and pretended to consider the question. Franny swatted his arm with her tea towel. He smiled and said, "I reckon any woman would love it, Jemmy."

Jemmy admired the locket on its bed of pink satin a moment longer before closing the jewelry box. "I surely hope so. I mean to convince her to marry me, though I don't know why such a fine woman would settle for a gimp like me." Jemmy patted the stump of his right leg.

"Of course she'll marry you. You're a hero, Jem Turner," Reuben said. "And you got a medal to prove it from Colonel Miles."

"Just 'cause the Rebs done blew my leg off don't make me no hero, Rube. But I was proud to serve next to the colonel and your pa in the 27th."

"Jemmy, you were a hero before you ever went to

war," Franny said. "Why, you helped Reuben save dozens of lives."

"You'ins hid 'em and fed 'em. I just walked 'em to the next stop along the way."

Franny's eyes twinkled. "To Colonel Miles' house, where a certain Miss Lucinda Brown was dedicated to the same cause?"

Jemmy grinned. "She sure was a sight for sore eyes after a long walk through the night. I hope you're right 'bout her takin' me on as husband."

"Well if you don't get your carcass on the stage, you'll never know, will you?" Reuben said. "I hear it coming."

And then Franny heard the wheels and pounding hooves. "Oh dear!" She hurried to wave her tea towel out the door as Jemmy struggled to rise from his chair.

Abby blinked, stifled a yawn, and then smiled when she saw that John's hair was sticking up all over. He'd been running his hands through it again, either in fatigue or distraction. In spite of that, his face was lit with excitement.

"So this was a stop on the Underground Railroad," he said. "I knew there were several in Alton. There's supposed to be tunnels under the—"

"Yes, but, John, did you get it? They were talking about Charlotte and Colonel Miles. Franny and Reuben know them...I mean knew them. I can't wait to tell Merri."

"It's about seven or eight miles to Miles Station." he said. "Not far to drive. But that Jemmy guy and the slaves walked it at night."

"And Reuben? How could such a good man turn out to be a murderer?"

"They say war does bad things to a guy's head," he said.

"Maybe. But I just know he didn't do it."

"Okay. Let's keep looking."

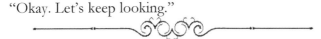

Franny set the plate of muffins on the table and smiled in satisfaction. It was good to get out her mother's china from time to time even if there were a thousand chores still to do. Now if only Mrs. White would have the courage to come. There was a rustle on the porch and then a timid knock and she hurried to open the door. Mrs. White was there in her usual drab gray bombazine dress.

"You came. I'm so glad."

Smiling shyly, Mrs. White glanced back toward her own home across the road and then to a point somewhere to the left of Franny's face. "I thank you for inviting me."

Franny gently took her by the arm and led her into the kitchen. "Everything's ready and the kettle's about to boil."

When Mrs. White saw the table, her smile grew larger. The cream-colored teacups were rimmed with pink roses and a green Mason jar of purple irises sat in the center of the table. "It's beautiful, but I don't want to be a bother."

"I'm glad for the company. I don't get to use my mother's china nearly often enough."

Mrs. White sat stiffly at the edge of her seat while Franny poured boiling water into the teapot and then took the kettle back to the stove.

"I've been studying in Ephesians."

Mrs. White contemplated her hands where they lay in her lap. "I reckon that's the part about submitting to your husband."

"So you're familiar with Ephesians, then?" Franny sat at the table and opened her Bible.

"It's Mr. White's favorite book of the Bible."

Franny smiled. "The men love that part, don't they? But look at verse twenty-one. It says, for

169

'*everyone* to submit to one another out of reverence for Christ.' I imagine you never heard that preached on, did you?"

"No, I never did."

"Or how about this verse, 'Husbands, love your wives, just as Christ loved the church and gave himself up for her.' Don't you suppose that means women are important to God too? That he loves them as much as he does the men?"

Mrs. White frowned in confusion and then looked down at her hands again. "I don't know. Mr. White says man was made in the image of God, not woman. She was made in the image of man."

"But that would make women something less than fully human," Franny said indignantly. She handed the plate of muffins to Mrs. White, who timidly stretched out a hand to take one. As she did, her sleeve retreated, revealing finger-shaped bruises on the pale skin of her wrist. She quickly tugged her sleeve back down, and Franny turned away until she could school her face to a pleasant smile.

Then she turned in her Bible to Genesis. "See what it says here in chapter five," she said gently. "Right there? 'When God created man, he made him in the likeness of God. He created them male and female...and when they were created, he called them 'man.' What do you think? Doesn't that mean Eve was made in God's image too?"

Mrs. White looked up, her face a mixture of surprise and uncertainty.

Praying constantly, Franny continued to lead Mrs. White to a fuller understanding of the Scripture. It would take time to break through the fear and error, but she seemed receptive. The morning passed quickly and Mrs. White smiled more and more freely until Franny said, "Where did the time go? Here it is almost noon and I told

Reuben I'd bring him his dinner."

The smile on Mrs. White's face drained away quickly. "Oh, no!" She bolted from her chair. "I've got to go now. Mr. White will be back from town soon." When she was on the porch, she paused. "I'm sorry I can't help with the dishes."

"Don't worry about that," Franny said, smiling. "Just say you'll come back again."

"I'd like that so much. I'll come…if I can."

Franny watched sadly from the window for a bit. Mrs. White was fairly running home as if the Devil were after her. She had only meant to bring a bit of sunshine into her life—not cause more trouble.

Franny wrapped a piece of last night's cornbread and this morning's bacon in a tea towel and put it into the muslin feed sack she kept ready. Then, putting on her bonnet she took the feed sack and a clean mason jar and went out to the well in the back yard. It took a bit of maneuvering, but she managed to lean over and grab the damp rope. Then she pulled, hand over hand, until she could grab the handle of the brown stoneware jug that was suspended from it and lug it over the top. After uncorking it, she tipped the heavy jug and poured icy cold buttermilk into the mason jar. She capped the jar tight and then recorked the jug and lowered it carefully back down into the spring-fed well. It took a lot of time and effort, but Reuben was sure to be hot and tired and he loved cold buttermilk better than just about anything.

The smell of fresh-turned earth and the sound of birds happily discussing their nest-building work filled the air as Franny made her way down the road to the field where Reuben was planting corn. She crossed the ditch beside the road and then entered the field through a break in the hedgerow. Reuben's horse Benny woke from a nap and whickered a greeting. Benny and the farm cart were pulled up in the shade of some Osage orange trees that Reuben's father had planted in his youth. She set her sack on the cart, and holding her hand to shade her face, looked across to see Reuben just coming over a small rise that had up until then hidden him from her view. Even though he carried a heavy sack of seed corn over his shoulder, he seemed unaffected by it. He was walking steadily, in an arrow-straight row, operating the planting drill. When he saw her, he set it down, took off his wide-brimmed hat, and then lowered the sack to the ground. He smiled, his teeth a bright contrast to his tanned and dirty face, and then put his hat back on and started toward her.

By the time he crossed the field, Franny, had laid out his meal on the floor of the cart and hitched herself up to sit beside it.

"What a sight for my poor eyes." Reuben said.

"What? Me or the cornbread?"

Pretending to consider the question, he pushed her bonnet back and grinned. "Hmm. You'll just have to guess which I love more." He lowered his mouth to hers. "Thank you, darlin,' for bringing me my dinner."

Franny patted Reuben's dirty face tenderly. "Thank you, husband, for all the work you do. I just wish it didn't have to be so hard." She gestured to the north where Mr. White's hired hand Jemmy was planting his field with the help of his new horse-drawn planting machine. I asked the Lord to give you one of those so you can sit instead walking your acres."

"Ah, Franny. I'd just get soft if I rode around while Benny did all the work."

"But, Rube—"

"You know with only forty acres we can't afford to buy all the new-fangled contraptions that come along."

Franny smiled at the way Reuben was making short work of the cornbread and bacon. "Well, it won't hurt to pray."

Reuben just shook his head. "How did it go with Mrs. White?"

"She didn't say much, but she listened. And smiled. But I don't know what she's thinking."

Reuben wiped his face with the tea towel. "Well, darlin', all you can do is sow the seed and trust the Lord to make it grow. And speaking of sowing seed…"

"That does it," Abby said. "Reuben can't be guilty."

John huffed and rolled his eyes. "You mean because he's a Christian?"

"Yeah. Don't look at me like that, John. I know Christians sin. We sin all the time. Even nice people. I mean think of what Beulah did. But still—murder?"

"He sure doesn't seem the type, but we need to find solid proof one way or the other," he said. "Make it go forward more. We were just in spring planting time. The fire was in the winter, or late fall."

"And she didn't look pregnant yet," Abby said. "But, John, did you see that china?"

"No, can't say I noticed the china, Abby."

"It's the same pink rose pattern. I'd bet on it. If it's Franny's mother's china, it's *at least* 160 years old."

"There are a ton of antique stores downtown. I bet they could get—"

"Don't be silly. They'd never give up their great, great grandmother's china."

"I'm just saying."

"Here, let me take it for a while," Abby said. John shifted the laptop from his knees to hers. Abby adjusted the settings and said, "There. That's better. We should be getting close."

After only a moment, John put up his hand. "Right there. Stop. Do you smell it?"

The smell of burning brush was heavy in the air, even in Franny's kitchen with the windows closed against it. Mrs. White was reading the Bible passage Franny had pointed to. "Believe in the Lord Jesus Christ and you shall be saved…"

"Do you see how easy it is?" Franny leaned as close as she could with her big belly and looked directly into Mrs. White's eyes, hoping to see understanding and acceptance. Instead she saw sorrow. Mrs. White had come a long way since they had started having Bible study in the spring. More and more, she was happy and smiling, although she had seldom volunteered her thoughts or opinions. No doubt, she had long been discouraged from having any, Franny thought with sadness.

"But I'm a terrible person, Franny. Inside my heart I think the most awful things. Things you couldn't imagine. Why just this morning I was thinking… Well, it's no wonder when Mr. Buchanan started burning the hedgerows and I smelled the smoke I thought, that's where you'll go—you're going to the Lake of Fire, just like Reverend Jaynes said.

"But you can call on the name—"

"But don't you see? I can't be a Christian like you. I don't do the good things that you do. I don't visit the sick or write sweet letters of encouragement. I can't even get my chores done on time and I don't submit to my husband like the Bible says I should. And Mr. White won't let me go to church or give money now that they have that new preacher. So how am I ever going to be a Christian?"

"But that's the good news—that's what the Gospel is

all about. You don't have to do anything. Nothing at all. Jesus did it all. He took the punishment for our sins so we wouldn't have to be punished—not ever again."

"But that's too easy."

"So easy all you have to do is believe. Would you like to pray and tell the Lord you believe?"

"Oh, I would!" Mrs. White said in a rush. All the tension on her face melted away and she laid her head on the table before her.

Franny took Mrs. White's hands into her own and bowed her head. When they finished praying together Mrs. White's face was radiant.

"Thank you for showing me, Franny."

"I'm so happy for you." Franny patted Mrs. White's hand. "You come back and we'll study—"

A loud banging interrupted them and both women looked at the door, Franny in surprise, Mrs. White in terror. It flew open and slammed against the wall and Bertram White stormed in, breathing out a poisonous rage that seemed to fill the room.

"There you are! I told you I don't want you hanging around with this troublemaker, do you hear me?"

"Yes. I was just about to leave," Mrs. White said. She looked at Franny in apology. She gathered her courage and said, "Franny didn't do anything wrong. It was me."

"She's teaching you her rebellious ways!" Mr. White's voice filled the whole house. He sneered at the open Bible on the table. She doesn't obey the Bible any more than you do."

Mrs. White clasped her husband's coat sleeve. "I'll go home right now."

"See that you do. I'll be there directly."

Mr. White grabbed Franny's arm. His face was beet red, his eyes murderous. "You stay away from my wife, you hear?" Spittle hit her in the face. He pushed her and Franny fell back, the table blocking her fall. Mr. White stormed out of the house as angrily as he had entered it. Franny hurried to close and lock the door. She went to the window and saw that Mr. White had caught up to his wife and now held her by the arm, swatting her rear with every step as if she were a child that had done some naughty thing.

Rubbing her own arm where he had grabbed her and then, protectively, her belly, Franny began to cry. Amidst her tears she began to pray, sometimes aloud and sometimes beneath her breath, all the while pacing through the four rooms of her house. If only it were time for Reuben to come in. *I want my Reuben*, she thought. And then, amazingly, Reuben was there even though it was only three o'clock and not nearly time for supper. Franny went to unlock the door when she heard him struggling with it.

Reuben, wearing a sooty face and smoky clothes, came through the back door. "I forgot my...Franny! What's wrong, darlin'? Is it time? Is the baby coming? Are you having pains? Should I go get—?"

Franny put her arms around his neck. "Shhh. Don't worry so. I'm all right. It's just Mrs. White—"

When Reuben saw the marks on Franny's wrist, the same finger-shaped marks that Mrs. White so often had, he saw red. He gently put her away from himself and looked into her eyes. "Tell me," he said simply.

And she did, although she wasn't even finished with the story when Reuben began taking off his hat and coat. These, he hung up on his way out the door. Throughout he had not said a word.

Once again she watched out the window and prayed.

"Bertram White was a miserable excuse for a human being," John said.

"Wasn't he?"

"No wonder Reuben burned his house down!" John said. "If someone shoved my wife around, especially when she was pregnant..."

"But we still don't know that Reuben set the fire," Abby said. "I need to speed it up more. We can't be out here all night waiting for it to happen in real time." Abby set it on fast forward and they watched Franny race-walking around the house and then Reuben race-walking back across the road and into his own house. Franny and Rube did a lot of walking and talking, although Abby and John could not understand at the speed setting they were on. When the couple got into bed and covered themselves with a blue and green patchwork quilt, Abby looked up questioningly. "Should we skip past...I mean the rule was..."

"I know." John's face was a bit pink and he didn't look at Abby. "But this is probably the crucial night. Let's go on a bit more."

The night passed quietly, except for a few snores coming from Reuben from time to time. But then Franny sat upright in bed, startling Abby and John as much as she did Reuben.

"Wake up, Rube. I smell smoke."

"Of course you do, darlin'. The hedgerows are still smoldering."

"No. I mean I really smell smoke."

"I don't smell anything."

"That's because your nose is so used to the smell." Franny pushed the quilt away and, struggling, got out of bed and waddled out to the front room. "Oh, no! Reuben come see!"

Reuben came stumbling through the bedroom door in his long johns and hurried over to the window.

Across the road orange flames were shooting from the White's upper windows. Without a word or a second thought, Reuben hurried back to the bedroom to pull on his trousers and boots. Then taking his coat from the peg by the back door, he said, "Stay in the house, Franny," and ran outside.

Franny watched from the doorway as Reuben went to the barn and then came hurrying out with several horse blankets. He took them to the well and pulled up bucket after bucket of water to wet them down. Then carrying the water-logged blankets he started across the yard and around the house, his coat billowing out behind him. The wind was stronger than when they went to bed and Franny knew that would make everything so much worse.

Closing the back door, she hurried to the front room window to follow his progress across the road and up to the White's house, which was even more engulfed with flames. Reuben covered his head and arms with the wet blanket and went up the porch steps and through the front door.

Watching her husband disappear into the fiery inferno, Franny gasped in dismay and began to pray very loudly, not because the Lord was hard of hearing, but because she needed to. "Oh, Lord," she said over and over. "Keep him safe."

After what seemed like an eternity, Reuben came back out and then bent over, hands on knees, and coughed horribly, the sound traveling back to Franny on the wind. Reuben straightened and then started back into the White's house carrying his wet horse blankets. He was gone for a long time. She didn't know how long because she couldn't bear to pull herself away from the window to go check the clock. She would have to disobey Reuben. She didn't like to do that, but she couldn't stay in her house knowing he was in the burning house across the road.

But then Reuben came back into sight accompanied by another person also wearing a blanket of some sort. Franny's heart did a happy somersault, and then she realized it was not Mrs. White after all, but her loathsome husband who walked with Reuben into the front yard. Both men collapsed onto the grass and shook with the violence of their coughs.

Franny could restrain her need to be with Reuben no longer. She put on her long cloak and went out the front door. A light rain tapped on her hood as she hurried across the road as fast as she could safely go.

"He didn't do it!" Abby said. "I knew it!"

Smiling, John handed the laptop to her and then rose from the step and stretched. "Not only that—he tried to help get Mr. and Mrs. White out of the house."

"I can't wait to tell the Old Dears. They'll be so happy. And I'm going to tell them about their tea set. That will cheer them up a little even if we can't prove he didn't ..." She trailed off and stopped. "But how *did* the fire start?"

"Maybe the smoldering hedgerows flamed up. If so, you'd have to agree that it is Reuben's fault—at least partially."

"Oh," Abby said dejectedly. "Then we aren't really that much improved, are we? He still would have been charged with a crime—even if not murder."

"Something like reckless endangerment or even second degree murder."

"Which would explain why they sent him to prison instead of hanging him," Abby said. "So the Old Dears still won't feel much like giving him an apple, will they? Even if they believe us about it being an accident."

"And surely they will believe us." John ran his hands tiredly through his hair.

"How can they? If we could only show them. Do you think we should—?"

"No, I still think this shouldn't get out—at least until we're sure what we have here."

"I guess you're right," Abby said. "The media would go nuts if they got word of this."

"Come on. Let's keep going a bit more," John said and sat back down beside her.

Abby adjusted the vantage point so that they could look out the kitchen window toward the White's house and then sped up the time so that the nighttime hours raced by. Once an owl swooped into their line of sight but otherwise all was quiet and dark. Until it wasn't when an orange light bloomed in an upper window.

"There it is." Abby grabbed John's arm. "See! Reuben wasn't anywhere near the house when the fire broke out."

"Seeing it from this perspective, it's obvious no smoldering hedgerow could have started that fire or it wouldn't have lit up that room from within so suddenly."

"Yeah, if only that sheriff could have seen what we just saw." Abby felt a wave of sadness lodge in her throat and swallowed the lump that made it difficult to speak. "It's great to know the truth finally, but it makes me sick thinking of how unfair it was for Reuben—and Franny and the baby. Well, for the whole family including the Old Dears, for that matter."

"I know. Just think of the legal application of this program. If judges and juries could see crimes from different perspectives…"

"So then, what did start the fire?" Abby asked.

"We'd have to get inside the White's house to know for sure. And to do that we'd have to set up over at the museum." He stopped and studied Abby's face. "I know it's getting really late," he said. "And you must be tired."

"No, I'm okay. I don't care if it takes all night. I want to be able to tell the Old Dears how the fire did start. Just let me check on Merri first."

The twins' phone rang for a long time, and finally Merri herself answered, her *hello* rusty and sleep-clogged.

"Oh, Merri, I'm sorry. I didn't mean to wake you."

"No, I woke up a little while ago."

"How do you feel?"

"Kind of numb. We're watching some weird antique TV show. Some old dude playing an accordion. Unless I'm still asleep and dreaming this. Where are you?"

"We're at Shake Rag Corner. And guess what? It wasn't Reuben's fault!"

"You mean he didn't do it on purpose?"

"I mean he didn't do it at all. We're going to get inside the White's house to see how the fire started. You want us to come pick you up?"

"No, that's okay. I don't think I could stand getting inside that guy's head again...or watching Mrs. White turn into barbecue. Besides, Grandma Beulah's making me chocolate milk."

Abby laughed. "Okay, kiddo. I'll see you tomorrow. You take it easy, okay? And, Merri? I'm praying for you and your family."

Merri's voice was so soft Abby had to strain to hear it. "Thanks."

CHAPTER 16

Abby leaned against the brick wall of the museum, still warm from earlier sunlight, watching John set up the computer. "I just hope we're close enough to get a strong signal from here."

"We may have to wait until tomorrow when the museum's open," John said.

The White's house popped into view on the screen and they smiled at each other.

"Houston, we have liftoff," Abby said.

"Here," he said, come here and take the controls. "You're still much better than I am at fine-tuning the time."

She eased down next to him and took the laptop. "I'll try." She sped through several days and then weeks in fast speed, slowing only occasionally for a closer look as the White's led what seemed uneventful, boring lives. And then finally, she knew she had reached the right night when a fiery orange light filled the screen.

"That's it!" John said. "Slow down and back up."

"Okay, I'm going to lock onto Mr. White. If I start vomiting, call an ambulance, okay?"

"Okay," John said grimly.

"I told you to stay away from that she-dog." Bertram White's face was red with rage, spittle spewing from his mouth onto his wife curled on the floor at his feet.

"I just…"

"Shut up," he said and kicked her side again. "If you would just shut up I could stop!" There was a pounding noise and then the front door flew open and his stupid oaf of a neighbor stood glaring at him in his own house.

"This doesn't concern you, Rube."

"I'm afraid it does, Bert." Reuben started toward Mr. White. "You need to back away."

"How dare you interfere with a man disciplining his wife. Is this what this country is coming to?" He raised his foot to kick her again, but suddenly he was on the floor beside her, pain blooming inside his skull. He raised a hand to his nose and came away with blood on it. "You broke my nose! he said, scrabbling backwards across the floor. "Stay away from me."

Reuben bent down and took Mrs. White by the hand. She groaned with pain as he gently lifted her to her feet.

"Come with me, ma'am, and Franny will take care of you. You may have broken ribs." Her eyes darted from his to her husband's in obvious terror.

"I'm fine. I'm fine. You just go on home now."

"I'm not going to leave you with him." He lifted his hand to put it on her shoulder and she flinched.

"You'll just make it worse," she whispered. "He'll

calm down now and it'll be all right."

Reuben wanted to drag her home with him, but he figured she didn't need any more bullies in her life. He contented himself by going to glare at Bertram White where he lay on the floor, holding his bleeding face. "I'll be watching," Reuben said and turned to go, nodding to Mrs. White on his way out.

She limped from the room and down the hall to the kitchen. She would make his supper, something special to please him. But first she'd have to be able to see, so she opened the icebox, chipped off a bit of ice, and held it to her swelling eye. She took the chicken Jemmy had cleaned for her that morning from the icebox and cut it and dredged the pieces in flour. Lifting the heavy iron skillet made a sharp pain in her right side and she wondered if Mr. Buchanan was right about her ribs. She peeled potatoes, stopping from time to time to clutch her side or to hold the ice to her eye. She had string beans from last summer's garden, but for once she didn't have the strength to open the Mason jar. Finally, she gave up and broke the jar with her meat mallet. Bertram would be furious at the wasted jar if he knew, but then he would also be furious if there were no beans to go along with the chicken. She would have to hide the broken glass later. When everything was done she prepared a tray and started down the hall. Her left eye was swollen shut now and the heavy tray caused more sharp pains in her side. But she held in the groans that threatened to spill out.

The hall was silent except for the soft shuffling of her shoes. There had been no sound in all the time she had prepared the meal except for once, when she could hear him going to his study. She wondered if maybe he had fallen asleep after his rampage.

She knew it was a ridiculous and irrational hope, and it

died even before she entered the room and saw him in his chair, clutching a bottle of bourbon in his lap. He didn't straighten from his slump, only glared evilly at her from the swollen slits of his eyes. She walked slowly, timidly, toward him until she was close enough to set the tray down on his desk. There was always the chance that he would pass out before he got back to punishing her, but that hope too was dashed when he very deliberately wiped the tray off the desk with the hand not holding the bottle.

Then he rose from his chair, not at all incapacitated from the drink, and lunged for her. This time no neighbors came to investigate the noises. This time he didn't stop until, red-faced and chest heaving, he stood over his wife's still body. Nudging her with one well-polished boot, he shouted for her to get up. When she didn't obey, he squatted beside her and looked dispassionately at her bleeding, battered face. He slapped her lightly and then again harder. He put his fingers to her neck. When he didn't find a pulse, he rose quickly to his feet, his face a mask of horrible shock, the whites of his eyes showing like those of a terrified horse. He looked around the room to assure himself no one had witnessed the punishment he had meted out. Then he went to the windows and pulled the curtains shut, muttering about his foolishness in not doing so earlier. He went to lock the front door, too, cursing Reuben Buchanan and his she-dog of a wife. It was her fault for all of this. She had made him do it.

He went back and looked at his wife, so still on the floor. No sense feeling sorry for himself. The thing to do was come up with a plan. Happily, an idea came to him right away and he knew what must be done. He gathered her to his chest and carried her up the stairs in a gentle embrace. He put her onto their bed and then lit the lamp on the dresser to give himself the light he needed. He set about gathering various small items from her dresser and his chest of drawers and armoire—a few items of clothing, some bills and coins, his wife's jewelry, a small framed photograph of the two of them. He tossed it all onto the bed. Some of it landed beside her and some onto her cooling body. When he had selected all that he could reasonably carry away, he began looking for something in which to carry it. Finally, he remembered the carpet bag under the bed. He scooped up the things from the bed and stuffed them in no particular order into the bag. He went to the window and pulled back the curtain. It was dark enough now.

After one backward glance at his wife, he carried the carpet bag down the stairs, down the hall, through the kitchen and out into the yard. Looking nervously around, he made his way to the barn. He walked confidently into the gloom and put the carpet bag under the seat of his buggy, covering it with a canvas he used in inclement weather. The next part was the trickiest. He stumbled across the dark, rutted road, and then crept on to Reuben's barn. The door made a tremendous squeaking noise, enough to wake the dead, he thought, and then laughed softly at his own joke. As usual, Reuben had set the bottle of kerosene he had been using to burn the hedgerows just inside the door. He carried it out of the barn and then shut and latched the door. A light came on in the Buchanan's back room, and he froze. But then he realized they wouldn't see him if even if they happened to look out. He scuttled along back toward his house, carrying the corked bottle of kerosene.

He slunk back into his own house like a thief, carefully and quietly shutting the back door as if not to wake his wife from her slumbers. Then he went to the parlor, put the bottle down, and sat by the window, looking at the

Buchanan's Shake Rag Corner stage house as his wife liked to do. It was quiet, and he had expended a huge amount of energy in disciplining his wife, so he rested his head on the window sill to wait. When finally the last light went out at the Buchanans he waited some more. He waited until he was sure they were sound asleep.

He may have slept a little himself, because he noticed that the moon was high in the sky and its light was streaming in through the window, enough to cast shadowed bars across his face. Then, taking up the bottle of kerosene, he rose and went up the stairs and into the bedroom where his wife was still dead. The moon had wrapped her in its light and she looked beautiful—younger even. There was enough shadow that he could ignore the blood on her face. He undressed and put on his nightshirt, nightcap, and robe, leaving on his shoes and stockings. It would be cold out there.

He looked again, sorrowfully, toward his wife. He had tried and tried to make her into the kind of wife God commanded her to be. Still the Lord knew best. God had taken her from him and after He punished her, He would give her a new sinless body, one that would be capable of womanly obedience. Really, he was the one to be pitied. Now, he would have to continue on life's road, knowing that he had not been up to his husbandly duty. Now he would have to look for another helpmeet for his needs. This time he would choose more carefully.

Sighing in sorrow, he uncorked the bottle and sprinkled a little of the kerosene over his wife's plain gray dress, careful not to let any splatter on his own clothes. Next, he sprinkled the kerosene over the coverlet and throughout the room. He chuckled, thinking he must look like a Catholic priest sprinkling holy water. When he was satisfied with his work, satisfied there was enough for a purifying effect, he scratched a wooden match on the sole of his shoe and cast it into the room. After just one quick look at the bloom of beautiful orange color, he shut the door and went downstairs and out into the night.

Abby couldn't seem to stop crying. John tucked her head against his shoulder. "I told you not to look," he said, "but you didn't seem to hear me, which is good because I may have cursed a little. Okay, a lot. Your eyes were all huge and glassy and you were staring at the screen. Good thing the battery ran out."

"The flames just devoured her body," Abby said, heaving in a breath of fresh night air. "I couldn't breathe. For a minute there, I couldn't get enough oxygen." She burrowed her head a little more into his comforting shoulder, then remembering the insane gleam in Bertram White's eyes, tilted her head up so she could see John's face—his handsome, kind, sane face. "He was a monster, John. He just kept on hitting her. I'll never forget the sound of her neck snapping. That was one hundred times worse than the most violent movie I've ever seen."

"As bad as the physical abuse was...," John said slowly. "Well, in my opinion, the worst part was the way he warped the Bible to give himself an excuse to bully his wife."

"And he felt so...so...righteous doing it."

John leaned back against the museum wall, his arms resting on his bent knees. "Do you think God watches our lives like we're watching Reuben and Franny and the others?"

"I guess it's sort of like that."

"Well, how can he just stand by and do nothing when

a guy pounds his wife to death? And while Reuben rots in prison for a crime he didn't commit?"

"I don't know, John. When we watched Charlotte's life, we could see the good that was coming out of the bad stuff. But this? I don't see it. Then again, I'm not God."

"It's a rotten world we live in. Let's get out of here. We never did get dinner."

Abby raised her head to look at John. "How can you think about eating after that?"

"Sorry. It's not that I don't care. It's just that I'm really, really hungry."

CHAPTER 17

Merri and the twins were dispiritedly pushing Cheerios around in their bowls when Abby entered the Old Dears' cozy kitchen carrying the Alton Telegraph the next morning.

The morning sun cast a cheerful glow over the room, and they'd set the table beautifully, the cloth covering it a cheerful print of rose and blue flowers almost identical to the ladies' blouses. In spite of their efforts, the atmosphere was grim.

Merri only glanced up before she returned to staring at her cereal bowl. Abby wracked her brain for what to say to comfort a girl whose father had just been carried off to prison. Nothing good came to her. An image of her own father dressed in an orange jump suit looking imploringly at her from behind bars appeared in her head and she wished— not for the first time—that she didn't have such a good imagination.

"I see you're pretending to eat breakfast," Abby said, handing the paper to Eulah.

"Would you like some?" Beulah said, starting to rise from the table.

Abby put a hand on Beulah's shoulder. "No, don't get up. I already pretended to eat toast." Abby sat down next to Merri. "Any word about your dad?"

Merri pushed her cereal bowl away and laid her head down on her arms. "No, and Mom's not answering her phone."

Beulah stroked Merri's hair and looked up at Abby, her face a study in misery. "We were just talking about the party, weren't we dear?" Merri didn't answer.

"A party?" Abby asked.

"Yes. We're having a Fourth of July party right here tomorrow for the whole family. It'll be just the thing to get us all bright-eyed and bushy-tailed. You can invite your mom, Merri."

"Thanks, Grandma Beulah." Merri's voice was muffled and low. "But she will probably be too busy, as usual. And I can't come to your party because I have to find a way to go see my dad. Mom will be too busy for that too." Merri looked up. "But, Abby, you could take me."

"I don't know…" Abby said. Would they even let kids visit the prison? Would Merri be in danger if she did? And what would it do to her to see her dad in such a setting?

"But I have to go make sure…that he's not…you know…pooping."

"That he doesn't have dysentery?"

"Yeah, that."

"Oh, honey, prisoners don't get that now." Abby stroked Merri's hair. "Modern prisons are not like the old Alton Prison. But if they'll let us, John and I will take you to see him, I promise."

Merri was silent for a long while. "No, that's all right. I'll talk Mom into taking me. I wouldn't want you to have to go there. I mean it'll be all weird going to the prison...and...you and John...well, I'm sure none of your relatives have ever been criminals.

"Oh, Merri," Abby said, "we'll take you."

"After all," Beulah said, sniffing into her handkerchief, "the Good Lord said blessed are they that visit the afflicted in prison. Eulah, is that in Luke or John?"

"So would I, like, get points, or something, for visiting Dad?"

"Oh, honey, that's not the way it works."

"Well, that stinks then," Merri said sadly. "I'll never make it with a family like mine."

Abby squeezed Merri's hand. "Oh, honey, God loves you no matter what kind of family you come from."

"Even if your family didn't come over on the Mayflower," Beulah said, "or qualify for the D.A.R."

"Even if your great-grandfather was a murderer," Eulah said.

"And arsonist," Beulah added.

"Don't you remember what Franny told Mrs. White?" Abby said and then frowned. "No, I guess you weren't there."

"Of course she wasn't, dear. That was 150 years ago," Beulah said.

Merri's glance slid to meet Abby's. "But if I had been there, what would I have heard?"

"That we can't ever be good enough."

"If you're trying to be encouraging, it's not working."

"What I mean is, we can't make it to Heaven by what *we* do. It's what Christ did. We only need to accept his gift."

"Well, I did that," Merri said simply.

Abby squeezed Merri tightly. "Oh, honey, I'm so glad."

"God's going to bless you, Merri—and the family you'll have one day," Eulah said. "The Bible says God shows 'love to a thousand generations of those who love him and keep his commandments.'"

Beulah put her arms around Merri and kissed the top of her head. "Why, I think God gets a kick out of rescuing the most miserable creatures. Not that you are," she added quickly, "but still…"

"I imagine you're wondering, like we all do from time to time," Eulah said, "why God allows bad things to happen. But if only we could see our lives from a distance, I'm sure we'd understand."

"But we can't think like God with our puny brains, can we?" Beulah added.

Merri smiled wryly at Abby. "They get it and they haven't even met Charlotte."

"Charlotte? Is that a friend of yours, dear?" Eulah said.

The doorbell sounded and Abby jumped to her feet. "I'll get it. You just stay here." She went to open the front door and found Pat, looking tired, but dressed for work in a summer-weight suit.

"Come on in," Abby said. "Merri's in the kitchen. Any news about her dad?"

"A little." Pat's heels clicked behind her in rhythm with the shuffle of Abby's sandals. She sat down next to Merri and patted her arm. "Hi, sweetie. I talked to Sylvia." She turned to the twins and explained, "That's Brad's girlfriend."

"Yes, Merri told us about her." Eulah's lips closed tightly after she got the clipped words out.

"She said they took your dad back to Chicago. There's

a hearing on Monday. His lawyer's going to try to get him out on bail."

"Try?" Merri said.

"It's really serious, honey," Pat said. "He may have to stay in jail until he goes to trial."

"Can we go see him?"

Pat pushed a strand of hair from Merri's forehead. "Sure, sweetie, but we'll have to wait until I find out how to do that. Right now, I'm so furious with him for putting you through this, I could spit nails. Meanwhile, I'll take you home. Let's go and I'll help you pack, honey."

Merri lifted her head. "I told you, Mom, I can't leave yet. Lucy doesn't get home until tomorrow night."

"I could stay here, if you want to go with your mom," Abby said.

"But you're my heartless tutor, remember? You've got to help me with my report."

"That can wait, Merrideth," Pat said. "After all, it is Saturday."

"That's all right, Mom. It'll take my mind off Dad."

Abby and Merri followed Pat onto the front porch. "Okay, honey, if you're sure," Pat said. "Then I'll go ahead with my meeting." She sighed. "The Sanfords want to see the house on Laurel Drive one more time. That makes four visits. But I think they're finally going to sign. Wish me luck."

When Pat was gone Abby sat down on the porch step next to Merri. The morning sun was already strong and she reminded herself to water the Old Dears' petunias before she got caught up in the day. "You really want to work on your report on a Saturday?"

"Duh. Of course I don't want to. Let's go to Shake Rag Corner. Even if my family is the pits, I want to help the grandmas prove theirs isn't."

"We'll go tonight when John gets here." A picture of Bertram White kicking his wife popped into her head and Abby shivered in the July heat. "But you don't want to see what John and I saw last night. Oh, Merri, it was awful."

"So who started the fire?"

"Mr. White did it," Abby said. "He murdered his wife and then set the house on fire to cover it up."

"I knew he was a creep, but wow. So why didn't you tell Grandma Beulah and Eulah that Reuben was innocent?"

"Why should they believe me?"

"I think we should just show them," Merri said.

"But we agreed we wouldn't let this get out."

"But the grandmas need to know. And they won't tell anyone."

"It's not like they'd really understand about the software, I guess," Abby said.

"You wouldn't even have to show them the fire. We could show them the good parts—like how Reuben and Franny loved each other."

"Okay. I'm in." Abby stood and brushed off the seat of her shorts. "When John gets here we'll get his vote. But meanwhile, we'd better work on that report so you won't be lying to your mom. Right?"

"Oh, all right."

"The End." Merri bowed and Abby, John, and the ladies clapped loudly. Dr. Bob pranced around Merri, barking his approval.

"Oh my!" Beulah said. "That was marvelous."

"And so informative," Eulah added.

"It was great, kiddo. Much better after you narrowed

your topic to just the Indian tribes Lewis and Clark met," Abby said.

"Way to go, squirt." John pulled gently on a lock of Merri's hair. "That was very interesting about the Peace Medals they gave the Indians."

"I've got a picture." Merri went to the table and picked up one of the library books lying there. After thumbing to the right page she said, "See? They had a picture of President Jefferson on them."

"That's cool." John started to take the book from her, but she whipped it back and scrutinized the photograph. When she looked up from the photo, Merri's blue eyes were sparkling with some suppressed excitement. "Grandma Eulah and Beulah, could we see your father's pocket watch again? John hasn't seen it before."

"Of course you may. I'll go get it," Eulah said, shuffling toward the dining room.

"Bring the polish, too, Yoo," Beulah called after her sister. "Father's watch is real gold," Beulah said proudly to Abby and the others. "We never have to polish it, but oh the fob! We polish it along with Mother's silver every month."

When Eulah returned she sat on the sofa next to Merri and began to rub silver polish onto the old watch fob. Abby leaned over Eulah's shoulder to watch, but Merri's head kept getting in the way as she watched her every move. From what Abby could see, the fob looked like a coin, but larger than any she knew of.

"I think that's good enough, Grandma," Merri said. "Could I hold it now?"

Eulah handed it to her and after only a second Merri's face lit up with a thousand-megawatt smile.

Handing it to John, she said, "What do you see?"

John's head snapped up and he stared at Merri.

"What? What is it?" Abby said, trying to get a closer look.

Merri started to answer, but John put a finger to her mouth. "Shh. Not yet. We'll explain later." He handed the watch and fob back to the twins and said, "Thank you, ladies. We have to go now," as he hurried to the door.

They each carried high-powered flashlights, and their three beams of light diverged and intersected on the walls and floor. "This is creepy," Merri said, wiping cobwebs out of her hair. "Do you think it's haunted?"

"No, just has a lot of soul—like your house in Miles Station," Abby said.

"Watch out, Merri," John said, pointing to the infamous hole in the floor. "There's where Abby fell in."

"Maybe we'd better not go any farther," Merri said.

"There's only water damage in that one spot. Just stay away from the hole."

Merri shone her flashlight around the perimeter of the room. "I don't see a fireplace anywhere. Where do you think the Hulk was getting the stones?"

"I think I know. This way." Abby beckoned for Merri to follow her. When they got to the dining room, Abby saw a small door on the left that she hadn't noticed before. When she opened it, a wave of musty air hit her. Broken steps led down into the darkness. "Oh, yuck. This must be the basement."

"If it's down there, I'm not going," Merri said.

"Well, that's good, because I wouldn't have kept you company if you wanted to go," John said.

Abby grinned and shut the door. "No, I think the Hulk got them from the old kitchen."

They passed through the *new* kitchen and then at the threshold took the step down into the original kitchen. "That's where," John said, pointing to the stone chimney.

A sledgehammer leaned against it and scars in the stonework sparkled as Abby ran her light over it. "You can see where he's chipped out some of the stones. But why?"

"Maybe he grinds them for bread," John said. "You know, stones instead of bones.

Fee Fi Fo Fum.
I smell the blood of an Englishman.
Be he alive, or be he dead,
I'll grind his bones to make my bread"

"Thank you very much, John," Merri said. "It was bad enough just thinking of him as the Incredible Hulk. Let's hurry. I don't want to be here if a giant cannibal comes back."

"Okay," John said. "I'll get set up and you tune us in to the right time, Abby."

"I still don't know what we're doing here. I don't want Merri to see the violence and— "

"I know. Me neither. Just see if you can find a time Reuben's wearing his watch. It would have to be some time he's dressed up, like for church or something. I'm sure he wouldn't wear it when he was outside working."

"Okay, I'll try."

"Merri, you keep watch at the front door, and I'll take the back. Just yell if you see or hear anything," John said.

"Oh, I'll yell, all right."

As they shuffled away, Abby set the time and adjusted the speed so she could view Reuben and Franny as they went about their lives. When she started to feel like a peeping tom, she sped up so that she couldn't see the details, then slowed again periodically to check. It took nearly thirty minutes before she saw Reuben wearing something besides his buckskins or other rough work clothes. "I found it!" she shouted. "Come here, you guys."

Franny held Reuben's Sunday shirt carefully so it wouldn't wrinkle. He checked his face in the mirror and then rinsed his straight razor in the basin and set it on the shelf below the mirror. He toweled the last of the lather off his face and turned to face her. "I'll take that now."

Wordlessly, she handed him his shirt and then clasped her hands together to keep them from shaking.

"There's plenty of firewood stacked out on the porch and kindling in the box," he said, buttoning his shirt. "Jemmy's going to feed the stock. So, promise me you won't go outside."

"I promise." She had also promised herself she wouldn't cry, but a tear fell anyway without her permission. She lifted her apron to wipe it away then reached a hand up to touch Reuben's cheek. He drew her close and she breathed in the scent of his shaving soap.

Franny heard horses on the road out front and tightened her hold on her husband.

"Sheriff's here and I've got to go now, darlin'." Reuben released her and reached for his suit coat. "But don't worry. I'll be back soon as I straighten this out. Tomorrow, probably. At least by Thursday."

Franny wiped angrily at another tear. "Any fool knows you would never do something like that."

"Course not." He knelt in front of her and tenderly rubbed her belly. "I love you, little babe. You keep your mama company while I'm gone." Then he stood and turned for the door.

"Wait! You forgot." Franny hurried to the bedroom and came back with Reuben's pocket watch.

A smile flitting across his face, he slipped it into his coat pocket and opened the door. "Don't forget to bar the door."

After Franny tugged the bar into place she hurried to the window. Anxious for a last glimpse of Reuben, her eyes nevertheless were first drawn across the road to the charred remains of the Whites' house. Then she saw that Reuben had already mounted his horse. He and the sheriff broke into a trot. When they reached the curve in the road, the trees hid them and she couldn't see him anymore.

"That was so sad," Abby said. "How horrible for her to watch the sheriff take him away."

"But how about Reuben's pocket watch?" John said, gripping her arm in his excitement.

"John, I hate to tell you this, but that wasn't the same pocket watch—definitely not gold like the Old Dears'."

"Not the watch," Merri said. "John means the watch fob."

"But I don't see—" Abby began.

"Let's go forward in time," John said. "Wouldn't it be cool to see Reuben and Franny's son Albert William with it?"

"I don't know, John," Merri said doubtfully. "If we go forward too far, we're going to take the chance of seeing things we don't want to."

"I just want to trace the watch fob," John said. "No big deal."

"You don't know what it's like," Merri said. "If you

had seen Charlotte like we did—."

"What we saw last night was way worse," Abby said. "Merri, you go keep watch. I'll call you if we find something."

Franny heard her mother's voice. Or maybe it was a bumblebee. She thought about opening her eyes to look. But it would be safer to keep them shut so the sun wouldn't burn them right out of her head. So hot. If only Mama would let her go down to the creek, she'd stay in until supper time. The bumblebees buzzed again, closer this time. She mustn't let them get her baby. She wanted to shoo them away but her arm was too heavy to lift.

"Franny? Honey, you've got to feed the baby."

Franny's eyes shot open. "Don't let them sting him!"

Franny's mother sat down on the edge of her bed and carefully laid the baby next to her. "Hush, Franny. Nothing and nobody is going to hurt your baby." Her mother helped the baby find what he was so urgently wanting. "There now. He's happy now."

Franny's face was chalk white and beaded with perspiration, but she smiled weakly down at her nursing baby. "Isn't he beautiful, Mama?"

"He has your eyes, Franny."

"He's going to look…like his father…I just know it."

Franny's mother wrung out the wet cloth in the basin by the bed and gently wiped her face. Franny sighed in relief and let her eyes fall shut again.

"That's right, honey. You just sleep. Albert William knows what to do."

"Mama, let me hold it again."

Her mother picked up the watch and fob on the

nightstand. When she put it into Franny's palm her fingers closed around it and she smiled.

"See, baby boy? Your papa's watch. Mama, promise me..." Franny's eyes were so heavy, but she held them open. "Promise me you'll give this to Albert William...when he's old enough."

Her mother put her hand to her mouth to hold back a sob. "Oh, Franny, don't talk that way. Your father and I will take you home and you'll get better. Now you just rest and I'll go get you some nice beef broth. The doctor said you—"

"Promise...Mama."

"I promise. Of course I do."

Abby shut down the program and wiped her eyes with her sleeves. "I can't take any more."

John put a comforting hand on her arm. "No need, anyway. That baby was Albert William, the twins' grandfather. He passes the watch down to his son, Henry."

Abby jerked away from him and scrubbed harder at her eyes. "Don't you care that Franny was dying? Who cares about the stupid watch?"

"Of course I care about Franny. That was really sad."

"You're not crying."

"Well...I am inside."

"Still..."

"But, see, now we've established a clear line of descent between Reuben and Eulah and Beulah. Funny, I never noticed how similar their names are. Anyway, now we can trace the watch—well the fob anyway—back."

Merri stood at the doorway. "Did you find anything?"

Abby plastered on a smile. "Yes, we found the fob,

although I still don't see that it matters much. So it's old. So is the china and you weren't excited about that, John."

John smiled. "If I'm right, we'll all be excited. Now, let's try to go back in time—way back. Here, get up and let me try."

"You're welcome to it."

"What year was Reuben born?"

"The tombstone said he died in 1873 when he was twenty-two," Abby said.

"Okay, that means he was born in 1851. Let's assume his father was approximately twenty years old when he was born. If so, that would have been in the 1820s or early 1830s. So I'll search between those parameters."

"Good luck," Abby said. "You'll have to go fairly fast or we'll never get out of here. But then you have to slow down or you won't be able to notice anything as small as a watch."

"I know. Okay, you guys go keep watch."

"That's funny," Merri said. "Keep *watch*."

"I'll call you if I find anything." John adjusted the settings and soon the screen was a blur of color and movement beyond what they could recognize.

"You take the front, Merri. But if you see anything, come back inside." Abby paused to yawn and stretch. "I'll stand guard on the back porch."

Sue P., Assistant Librarian, was smirking as usual. "Only D.A.R. members are allowed to use the computers," she said.

"But I have to help the Old Dears," Abby explained. "It won't take me long."

"Sorry, but I'm superior and you're not."

Abby could tell she wasn't sorry at all, and besides, her name wasn't really Superior. Why was she trying to fool her? Then the computer started making a thumping noise and she realized it wasn't going to work even if she could get permission. It was hopeless.

Abby's eyes flew open and she sat blinking in the dark until she remembered where she was. The thumping noise came again. "What on earth is he doing?" She rose, yawning, from the porch floor and stumbled to the back door.

In Franny's old kitchen, John was kneeling beside the chimney studying the wall where it met the edge of the stone. "It should be right about here. Stand back." He picked up the sledgehammer the Hulk had left leaning there and swung it against the spot. Plaster fell away from the wall, sending up a cloud of dust that swirled in the lamp light.

Abby coughed and said, "John! What are you doing? You can't tear up the wall."

Ignoring her, he dropped the sledgehammer and then knelt and began pulling away chunks of plaster. "Here, shine your light this way."

Abby made her way around the debris toward John. "I was okay trespassing, even though there's a sign clearly posted, because after all, as you yourself pointed out, we're not vandals."

"Could you just shine your light this way?" John said again. "Please."

"What on earth are you looking for?"

John studied the hole in the wall. "I just need to make the hole a little bigger and then I can get it out." He picked up the sledgehammer and swung it at the wall again.

Her light bouncing along in front of her, Merri came running into the old kitchen. "The Hulk's here!" she squealed. "He's coming around the back."

"Blast it. I'm so close," John said.

"We've got to get out of here," Abby said.

"Okay, I'm going." John put the sledgehammer down and herded them toward the door.

"We are so going to get arrested," Merri muttered, and then added, "But, hey, maybe they'll give me a cell near Dad."

CHAPTER 18

They stood in the deep shadows of the museum's porch overhang, peering across the street at the old house. The Hulk's lantern still bobbed around crazily and the sound of steel on stone continued to drift to them faintly on the warm night air.

"Is he ever going to leave?" Merri said.

"This is killing me," John said, pacing in the darkness. "If he finds it, who knows what he'll do with it?"

"It? What it?" Abby said. John didn't answer her question. He was in the zone again and probably hadn't even heard her. She had a strong urge to pull her hair out.

"I'm going over there," he said.

"Are you kidding?" Merri said. "The Hulk will grind your bones for bread!"

"You two do realize that guy's not really a man-eating giant?" John said with a grin. "I'm just going to take a peek at what he's doing. He won't even see me."

"Of course we know that," Merri said indignantly.

"And we realize he's not really the Hulk either, John," Abby said. "But what if he calls the police?"

"I don't know what his deal is, but I don't think he's in any position to call the cops or he wouldn't be slinking around here at night."

Abby put a hand on John's arm. "Let's come back when he's gone."

"It'll be too late," he said. "He'll find it soon. I've got to get it before he does."

Even in the dark Abby could see his determination. "Okay, then," she said briskly. "Merri, you wait here and we'll—"

"No." John took her by the shoulders and gently shook her. "Please. Wait here with Merri. It'll be quicker and quieter if I go alone."

Letting out a frustrated huff, Abby squinted her eyes and glared up at him. "Oh, all right. But, you owe me for this."

"Why don't you do some surfing here while you're waiting?"

"Are you kidding?" Abby said. "I don't want to ever go into the Whites' house again."

John started across the dark street, and then turned and called softly, "Go back farther—before the Whites' house."

Abby frowned in annoyance. Then her brain cleared and she said, "He's right, Merri. I've been so focused on Franny and Reuben..." Abby hurried to John's laptop where it lay on the museum's porch and began booting up the program.

"The fort," Merri said. "I forgot all about it."

"Right. The house was built over the fort. Maybe we can tune in to it. Hey, maybe we'll find some cool stuff for you to add to your report."

"Or not."

Sergeant Ordway sat pondering the paper on the table before him. Finally, he picked up his quill pen, dipped it into the pot of ink, and began to write. He dictated to himself as he wrote, his muttered words and the scratching of the quill on the paper the only sounds in the dimness of the cabin.

February 8, 1804

Honored Parents,

I now take this opportunity of writing to you once more to let you know where I am and where I am going. I am well, thank God, and in high spirits. I am now on an expedition to the west with Capt. Lewis and Capt. Clark, who are appointed by the President of the United States to go through the interior parts of North America. We are to ascend the Missouri River with a boat, as far as it is navigable, and then to go on by land to the western ocean if nothing prevents it. The party consists of 30 or so men of the army & country round about and I am so happy to be one of the army men picked. We expect to be gone 18 months or two years. This place—our winter quarters— is on the Mississippi River opposite to the mouth of the Missouri River, which we will ascend in the spring.

We are to receive our discharge and a great reward for

this expedition if we make it back to the United States. They will give me 15 dollars per month and at least 400 acres of first rate land. And if we make great discoveries, as all expect, the United States has promised to give us even greater rewards. For fear of accidents, I wish to inform you that I left 200 dollars in cash at Kaskaskia with a financial man named Charles Smith who will put it on interest. And if I should not live to return, my heirs can get that money and all pay due me by applying to the U.S. government.

I have had no letters since Betsy's but I will write again next winter if I have the chance.

Yours sincerely,

John Ordway

He set the paper to dry and closed up the ink bottle tightly. The captains were gone to St. Louis gathering more supplies and for some political fizzlegig he only half understood, and so it fell to him to keep Camp Dubois running. There was much to do, if they were to keep to their scheduled departure date in the spring.

He took his coat from the peg, donned it and his fur hat, and shouldered his flint-lock rifle. Extinguishing the candles, he opened the door to the first rays of the morning sun. Spring was still a long way off, and the cold wind nearly took the door off. His boots crunched through the patches of refrozen ice on the well-worn path from the cabin's door to the stockade gate. At the guardhouse, Private Newman saluted and "sirred" him, and he returned the greeting.

"It's time to get them up, Newman," Sergeant Ordway said.

"Yes, sir." Private Newman took up his bugle and played reveille. When he was finished, he set about raising the stars and stripes over the fort.

The flag flapping wildly above him, Ordway struggled against the wind to open the stockade gate for the day. He stepped out into the morning and, as always, was struck by the beauty of the land upon which they had built their encampment. The captains had sited it beside the Dubois River, where it fed into the Mississippi just south of the mouth of the Missouri. It was a rich bottom land only thinly timbered with oak. It wouldn't take much to clear, he thought, and would yield good crops once a man set a plow to it. But they—President Jefferson called them *The Corps of Discovery*—would leave in the spring before it was time to work this land. He liked to imagine the 400 acres he would receive, rich just like this, he hoped, with a little cabin that he had built himself, and a wife and babies. If he made it back.

Newman called down from his perch. "Old Chief Kanakuk on the river, sir."

Ordway looked toward the Mississippi in the distance and saw a regal Kickapoo sitting tall in his canoe, his porcupine headdress waving in the wind. The morning sun reflected off the shell beads on the chief's cape. The two braves with him paddled strongly against the current, presumably to their camp four miles up the river.

"Carry on, Newman," he said. "Keep sharp."

When he went back inside, the men of Camp Dubois, except for those on guard and cook duty, had assembled in the yard. Thirty-five young men, many of them rough frontiersmen new to military life, stood there bundled up in their coats more or less at attention. They had been chosen for their hardiness and survival skills, and Captain Clark was bent on honing and harnessing those for the journey ahead.

"At ease, men," Sergeant Ordway called out. He received informal reports and made assignments for the day. Some of the men, following Captain Lewis' instructions, would continue with the work of attaching weapons to the river vessels. There was a brass cannon on a swivel for the bow of the keelboat and guns for mounting on its sides. The pirogues, too, would be outfitted with guns. Other men would continue the sorting, cataloging, and packing of their supplies, most of which would be secured in barrels and oiled leather against threat of water damage. The cook's crew, in addition to preparing their day-to-day camp meals, would continue to render lard and make hard tack biscuits for the journey.

Ordway assigned men to accompany George Drouillard, the camp's chief huntsman, on the perpetual task of keeping them supplied with meat. The men who usually made up Drouillard's hunting party, Privates John Collins, Peter Weiser, John Robertson, and John Boley, had lost the honor two weeks before when they had sneaked off while supposedly hunting to go buy whiskey from a nearby settler. They had proceeded to get drunk and knock the living daylights out of each other until Captain Clark had broken up the fight.

Sergeant Ordway glared at the four shamefaced privates. "You four fools, carry on with your work. Captain Clark expects you to be done before he gets back." Ordway concluded his orders to the assembled men by saying, "Work hard, men, and there'll be a shootin' contest before supper. An extra gill of whiskey to the winners."

After eating the salt pork and cornmeal mush Cook had prepared for them to break their fast, Ordway inspected the work on the boats. Then he decided he'd best check on the privates before he did any of the many other tasks he had set for himself. He didn't want Captain Clark to be disappointed to find the work unfinished, and truth be told, he didn't want to see the four fools get lashed for it. They weren't bad men, just young—Boley was only 19—and foolish. Some days he wondered if Captain Clark would get them whipped into shape enough when it came time to choose the final roster for the expedition.

The privates were laboring in the cold wind to finish the little cabin they had begun two weeks before for the widow-woman who was to come wash and sew for the camp. As Ordway approached, he heard them cussing, but only in a friendly sort of way. At least they weren't fighting again.

"Hallo!" Collins called out from the roof where he was daubing the chimney with mud. "Men, straighten up and fly right. The sergeant's come to inspect."

Sergeant Ordway refrained from smiling. "Looks like you're near to finishing the widow's cabin."

"Yes, sir," Private Weiser said. He was hammering the last leather hinge onto the cabin's door. "We've near froze our privates off, but it'll be ready for her to wash our dirty socks and sew the captains' buttons before nightfall."

Boley pulled his shirt away from his chest and sniffed his armpits. "Whew! And our long johns, too, don't forget."

Collins called down from the roof, "Company coming, sir." He pointed to the south down the grassy trail that led to Cahokia and then on to Kaskaskia, the nearest thing to a town in the Illinois country.

"Who is it?" Ordway held his rifle close and watched with approval as Boley and Robertson picked theirs up to the ready. They may be fools about whiskey, he thought, but they knew how to handle their guns.

"Can't tell for sure," Collins said. "It's five men on horses and a mule pulling a sledge."

"Then mind your foul mouths," Ordway said. "Sounds like the Whitesides are here with the washer woman."

Curious about the expedition, Samuel Whiteside, along with others from their settlement called Goshen twenty miles to the east, had already visited Camp Dubois several times. Ordway had heard that Whiteside and his brothers, sisters, and their families, along with several other strong pioneer families, had originally come up from Kentucky in 1791, settling a few miles south of Cahokia and there rebuilding an abandoned blockhouse fort they named Whiteside Station. Then in 1801, Samuel and some of the others, having begun to feel crowded, struck out on their own.

"Greetings from the Land of Goshen," Whiteside called cheerfully. "Looks like we arrived at a propitious time."

"Yes, the men here are just finishing up."

Widow Buchanan's face was all smiles. "Why, that cabin looks right cozy, boys."

Ordway saw the men swell with pride at her compliment and grinned. "Privates, you carry on with your fine work." And then, tipping his hat to the woman, he said, "We're mighty glad to have you here to do for us, ma'am."

"I'm proud to do it." Smiling, she got down from her mule and hurried to admire the cabin.

Ordway didn't recognize the three others with Whiteside, but they all seemed friendly. They greeted Ordway and the privates pleasantly, dismounted, and then wasted no time getting to work untying the ropes that bound the supplies on the sledge.

The woman came out of the cabin and went to the sledge. "I'll carry that one, Nathan," she said, taking a bundle from one of the men. "I brought some bread for the men," she told Ordway. "It's not fresh of course, but there's butter."

"Butter?" Boley laughed like a small boy who had just been given a St. Nicholas treat. "Did you hear that, Robertson? Real bread and butter."

"And there's turnips, too, if you have a mind for them, for supper."

"That's neighborly of you," Ordway said. "The men really appreciate something fresh."

"Nathan, set those down in front of the cabin, all handy."

"Yes, Ma." The tall sandy-haired young man took a large wash kettle in each hand and then, seeming not to notice he was lugging 150 pounds of iron, carried them to the cabin.

Whiteside pulled Ordway to the side and said quietly, "What do you think of my young bucks? You can see they're likely fellows, strong and healthy."

"Hard workers, too, from the looks of 'em," Ordway said. "But if you're hinting at what I think you are…"

"They really want to go. They've been bending my ear about it ever since they heard about this grand adventure y'all are going on."

The four young newcomers unloading the widow's goods kept glancing over at Sergeant Ordway and Samuel Whiteside like pups hoping for a meaty bone.

"You're welcome to stay until the captains get back," Ordway said. "Captain Clark is in charge of recruiting, not me. And he's mighty particular."

"Fair enough," Whiteside said. "I promised the lads

I'd ask."

"We're having a shootin' match later on. Care to join us? My men always love to get the chance to test themselves."

Whiteside's smile was smug. "I was going to suggest it myself. Wait 'til you see 'em. The widow's boy, Nathan there, can trim the fuzz off a squirrel's ear at 50 yards."

"Abby?"

She jumped, Merri let out a shriek, and John jerked back. "Sorry. I didn't mean to scare you. You were really concentrating." John put his hands on her shoulders and leaned in to look at the computer screen, its glow reflecting off the museum's glass door where she and Merri sat.

"Don't sneak up on us when we're time-surfing," Abby said, putting her hand to her chest to calm her galloping heart. When she had her breath back she smiled and said, "John, it was so cool. We saw Camp Dubois."

"But Mr. Rohst needs to change a few things in the replica of the fort he's got out back," Merri said.

"So what were Lewis and Clark like?"

"Unfortunately, they weren't there," Abby said.

Merri tugged on her arm impatiently. "Abby, surf to the day when they get back from St. Louis."

"It's so late, squirt," John said. "We'll come back to the fort another time." He pointed to the low-battery message that had popped up on the screen. "Besides, you're almost out of juice, anyway."

Abby closed the laptop and handed it up to John. "Give me a hand, will you? I've been sitting on the sidewalk too long." John pulled her to her feet. Then Abby did the same for Merri.

"I take it our mysterious guy didn't find your mysterious *it*," Abby said.

"He hauled out fifteen or sixteen more stones to his truck, for whatever reason. But he didn't find it. Yet. He just left."

"Well," Abby said, "where is it?"

"I left it there. You were right, Abby. I can't just tear up the wall—especially knowing it's…well…Anyway, I'll bring something to cut it out with. We can come back tomorrow. And I think it's time we brought the Old Dears."

"Then you vote yes?" Abby said.

"I vote yes."

CHAPTER 19

"Here it comes, Michael!" Beulah said. "Get ready, Merri."

"I've always loved a parade," Eulah announced for the third time to no one in particular.

At Merri's suggestion, they had gone out to Miles Station earlier to pick up Michael, and now he was beaming happily beside the Old Dears, who sat in lawn chairs on their front sidewalk, wearing the same matching T-shirts emblazoned with rhinestone American flags they had worn to church that morning.

Abby had always loved a good parade too, even when she became a teenager and her friends had declared them passé. But at the moment she wasn't in the mood. She stood behind the twins between Merri and John and poked John's arm again. Hard. "Tell me what *it* is."

"Hey, that hurt." He put his hands into the pockets of his shorts. "You might as well stop asking. I'm not saying anything until after the parade."

Abby turned to glare at Merri, who only said, "Don't

look at me. He made me swear not to tell."

Abby crossed her arms over her chest and watched as a vintage fire engine, honking like a fog horn, made its way slowly up their street.

John leaned down to whisper in her ear. "Abby, don't be mad, darlin'."

"Don't 'darling' me, John. Wait a minute. Were you trying to sound like Reuben?"

Abby pulled away, but John just grinned and stepped closer to close the gap between them. "I want to give you a surprise. You like surprises, don't you?"

"Oh, all right. But as soon as this parade is over."

"I promise," John said.

Men from the local department clung to the sides of the fire engine, throwing wrapped candies for the children on both sides of the street.

"There, Michael," Beulah said. "Get those Tootsie Rolls over there."

Michael looked uncertain until he saw the other children dart out to gather the candy. Grinning, he hurried to pick up as many as he could and then brought them to Beulah.

"Aren't you a dear boy?" she said, hugging his thin shoulders. "I'm so glad you came today."

"You know, Michael will be visiting Lucy quite often," Abby said. "And I bet he could use a pretend grandmother too."

"Good idea!" Beulah said. "We'll have lots of fun. Do you like ice cream cones, Michael?"

Nodding shyly, Michael unwrapped a Tootsie Roll and popped it into his mouth.

A white convertible purred past with two women waving and tossing peppermints. The hand-lettered sign affixed to the side of the car said, "Dolly's House of Hair

Styles."

Merri looked left and right and paused as if trying to decide whether she was too sophisticated to scramble with the other kids. Finally, she sprinted out into the street with Michael and grabbed a handful of candy.

A marching band high-stepped down the middle of the street, enthusiastically laboring over a piece that Abby didn't recognize.

"What are they playing?" she shouted over the music to John.

"Sounds like a cross between *Proud Mary* and the theme from *Star Wars,*" he shouted back with a laugh. "But I think it's the school fight song."

Cheerleaders in red and white uniforms posed daintily on a float sponsored by Sunset Ford. One of the kids on the street called out, "Hey, where's the candy?" The cheerleaders continued to smile and wave, except for one who turned and glared at the boy.

But after that, the parade participants showered the kids with candy and prizes until the bag Beulah had brought for them to put it in began to get heavy. The Old Dears seemed to like each entry better than the last. They crowed with delight when eight children from the Tumbling Tots Club walked in formation as a waving flag, with Uncle Sam tottering along on stilts behind them. They were thrilled to get little calendars handed out by the Wreck 'n Roll Auto Body Shop.

"Oh, get two," Beulah said. "There's a coupon on the back." Abby sent up a little prayer that they would never find themselves in a position to need the coupons.

The Old Dears sang along with the Waterloo German Band, who wore Alpine costumes and played *Roll Out the Barrel* from an elaborate float made to look like a Bavarian cuckoo clock.

"Here come the Shriners," Beulah said breathlessly. "That's our favorite part."

Six men wearing burgundy cone-shaped hats put-putted up on their little go-carts, then stopped and performed an elaborate pattern of figure eights before going on down the street.

Beulah and Eulah clapped furiously. When their clapping stopped suddenly, Abby looked down and saw they were struggling to get out of their lawn chairs. She leaned toward them and asked over the noise, "What's wrong?"

"Help us up, sweetie. Here comes Old Glory."

John stepped forward to help, and then the Old Dears stood crookedly at attention, wrinkled hands over hearts, as the local branch of the V.F.W. went by in their white shirts and blue ties, carrying a huge flag. Abby felt a flutter in her stomach to see people coming to their feet all along the way. She placed her hand over her heart and saw that John and Merri had done so as well. Michael, seeing that John had taken off his cap, quickly removed his own, put his hand over his heart, and stood at attention.

When the honor guard was past, Beulah started to sit, but Eulah sighed and took her arm. "You might as well stay up. I see the horses."

"Oh no, there they are," Beulah said.

"Don't you like horses?" Merri asked.

"We love horses," Eulah said, "but they always signal the end of the parade."

Six riders on six gleaming horses of various colors drew abreast of them and stopped to wait for the float in front of them to move on.

"Why do the horses always come last?" Merri asked

"Stand back!" John called, laughing. "You're about to find out why."

A big black horse with white markings lifted his tail and deposited a malodorous heap on the street.

"Ewwww!" Merri said, but Michael laughed uproariously.

"Okay, everyone," John said. "are you ready for the surprise?"

Eyes gleaming, Eulah and Beulah nodded their heads in unison.

"It's about time," Abby muttered with an annoyed look at John.

"Wait here and I'll bring my car around," he said.

"And I'll get mine," Abby said.

"Why don't we take our Lincoln?" Eulah said. "We can all fit in it."

"Sweet!" John said. "I've been itching to get my hands on that beauty."

Michael set the lawn chair he was carrying down on the Shake Rag Corner front porch and went to peer curiously through a grimy window.

"But isn't this trespassing, dear?" Eulah said between breaths as she hauled herself up onto the old porch on Abby's arm.

Beulah huffed along on Merri's arm behind her sister.

"Yeah, John," Merri said, "what if the Hulk comes back?"

"I'm betting he won't dare in broad daylight and we'll only be a minute." John was carrying five lawn chairs in his right hand and a small folding table in his left. "Besides, you ladies have a certain right to be here."

"We do?" Beulah said.

"Yep," John said as he wrestled the front door open.

And surely, even the Hulk wouldn't harm elderly ladies, Abby thought as she led Eulah into the house. The old house looked totally different in the daylight. She studied the peeling vintage wallpaper and the carved moldings around the doors and windows. "Isn't it amazing?"

"Yuck! What's that all over the floor?" Merri said.

"You mean besides about a million years' worth of dust?" Abby answered. "It looks like bird droppings. And look! There's a nest on the window sill."

"Ewww!" Merri said. "If I had known how bad this was, I would never have come in here at night."

"A little bird poo never hurt anyone," Beulah said. "Where's the surprise?"

"Actually," Eulah said, "bird droppings can sometimes carry—"

"Right this way," John interrupted. He led them through the dining room and into the room that had once been Franny and Rueben's kitchen. Abby and Merri set up the table and chairs and helped the twins into them while John went back to the car for his laptop. When he came back, he set it up on the table and soon the program whirred to life, filling the screen with the familiar colorful logo.

"Are we going to go on the World Wide Web?" Beulah said.

"We sure are." John took out a piece of paper and showed it to Abby. "Last time I jotted down some settings so it would be easier to get back where we wanted to go." He clicked and the image shuddered a little and then settled to the scene they had first come across where Franny was making breakfast for Reuben. "I'm not going to lock on anyone or go virtual," he explained to Abby and Merri. "That way we can explain along the way better."

"Oh what a sweet pioneer couple," Beulah said. "And look! She's got a tea set just like ours."

Abby smiled at John and he returned a grin. "Merri, Michael, drum roll, please." They pounded their hands on the table in front of them, and John said, "Ladies, may I present Reuben and Frances Buchanan, your great grandparents."

"Which is why," Abby said, "that actually *is* your tea set."

Eulah leaned toward the computer monitor for a closer look. "Well, I'll be!" she said in amazement. "You young people are so clever."

"Franny got that tea set from her mother, which means it's really old," Abby said.

"At least 160 years old," John added.

"Franny's pregnant with Albert William, your grandfather," Abby said.

"And that's Reuben—the murderer?" Eulah said. "He looks quite a bit like Father, don't you think, Beulah?"

"Oh, he does, doesn't he? And so nice, not at all like the bad guys on TV."

Abby took a twin's hand in each of hers and smiled at Eulah and then Beulah. "He *was* nice," she said. "He didn't do it."

"He didn't?" the twins asked in unison.

"Nope. Reuben wasn't anywhere near the house when it caught fire," John said. "And, we'll prove it to you. Here, watch."

"So after Franny died, they changed the baby's name to Edwards because they thought Reuben was a murderer," Eulah said.

"And arsonist," Beulah added.

"And Albert never knew that he was a Buchanan and that his father died in prison just across town for a crime he didn't commit," John said.

Eulah dabbed at her eyes with her hanky. "So he really was innocent. I feel bad for thinking all those mean thoughts about him. Thank you, John, for bringing us here to show us."

"That World Wide Web sure is something, isn't it?" Beulah said. "What will they think of next?"

"Oh, there's more—much more," he said. "Let's go forward just a bit." John navigated until he found the point where Reuben was dressing to leave with the sheriff and then paused the action. "Take a look at this scene. Do you recognize anything?"

"Well…not really," Eulah said, squinting at the screen. "Do you mean the watch? It looks inexpensive, not at all like Father's gold one."

"Look closer," John said, his eyes gleaming.

"The fob! It's Father's watch fob!" Beulah cried.

"Did you remember to bring it?" John said.

"It's right here," she said, digging in her purse. She set the watch with its fob on the table in front of them.

"It's definitely the same," Beulah said. "Oh, John, this was a grand surprise."

"That's not the surprise," John said. "Even Abby and Merri don't know the surprise."

"No, Abby does not know the surprise," Abby said crossly.

"I know the surprise," Merri said.

John tousled her hair and smiled smugly. "Not all of it." He consulted his paper again and then changed the settings.

"I started here where Reuben's putting on his watch

in 1871," John said, "and went back, back to when…well, you'll see."

Abby didn't see what date John set, but then the screen was filled with action as several bearded men race-walked across the screen carrying boards and hammers.

"Oh, cool. They're building the house," Abby said. "What's the date?"

"Spring of 1846," John said. "But, actually, they're not building this house. Just watch when I set the action to fast reverse." The men carrying tools and boards raced backwards and began undoing their work. The house deconstructed until at last, only a small log cabin stood in a clearing of tall trees.

"There was a log cabin here before this house?" Abby said.

"It's still here," John said. "They built onto it."

"Where?" Frowning, Abby scanned the room.

"I'll explain in a minute. Just keep watching," John said.

After a moment, a man in buckskins came from behind the cabin, carrying an axe over his shoulder.

"Who is it? Do you know?" Abby said.

"That is Benjamin Buchanan. I got the impression his middle name is Franklin, which would be cool. Ladies, he's Reuben's father— your great, great grandfather."

The man went to a pile of logs and began to split kindling. He stopped after a while and shrugged out of his shirt. Dropping it to the grass, he picked up his axe and started chopping again.

"Watch," John said. "Wait for it. Wait for it. Now." He paused the action and they saw a gleam of light on Benjamin's sweaty chest. John zoomed in closer until they saw that he was wearing a medallion on a leather cord.

"Do you recognize it?" John said.

"It's the same," Abby said. "That would make it—what? About one hundred seventy years old?"

"Oh, it's older than that," John said.

"Yeah," Merri said. "It's a—"

"Wait, squirt. Not yet," John said, grinning.

"Are you saying that's Father's watch fob?" Eulah said.

"Yep," John said.

"Oh, my!" Beulah pulled a hanky from her pocket and fanned her face with it.

"Okay, we're going back further." John consulted his paper and made changes to the settings. "And we're going virtual. Just watch this, ladies."

Nathan Hale Buchanan thought he had never seen a more beautiful sight than that which greeted him when he crested the last rise. His wife was sitting in a cheerful patch of violets in front of their cabin, her calico skirt fanned around her. Her hair was like a raven's wing in the sun as she crooned a Kickapoo lullaby to the baby—his little son—at her brown breast. No, nothing more beautiful, he thought, and that was saying a lot. After all, he'd seen great thundering waterfalls and towering snow-topped mountains. Wisps of black hair were fluttering around her face, having come loose from the braid that fell down her back.

And then she saw him. In an instant, she had replaced the baby with a rifle that she expertly held aimed at his heart. Although their son cried indignantly, her attention—and fierce frown—were only on him.

"Mary Anne," he cried, getting down from his horse. "Don't shoot. It's me."

"Husband," she gasped. She hurriedly set the rifle down, picked up their crying son, and rose gracefully to her feet.

And then they were in each other's arms, kissing frantically, as if they had been parted a year instead of only three weeks.

Nathan looked down at the baby snuggled between them and grinned. "He doesn't even care that we're near to flattening him."

"He is happy to have father home." She sniffed and grinned. "You smell of bear grease. Like real man."

He breathed in the scent of her hair and skin. "You smell like lavender. Just the way I've been remembering."

"Come inside," she said. "Now we celebrate."

"Yes, ma'am!" He took her arm and led her eagerly to the cabin door.

Smiling in amusement, Mary Anne pulled back. "Not that kind celebration."

The cabin door opened and his ma stepped out. "I reckon I allowed y'all enough time for kissin'. Now put your horse away and come in, Nathan. It's time for the boy's birthday celebration. Here, I'll take that little man, Mary Anne. You'd better go check on supper."

"It is? I mean, yes, I wouldn't miss it for the world." The days and nights had run together while he labored at the Half Moon salt spring with the other men. They had taken turns watching the boiling kettles and standing guard against the Shawnee who took exception to their intrusion on what had admittedly long been their operation. He sent up a silent prayer of thanks that he had, by dumb luck, managed to get back home on his son's first birthday. Whistling happily, he led his horse to the lean-to and set about caring for him.

When he stepped into the dim cabin, the smell of food

made him feel faint. It was his own fault. He could have stayed to eat breakfast with the rest of the men who were camped a few miles away, hoping to shoot a deer or two before returning. But he had been unable to wait another minute to be home. The men had teased him unmercifully, but Captain Whiteside had given him his share of the salt and told him to go on ahead. "You'd best get home to your little wife and papoose before you die of pining for them."

His stomach growling, Nathan put his rifle on the rack over the door and set his pack down. "I could eat a bear!" he declared. He stopped and said, "It's… not bear stew is it?"

His wife's eyes twinkled and her teeth gleamed in her dark face as she stirred the iron pot simmering over the fire. "Sorry, Husband. No bear stew today. Just venison."

He sighed with relief. "Good. I hope I never have to eat another bear in all my born days."

He sank wearily onto the bench and tried to wait patiently. Mary Anne brought bowls of steaming stew to the table and then, glory be, warm cornbread. His ma brought the jug and poured apple cider into a cup and handed it to him. Nathan smiled his thanks. "I saw lots of buds on your apple trees when I passed just now, Ma. I reckon it'll be a pink and white cloud over your cabin, come May."

"I figure they'll set forty bushels of apples this year. We'll have enough cider to sell in Cahokia."

Mary Anne stood politely in the shadows, planning to wait for him to finish eating, as was the Kickapoo way. He didn't want her to give up all her people's ways, but this was one custom he wouldn't allow to stand. "Come, sit beside me, sweetling, and we'll thank the Lord."

When they had eaten their fill, including the baby, who eagerly lapped up the broth from the wooden spoon his grandmother held to his mouth, Nathan went to his pack by the door and took out the leather bag of salt that was his share. "This should last us through the year, maybe longer," he said, proudly handing it to his wife. "And this is for the little man." He held out the whistle he had fashioned from a willow sapling, and the little boy took it and immediately put it in his mouth. "Look at how smart he is! He already knows what to do."

The women laughed, but then he realized they were laughing at him and he felt his face heat. He hoped he wasn't blushing like a girl.

"The baby's going to love the whistle, Nathan," his ma said, her eyes twinkling. "For gnawing on."

"It is fine gift, husband," Mary Ann said quickly. "Come, tell boy more stories of great adventure."

"Very well," Nathan said. He went to the hidey hole he had fashioned in the stonework of the fireplace. He used an old knife to lever out the stone and then reached in and took out two of his greatest material treasures. The first, his journal in its oiled leather pouch, he laid on the table. The second, a medallion on a blue ribbon, he held up for his wife and ma to see. "I reckon he's still too young for this too." They only shook their heads and smiled. But he put the medallion around his son's neck and stroked his soft cheek. "Someday, Thomas Jefferson Buchanan, this will be yours." Then he held out his hands to the boy in his mother's arms and said, "Come, sit on your father's knee, and I'm goin' to tell you stories you scarce will believe. Like the time I stood astride the great Missouri River where it trickles out of the mountain and…"

Abby felt her heart racing. "The watch fob. Oh, my gosh."

She stood and then just as suddenly sat back down. "That's the man Merri and I just saw last night at Camp Dubois. He was unloading the iron kettles for the widow. Her. His mother."

"Now, Merri, tell them," John said.

Merri smiled broadly at Eulah and Beulah. "Your father's watch fob is one of the Lewis and Clark peace medals. Like in my report. Captain Clark must have let that Nathan guy go on the Expedition in 1804. It was his Lewis and Clark medallion that got passed down in your family."

"Exactly," John said. "Abby, do you realize if we lock onto Nathan *we* could go too, see what it was really like?"

"You'll have to make an extra special apple for him," Merri said, patting Beulah's arm.

Beulah looked with wonder at the watch fob in her hand. "So, that was a story about our great, great grandfather, who went on the Lewis and Clark expedition?"

"Not a story about. That was really him," Merri said.

"And this," John said, indicating the room they stood in, "was Nathan's cabin. Part of it, anyway."

"We're in the log cabin?" Abby said.

"Yep. Which means," he said, going to the hole he had made in the wall next to the stone chimney, "that Nathan's so-called 'hidey hole' should be right about here."

Abby jerked around to stare at John. "The it!" she said, hurrying to his side. "How could I forget the it? Hurry, John. Get it out."

"So now you think you know what the *it* is?" John said, grinning. He dug in his pockets and took out a carpenter's utility knife. "I can't promise you anything since there wasn't any mention of it at the museum—"

"Just try."

Kneeling in the dust, John worked until he had cut a

neat rectangle about twelve inches by six inches in the wall. He tapped the rectangle twice and it came loose. Then he pried it out and looked into the opening. "I was right! Look!"

Merri squatted beside him. "Wow, John. It's a rock."

"Yes, isn't it great!" he said, smiling eagerly up at Abby. He tapped on the wall with his knuckles. "Behind this is more stonework. And a log wall."

"So, you mean someone—it'd have to be before Franny and Reuben's time—plastered over it," Abby said.

"Yep," John said. "If we took this plaster off, we'd find Nathan Hale Buchanan's fireplace. And his hidey hole."

John peered into the opening. "I'm not over far enough." He enlarged the opening and scraped away plaster with his knife. After what seemed to Abby a thousand hours, he finally called out, "I've got it."

Abby's heart hitched, but then she told herself to be prepared for disappointment. After all, what were the odds that anything was still in there?

Putting both hands into the opening, John lifted out the stone that had been covering Nathan Buchanan's hiding place for over two centuries. He laid it on the floor beside him and saying, "Cross your fingers," reached in again and carefully pulled out something that looked to Abby like a small saddle bag of dark brown oiled leather.

"What is it?" Eulah and Beulah said in near unison.

"Let me show you," John said. He took the leather bag to the table and they stood looking at it.

"I can't believe it," Abby said. "How did the family lose track of this…this…?"

"Treasure," Merri said. "It's like a buried treasure."

"I don't know why it got plastered over," John said. "Maybe later we can do a little time-surfing and find out.

But for now—" he looked first to Abby and then to Merri. "One of you open it. It's your adventure."

"Definitely another star for you," Abby whispered under her breath. "Merri?"

"You do it."

"Okay." Abby unbuckled the bag, gently lifted the leather flap, and then drew out an unadorned, obviously old, leather-bound book.

"That's it," Merri said. "It has to be."

"Open it carefully," John said. "It will be fragile."

"Maybe I shouldn't," Abby said. "Shouldn't we turn this over to the experts?"

"Just open the cover," John said. "That should be safe enough."

Carefully, she lifted the cover and read the words written there. For some reason, she had the urge to cry. "Come see what your great, great—how many greats, John?"

"Four, I think."

"Okay. Look what your four times great grandfather wrote." Then she stood back so that Eulah and Beulah could get a closer look. Eulah read it aloud:

This is the journal of Nathan Hale Buchanan, who along with Captains Lewis and Clark and 31 others, under order of the president of the United States, explored the interior of the continent to the western ocean and returned home September 23, 1806.

Turning to stare at her twin, Eulah said, "Oh my! It looks like we've found two heroes in one day, Boo."

"This is what the Hulk was looking for," Abby said.

"Somehow, he knew—"

A shadow fell over the table and a deep voice demanded, "Knew what?"

CHAPTER 20

The Hulk stood in the doorway glowering at them. "So now you've decided to move in, have you?" he growled, not giving them a chance to answer. "Maybe you thought it would be a good place to open up an old folks' home." He aimed a thumb at the twins.

Abby pulled Michael and Merri to her side and glared back at him.

"No, sir." John rose and went to stand in front of the others. "We didn't mean any harm."

"No harm? Well, you could get harmed when the place falls in on your heads. It's bad enough you're trespassing, but don't you have enough sense not to bring little kids—not to mention old ladies—into such a dangerous place?"

"Hey, I'm not a little—" Merri shut up when Abby squeezed her arm.

"I know," John said. "It's just that…well…"

Abby was thinking about how protective John had

been to put himself between them and the Hulk and reminding herself to add another star to his chart, which was why she hadn't noticed that Eulah and Beulah had gotten up from their chairs. But the Old Dears were standing in the Hulk's personal space, toe to toe with him—not, however, head to head, for their twin silver hairdos only came up to the middle of his chest.

Beulah glared up at him in a show of bad temper Abby had never seen from her. "Hold your horses, mister. This young man brought us here to show us our Buchanan relative on the World Wide Web."

"To prove he wasn't a murderer," Eulah said.

"You always forget arsonist, Yoo," Beulah said. "Dear John knows how strongly I feel about the apples."

Several expressions fluttered across the Hulk's face. He looked embarrassed to be confronting elderly ladies, but mostly, Abby thought, confused. He pointed at John and said, "He's a murderer?"

"Don't be ridiculous!" Eulah, arms crossed on her chest, stared up at the Hulk. "Rube Buchanan was the one everyone thought was a murderer—and arsonist."

The Hulk scratched his head and looked puzzled. "Buchanan?"

"Yes," Beulah said firmly. "This house belonged to our great grandparents Reuben and Frances Buchanan."

"So, we're related?" the Hulk asked.

"Well, I certainly hope we're not related to someone so rude," Eulah said. "Who are you and why are you trespassing?"

"I'm Doug Buchanan, ma'am, and I happen to own this heap."

"Well, I'm Beulah Buchanan Edwards and this is my sister Eulah—we're twins."

Doug Buchanan turned to John again. "What does she

mean about the *World Wide Web*?" he said, using air quotes. Abby wasn't sure, but thought his lips quirked a bit before he managed to resume his scowl.

"As I said before, we're doing research." John looked at Abby and Merri, silently asking their permission to go on. When they nodded, he continued. "We discovered a program that...well, I know you're going to think it's crazy, but...it takes you back in time."

"Only in a virtual way," Merri added helpfully.

Buchanan, back to his Hulk persona, huffed and then, sidestepping the Old Dears, got in John's face. "What is this? Some kind of scam you're pulling on old people?"

"Show him the World Wide Web," Beulah said. "That'll shut him up."

"Here, look." Abby reached over and clicked the mouse to get past the screen saver. "See," she said, staring up at him. "We told you."

"What? So there's a bunch of pictures of houses?"

Abby's eyes darted back down to the screen and she saw that Reuben and the cabin were no longer there. Only the usual *Beautiful Houses* slide show was scrolling past. "It's gone! Hey, you guys, the cabin's gone!"

"You'll have to reset it," John said.

Abby began clicking on the controls. "No. I'm telling you, it's gone."

"Oh, great," Merri said. "Here we go again. It's like the program doesn't want the Hulk—"

Abby glared at Merri, who stopped speaking when she got her telegraphed warning about not annoying Mr. Buchanan any more than they already had.

"Well, anyway," John said, turning back to Buchanan, "as soon as the program starts working again, we'll show you Eulah and Beulah's relatives who used to live here."

"What? Are you crazy?" Doug Buchanan pulled his

cell phone out of his pocket. "That's it! I'm calling the cops."

"Wait!" Abby picked up the journal and held it to her chest. "We found this."

"What is it?" Buchanan said.

John snorted in disgust. "As if you didn't know."

"I have no earthly idea what you're talking about."

"Yeah?" Merri pointed accusingly at the scarred stone chimney. "Then why were you stealing rocks from that?"

"I own those rocks!" he roared. And then seeming to realize he was shouting at kids and old ladies, he lowered his voice and said, "I was just trying to get some pretty stones for my mother. She wants them for her rock garden as a memento before they tear down this old place."

"Then why were you sneaking around here at night?" Abby said

"I could ask you kids the same question, couldn't I?" He ran a hand through his hair and heaved a sigh. "The city lawyers have been trying to run me down so they can serve me notice. Ever heard of eminent domain? They want to take this place and turn it into a parking lot. And I'm stalling, hoping to think of some way to—to do something," he said desperately.

"I doubt they'll be able to do that now," John said. "Show him, Abby."

Abby reluctantly held the journal out to Doug Buchanan. When it went from her hands into his she mentally grimaced, wondering if they had just made a huge mistake.

He carefully opened the journal to the first page and read aloud:

May 14, 1803. Captain Clark mustered the men and we commenced to board the keel boat. We left Camp Dubois at 9

O'clock and reached the mouth of the Missouri River at 4 O'clock.

Buchanan swore and looked up in shock. "Oh, sorry. Pardon my French. But this is unbelievable! Where did you find it?"

John showed him the hole he'd made in the wall next to the stone chimney.

Buchanan squatted next to John and studied Nathan's hiding place. "And to think it has been behind the wall all this time. There have been rumors in the family for years about a Lewis and Clark connection. Especially when everyone gets together for the reunion and some of the old biddies get to talking. But I never believed it." He snorted out a laugh. "Just like half the people in Illinois claim Lincoln slept in their houses, or that their ancestors came over on the Mayflower."

"Oh, how fun that must have been to go to family reunions!" Beulah said.

"I suppose so," he said. "How do you figure we're related?"

"Why don't you come over to our house and we'll show you what we know?" Eulah said.

"How about tonight?" Beulah said. "You can come to our Fourth of July party."

Doug Buchanan showed no signs of relinquishing Nathan's journal and Abby felt sick to her stomach. What if he took it away and they didn't get a chance to read it? What if he didn't understand its historical value and sold it on eBay?

As if he had been reading her mind, Buchanan said, "I'm going to put this in a safe place for now, but after that, I have no idea what to do with it. It'll have to go to someone that can take proper care of it."

"I know just the person," Abby said with a relieved sigh.

Beulah, wearing a cone-shaped birthday hat, came from the kitchen proudly bearing a large glass bowl of something colorful. "You forgot the Jello salad, Yoo."

"Don't call me that," Eulah muttered from her seat at the dining table.

Beulah set the bowl down in front of the ever-smiling Michael, who was also wearing a paper hat. The "salad" appeared to be cubes of red and blue gelatin mixed together with miniature marshmallows. Abby grinned at John and Merri across the table from her.

"Everything looks so…festive," John said. "With the red tablecloth and flag napkins and all." He sounded like he was trying not to laugh.

"Why, thank you, John," Beulah said, adjusting her red, white, and blue hat. "People tell me I have a flair for parties."

"It's the Fourth of July, not your birthday," Eulah groused from the end of the table. "Mine, either. I don't know why I have to wear this stupid hat."

Beulah had found only three hats in her store of party supplies and wanted to go back to Walmart "quick as a rabbit" and get enough for everyone. Thankfully, John had been able to talk her out of it.

"Thank you for inviting us," Doug Buchanan said from the place of honor at the end of the table.

Doug's wife Dora sat to his right. "Sorry our boys couldn't make it," she said. "Did Doug tell you they're twins?"

"Why, that's wonderful," Beulah said. "I hope they

can come the next time."

"Twins run in the Buchanan family, you know." Doug picked up the hamburger on his plate, and removing the tiny paper flag, started to take a bite. Then he quickly put it back on his plate when Beulah extended her hand to him.

When everyone was holding hands, she bowed her head and said, "Dear Lord, thank you that Cousin Doug and Dora could be here with us. And thank you for our grandchildren Merri, Michael, Abby, and John. I know they're just pretend, but they mean so much to us. And please be with Lovely Lucy and grant her traveling mercies tonight. And thank you for this food, Lord. Bless it to the nourishment of our bodies. Amen"

Abby contemplated the huge bowl of Cheesy Puffs in front of her and wondered if God would be willing to work a miracle to make junk food actually capable of nourishing their bodies. "Cheesy Puffs, anyone?" she said. "They're extra crunchy and extra cheesy."

"Don't mind if I do," Merri said, taking the bowl from her.

"Oh, I almost forgot the Kool-Aid," Eulah said, pushing herself to her feet. When she came back from the kitchen she was struggling with two pitchers. John nearly leapt across the room to take them from her just as they were slipping from her frail hands.

"Red or blue?" Eulah said.

"Uh, I'll have...red, I guess," Dora said.

Abby bit down into the hamburger and managed, after a while, to tear off a small piece of the meat. It was rather like beef jerky. Doug seemed to be struggling to swallow. Next to her, John was reaching under the table. Then Abby heard a happy snuffling sound and knew that Dr. Bob at least was enjoying his burger.

"Don't forget to save room for dessert," Beulah said

cheerfully.

"We got cake from the Walmart," Eulah cackled. "Looks just like a red, white, and blue flag."

While Abby and Merri cleared the table, Eulah enlisted John's help getting their family tree mosaic down from the wall. Beulah brought the box in which she had stored the glue gun and remaining apples. "That is so adorable," Dora said. "How fun."

"It is when you have enough apples to put on the tree," Eulah said.

"We'll have lots of Buchanan apples after today," Beulah said. "John, tell me those names again. The ones we found out this afternoon."

"I've got it," John said, taking a folded paper from his pocket. "First, Nathan Hale Buchanan, he's the one of Lewis and Clark fame. His son was Thomas Jefferson Buchanan. Then came Benjamin Franklin Buchanan."

"There's the connection," Doug said. "I think Benjamin was a brother to my great, great-grandfather."

John scrunched up his face in thought and then after a minute said, "I never could keep that kind of thing straight. Anyway, you're some kind of cousin."

"Then I'll put your apple right there, Doug," Beulah said, happily pointing to a branch on the tree.

"I guess you know we have a murderer in the family?" Doug said. "They say he died in prison."

"His name was Reuben Buchanan, and he was our great grandfather," Eulah said stiffly.

"And he was innocent," Beulah added.

"Oh, sorry," Doug said. "I guess every family has a skeleton or two in the closet."

"No, really," Merri said. "He was innocent. We can prove…well I guess we can't now, but—"

"I have good news," Abby said. "Actually, I found out

this afternoon that the program's still working. Here, at least," she said. "And maybe we'll be able to get it going again out at Shake Rag Corner for Doug and Dora."

"Really?" Merri looked thoughtful. After a moment she turned to Abby and said softly, "I've been thinking. You know how it stopped working with Charlotte at my house?"

"Yes," Abby said cautiously.

"Well, what it if wasn't the storm that stopped it? What if it just stopped because—"

Abby put a hand on Merri's arm in warning. "I don't know, Merri…that sounds…"

"And today at Shake Rag Corner it stopped again—like maybe that's all we were meant to see."

"Shhh," Abby said. "We can talk later."

Doug frowned like he was about to speak, and Abby wondered if he had overheard Merri's comment. If he had he would think they were crazy for sure. And if Kate heard that theory? Well, she could hear her laughing all the way from Springfield. Kate would really feel like she needed to do an intervention, the kind where they sent the guys in white coats.

Then Doug smiled and said something to his wife. Abby breathed again.

"Well," Beulah said, "It's time to put Reuben on the tree where he belongs." She selected a blank apple and wrote in silver ink, *Reuben Buchanan, born 1851, died 1873*, and then glued it on the tree. "There," she said with satisfaction.

Dora laughed wryly. "We've got a murderer in my family too. Someone actually wrote a song about it. He killed a man over a woman down in Bristol. The town straddles two states, so the song says he shot a man in Virginia, and he died in Tennessee."

John leaned back in his chair and put his hands in his pockets. "Lucy and I don't have a very illustrious family background either. We come from starving Irish immigrants who came to America during the potato famine in the 1840s."

"Humph!" Abby said. "That's nothing. I don't even know who my real family is."

"You never told me you were adopted," Merri said.

"I'm not. It's just that my mom's great grandfather changed the family's last name. Seems he stole a horse in Kentucky and only escaped hanging by crossing the Ohio River and sneaking off into the woods of southern Illinois. He changed his name to *Woods*, which wasn't all that original. We have no idea what his name really was, so there's no hope of tracing Mom's family tree."

"I have Indian blood on my mother's side," Doug said.

"Oh, you have Indian blood on both sides." Abby closed her mouth and mentally smacked herself.

Doug looked curiously at her. "How did you guys find out so much about the Buchanan family anyway? Really?"

If she mentioned the computer program he'd probably just get all riled up again. He might even start thinking of calling the police again. "Well...we uh..." Abby said.

Merri stood up from the table. "Oh, well, that's nothing. My dad's in prison right now."

"Oh, dear," Dora said. "You poor girl."

"That's all right, Merri." Abby patted her arm. "As you heard, we all have skeletons."

"I'm sure we have more than one skeleton in our tree...er...closet." Eulah coughed into her napkin. "No doubt there was other hanky panky going on."

Abby watched the color drain from Beulah's face, but Eulah went on. "Well, anyway, we can't think about the skeletons." She sniffed and then pulled out a red, white, and blue hanky. "We just have to get on with life, be glad for the family God gave us. Doug, tell us again about that Buchanan reunion."

"It's always the third weekend in August, over at the city park." Doug looked from Eulah to Beulah. "I hope you'll both come."

"I don't know why they have it in August," Dora said. "It's always hotter than Hades."

"That won't matter to us," Eulah said. "We've been waiting our whole lives to go to a family reunion."

Smiling again, Beulah pulled herself up from the table. "It's about time for the fireworks!" she said. "And Lucy's widow's walk is the best spot for seeing them in the whole city. Hurry everyone. We don't want to miss it."

"They never start before 9:00," Eulah said. "It's not dark enough."

"It will be by the time we haul ourselves up all those stairs," Beulah said.

They all trooped across the twins' yard and up the porch steps to Lucy's front door, Doug and John taking the twins' arms. "Right this way," John said. "You'll love it. You can see the river from here."

"How exciting!" Dora said. "I've always wanted to go up on one of these widow's walks."

"You're not planning to shove me off, are you?" Doug said with a wink.

"We'll be right there," Abby said to John. "The rest of you go on up. There's something I need to show Eulah and Beulah on the computer."

CHAPTER 21

Abby went to Lucy's dining table where John had left his laptop and started the program while Merri pulled out chairs for the twins. Abby set the date and began to search for the time she wanted to show the twins.

"I just love the World Wide Web," Beulah said.

"Me to," Eulah said.

"What's up, Abby?" Merri asked.

"Well, I got to thinking about something John and I talked about—how with Reuben and the fire we didn't know the truth until we saw it from a different perspective. So this afternoon I decided to…well, I may have sort of broken our rule about not time-surfing in this house."

"Yeah, and what about the part about not doing it alone? You know, all for one and one for all."

"Sorry, Merri, but I had an idea that I thought I should check out before I showed it to anyone." Abby studied the computer monitor where a young woman was playing the piano. Then she stopped the action and turned to look at Beulah and Eulah.

"That's me!" Beulah said.

"Abby! What are you doing?" Merri said, darting glances from her to the Old Dears. "Are you insane?"

"Don't worry. I know what I'm doing." Abby turned and looked closely at Eulah. "This is Beulah. Back in 1943. Remember how she liked to come over and play your piano?"

"Oh," Beulah sighed wistfully. "I was so pretty. And so young."

"And so foolish," Eulah said, frowning.

"Just watch," Abby said. "Watch carefully."

Of course, Beulah loved her parents, and got along with them just fine too. But when she thought about having to live with them forever she got a little panicky feeling in her stomach. Everyone had assumed she would marry too and there *had* been boys, after her father had decided she and Eulah were old enough to receive callers. But none of them worked out, for one reason or another. Now, almost all the men of marrying age were gone, off fighting in the War. All gone and she was twenty and had never been kissed.

She heard the front door shut, and then her sister's husband was standing motionless in the dimness, holding his duffel bag.

"You look so beautiful in the light," he said almost reverently. "Don't stop playing."

"Carl, you're home. We thought—"

"I only found out two days ago. I wanted to surprise you." He dropped the duffel where he stood, and taking off his cap, started eagerly toward her. That was when

Beulah realized his mistake. She stood quickly, shoving the piano bench away. There would have been enough time while he walked from the doorway to the piano for her to say "Welcome home, Carl. Eulah will be here soon," but the words somehow didn't come out. She could have stayed in the light so that he could see her more clearly, but somehow she found herself walking toward him into the darkness. In three steps it was forever too late to correct the error, because then she had allowed him to take her into his arms and rain kisses over her brow and cheeks. She closed her eyes and inhaled his scent, savored the feel of having a masculine body crushed to hers. And pretended. A part of her brain knew that there would be a steep penalty to pay when he realized his error, but another louder voice said, take the kiss while you can.

Eulah stood unseen in the dim parlor doorway, her face ravaged with the pain of betrayal—double betrayal. She gasped and held her hands to her chest, as if she could somehow hug her heart and stop it from hurting. She turned and stumbled back out to the kitchen. She had to get out. How could she stay one more minute to watch what was inevitably coming next? She would go somewhere. She'd drive somewhere…anywhere. "Oh, God," she cried. "The pain."

Tears were streaming down their cheeks, but the sisters sat there unmoving and silent. At last Beulah turned to her twin. "All this time…You knew all this time. Oh, Eulah, I'm so sorry. I wanted to undo it, but I couldn't. There was no way."

"But that's not all, is it, Beulah?" Abby sniffed and wiped her eyes with the back of her hands.

Eulah looked up sharply. "You don't have to show us anymore."

"I think you need to see this," Abby said. "Trust me." She un-paused the action and let the story play out.

Beulah pulled away and stumbled over the piano's leg. She would have fallen, but Carl reached out and grabbed her flailing arm. He spun her toward the light streaming down from the chandelier hanging in the stairway and studied her face. Once again she pulled away and then, saying nothing, turned and raced out the front door, while he stood there staring after her. After a moment, he went and closed the door she'd left open to the cold night air.

The room faded and was gone. The screen filled with colorful images of random houses scrolling by.

Merri clicked frantically on the controls. "It's gone again," Merri said in disgust. "It's not here anymore."

Abby put a hand on her shoulder to quiet her and then looked into Beulah's face.

"He hated me for a long time after that," Beulah said. "And I don't blame him. I wanted so badly to make time rewind, so I could fix it. Just that one minute, when I could have said…"

Eulah sat in shock, staring straight ahead. Then, a smile slowly spread across her face. "You didn't do it? You and Carl didn't…? All this time I thought…You didn't go through with it."

"Oh, Eulah, I could never betray you. But I thought about it for just a minute. Can you ever forgive me?"

Eulah reached a wrinkled hand up and gently stroked Beulah's wrinkled cheek. "I forgave you over sixty years ago, Beulah Mae."

Merri stared at the twins. Abby smiled a little at the look of surprise on her face.

"If Jesus could forgive all *my* sins," Eulah said, "I can forgive my sister and husband. After all, we're family."

A smile of amazement lit up Beulah's face and she squeezed her sister tight. "Oh, Yoo."

"Don't call me that," Eulah said. A whizzing sound followed by a loud bang came from outside and then light streaked into the dim room where they sat. "Come on. They've started now," she said and pulled herself and then her sister to their feet.

John and Doug helped the twins up all the stairs and through the little door onto the widow's walk. "Ooh, look... at that... one!" Beulah said. "It's like a... purple and orange... flower."

"You'd better...watch your feet...instead of the sky," Eulah said, trying to get her breath back. She was holding onto Beulah's arm, but Abby wasn't sure who was actually supporting whom.

Michael didn't seem to notice their arrival. He was watching the pyrotechnical display in the sky with rapt joy, as if he had never seen such a sight before. But then, maybe he never had. Abby nudged John and they smiled together at the little boy's happiness.

The fireworks were some of the best Abby had ever seen, and she'd never had such a perfect spot to view them from, but she was enjoying watching everyone's smiling faces almost more than the light show overhead. How had they all become so important to her in such a short time?

Then she saw that John was watching her and she felt her pulse leap. Above the sizzles, whizzes, and shrieks of the fireworks and the oohs and aahs of the spectators he said, "Come on."

He took her by the hand and led her along the walk around to the other side of the chimney. And at last, just as a red chrysanthemum of light bloomed over Alton, he pulled her into his arms.

It felt wonderful and Abby thought she could stay there forever. But then, with Herculean effort she took charge of her scrambled brains, pulled herself together, and glared up at him. "You're touching me, John."

"Well, I don't want to," he said grumpily.

"Well, thank you very much," she said, and tried to pull away.

John wouldn't let her. "Because I'm tired of calculating square roots," he mumbled into her hair, "and running through baseball stats, and redesigning the engine on my—"

"Uh, John?" she said. "I'd like to point out that you're still holding me."

"That's because we've got something we need to straighten out," he whispered almost angrily. "I figured this would be a safe enough place with everyone around."

"What did I do?" Abby said.

"Nothing. I just want you to know I'm happy to be Merri's big brother. Who wouldn't want to be? She's a neat kid. But just so you know, I'm not signing on to be yours." He looked into her eyes and pushed a curly lock of hair away from her forehead. "Because I'm definitely not thinking of you like a sister."

Heat started rising from her neck and she knew her blasted blush was back. At least it was dark this time and he wouldn't see it. Not-Like-A-Sister still reverberated in her head, bouncing off the goo that had been her brain. Not-Like-A-Sister was good, she thought, but there must be a caveat.

"Maybe a friend or a cousin then?" she said, laughing nervously.

"Only if it's a really, really distant cousin. A kissing cousin," he said solemnly, pulling her even closer.

Anytime, she thought and swallowed hard. Like right now. "Then you're not gay?" she blurted and immediately felt her face flame hotter. "I mean…er…Pat thinks you are, but I said just because you're nice and like the theater doesn't mean… It's just that…I thought you weren't attracted to me. I'll stop babbling now."

John closed his eyes for a second and groaned. "You think…I'm not… attracted to you?"

"Well," she said crossly, "You're always backing off like I have cooties."

"I'm trying to treat you with respect," he said just as crossly. "I knew if I touched you—"

"I trust you, John." She put her hand on his cheek and smiled into his eyes, while mentally adding a star for self-control to his chart. "I trust *us.*"

John snorted a laugh. "I'm glad you do, Abby…because…just so you won't be confused…" He lowered his mouth to within an inch of hers. "Or… have any more doubts…."

When his lips touched hers, Abby saw fireworks through her closed eyelids and thought, *wow!* She imagined another star on John's chart, and just this one time it wouldn't be for his sterling character. Another burst of light bloomed, and on the other side of the chimney everyone oohed and ahhed their delight. *My sentiments exactly*, she thought. And then Abby put her arms around his neck and kissed him back.

*E*PILOGUE

Abby's phone vibrated for the third time since Pastor Goodson had begun to pray. Thankfully, she had remembered to turn off the ringer before the graveside service began. She took her hand from John's and slipped the phone out of her pocket for a quick peek. There were three missed calls, all from Kate, who probably wanted to talk more about decorating their dorm room. Again. For crying out loud, Abby thought, hadn't they already discussed everything from fringes on the curtains to the color of the bulletin board on their door? There would be time enough to decide the final details before classes resumed in two weeks. She put her phone away and took John's hand again as Eulah and Beulah's pastor continued to pray.

Abby had been worried that the funeral would be a disappointment to the Old Dears. For one thing, the pastor didn't personally know the deceased. And then the fact that he was a convicted felon buried in 1873 in the Alton

Prison Cemetery could have been a damper. But Pastor Goodson had taken the twins' word for it that Reuben Buchanan had been a child of God and innocent of the charges against him. It occurred to Abby that it must be difficult to be called upon to preach a funeral sermon for an ungodly man like, say, Bertram White, for example, and she wondered briefly what had ever happened to him.

Pastor Goodson had chosen Psalm 37 for his text, emphasizing the parts about trusting in the Lord and not fretting "when men carry out their wicked schemes." It had seemed perfect for the occasion, and, although she had wept thinking of Reuben's unjust treatment, Abby had also been comforted to be reminded that the Great Judge would make it right one day.

And she would *try* not to fret, even though it looked unlikely that they'd ever be able to prove Reuben's innocence to the world, and more importantly to Doug and the rest of the Buchanan family. If only they had been able to get the computer program to work again out at the old house.

But even without proof, Doug had been amenable to holding the service for his infamous relative. He had just smiled indulgently at Eulah and Beulah and promised to be there. And he had done much more than just show up on time. He had arranged for the small canopy that shaded them from the August sun and had brought chairs for all the ladies. Most importantly, he had expedited the engraving for Reuben's new headstone so it would be ready in time. And then Doug and his twin sons Jason and Jackson, stoic in their suits and tugging at their ties, had stood loyally behind Eulah and Beulah's chairs throughout the funeral sermon. Dora was there too, teary-eyed in support next to the Old Dears.

Pastor Goodson prayed on. Abby thought of the

proud moment the family had seen Nathan Hale Buchanan's journal on display at the Lewis & Clark museum. Mr. Rohst had been thrilled to take custody of it until the state Historic Preservation Society could verify its authenticity. Even without that, the journal was already drawing crowds from across the region. And of course, all talk of turning Shake Rag Corner into a parking lot had ceased. Mr. Rohst had told them it would undoubtedly be placed on the state's registry of historic sites. And the twins were ecstatic that Abby had found, after more research, that their great, great, great, great, great-grandfather, James Henry Buchanan, had served in the Revolutionary War, qualifying them for membership in the D.A.R. after all. The Old Dears couldn't help but gloat a little. Watching Dragon Lady sputter was worth every hour Abby had spent under her watchful eye in the genealogy department.

Pastor Goodson prayed on. John shifted beside her and Abby sneaked a peak to find that he and Merri were grinning. She jabbed him in the side, but then grinned herself when she saw they were watching Beulah, who had pulled out her father's pocket watch and was checking the time.

Abby closed her eyes again and breathed deeply, hoping to suppress inappropriate laughter. The scent of the floral arrangements at Reuben's new headstone was a heady perfume in the heat and humidity. She and John had brought carnations and roses. Pat had generously contributed a bouquet on behalf of Merri and herself, even though she had no clue what was going on and couldn't make it to the funeral. Doug and Dora's family had brought stately white lilies with a blue ribbon draped across the bouquet that said "Cousins." And Eulah and Beulah had chosen daisies because that had been their father's favorite flower and they figured Reuben, who looked so much like him, might have liked them too. Earlier that morning they had brought similar arrangements to Franny's grave in the illustrious Edwards' family plot in the Edwardsville Cemetery.

At last, the pastor finished his prayer with a devout "amen" and smiled kindly at the gathering.

"It was a lovely service, Pastor Goodson," Eulah said.

"And so comforting," Beulah said.

Doug Buchanan, looking mightily relieved it was over, said, "I hope you'll join us at the reunion, Reverend. The Buchanan ladies always bring plenty of good food."

"I'd be honored. Just lead the way."

Abby's phone vibrated again and she saw that this time Kate had texted. She frowned.

"What's wrong?" John said.

"Oh, nothing. Kate's just being Kate," Abby said. "She's coming here after all."

"You don't seem too happy about it," Merri said. "I thought you wanted me to meet her."

"I do, kiddo. And we'll have fun. But it's weird. She wants to know if I'll go with her to Equality, wherever that is, for what she calls a *friend fest weekend* before school starts."

"As in Equality, *Illinois*?" John said.

"I think so. Do you know it?"

"It's a little Podunk town a couple of hours south of here. I gotta say it wouldn't be my first choice for a *friend fest weekend*," he said using ironic air quotes. "Why on earth does she want to go there?"

"I have no idea. But here's the weird thing. She wants me to bring your laptop. Would you mind?"

"Not a problem. You don't suppose she finally believes you about the program?"

"Do you think so?"

Eulah and Beulah, politely escorted by Pastor Goodson, came up to where they stood, wearing their best happy faces.

"Are you ready?" Doug said. "Just follow my car."

"Oh, Yoo, just think, our first Buchanan reunion!" Beulah said.

"Don't call me that," Eulah said.

Beulah smiled at Pastor Goodson. "And you can follow us. Abby and John are taking us in the Lincoln. You can't miss it."

"Come on," Merri said. "Let's go for a boat ride."

"Go on. We'll be right there," John said.

Abby and John watched as the four followed the Buchanans up the green hill and through the wrought iron gate.

John turned to Abby and cupped her face with his hands. "We did good, didn't we?"

"Yes we did. Now kiss me quick."

John lowered his lips to hers and she drank in the sweetness. It ended all too soon. But then John took her hand in his and together they looked down at Reuben's new headstone. "Finally at peace," he said. "Well, of course, he's always been at peace."

"And now we can be too."

Reuben Buchanan

b. 1849 d. 1873

Beloved Husband of Frances Edwards Buchanan
"The days of the blameless are known to the Lord."

The End

A Note from the Author

Domestic Violence in Unclaimed Legacy

It wasn't easy writing about domestic violence, but it is a part of daily life for so many families—even Christian ones—that I felt I couldn't shy away from it in telling Reuben and Franny's story. When we consider spousal abuse, we think most often of physical violence, and my heart goes out to the women who suffer beatings and broken bones as a matter of course in their marriages.

I believe there will be a special punishment for those bullies who, like Bertram White, use the Bible (misinterpreted and bent all out of recognition) to justify their actions.

I pray that if you are in a violent relationship you will be rescued from your misery. If Christians—even pastors— are telling you that you are obligated, as a good wife, to endure the beatings, I want you to know that I and many other Christians—even especially pastors—would tell you that you aren't. Flee to safety! The first step might be calling the National Domestic Hotline. 1-800-799-SAFE. Meanwhile, know that I'll be praying for you.

The History Behind the Story

For more about the real history check out the "About My Books" tab on my website. www.deborahheal.com If you're ever in the area, I hope you'll visit the real Lewis and Clark State Historic Site to learn more about the explorers' time in Illinois before embarking on one of the most exciting adventures in American history.

Let's Keep in Touch

I'd love to hear what you think of *Unclaimed Legacy*. If you enjoyed it, please write a review for it and post it on Amazon, Goodreads, or my website. (Authors need lots of reviews!)

> **www.deborahheal.com**
> **www.facebook.com/DeborahHeal**
> **www.twitter.com/DeborahHeal**
> **www.goodreads.com/deborahheal**

But the best way for us to keep in touch is by subscribing to my V.I.P. Readers List (on my website). You'll get lots of free stuff, including ***Charlotte's House***.

$\mathcal{E}$VERY $\mathcal{H}$ILL AND $\mathcal{M}$OUNTAIN

$\mathcal{B}$OOK 3

Their discovery on the third floor of Hickory Hill is almost too much to bear.

Since the *Beautiful Houses* computer software worked so well for the Old Dears' family tree project, Abby's college roommate Kate hopes the computer program will help her find out more about her ancestor Ned Greenfield.

Abby and John reluctantly agree to help Kate, but only on the condition that she and her fiancé Ryan promise to keep the program a secret, because if the government ever discovered they possessed a computer program that allows you to rewind and fast-forward the lives of people it would surely want to get its hands on it.

The two couples take a trip to the tiny town of Equality, set in the hills of southern Illinois and the breath-taking Shawnee National Forest. According to Kate's research, Ned Greenfield was born there at a place called Hickory Hill.

The mayor, police chief, and townspeople are hospitable and helpful—until the topic of Hickory Hill comes up. Then they are determined to keep them away. Eventually they find Hickory Hill on their own—both the mansion and the lonely hill it sits upon. And what a perfect old house to time-surf in!

Built in 1834, Hickory Hill stands sentinel over Half Moon Salt Mine where the original owner John Granger accumulated his blood-tainted fortune with the use of slave labor in the free state of Illinois—the Land of Lincoln.

Abby and her friends meet Miss Granger, Hickory Hill's current eccentric owner, and they eventually get the chance to run *Beautiful Houses* there. Their shocking discovery on the third floor concerning Kate's ancestor Ned Greenfield is almost too much to bear. What they learn sends them racing to the opposite end of the state to find the missing link in Kate's family tree. And there they are reminded that God is in the business of redemption—that one day he'll make all things new.

What Readers Are Saying...

"This is the first five star rating I've given in hundreds of books. The story plot is unusual and wonderful in so many ways."

"The characters are believable and endearing. I am about to finish the second series and hope more come out soon because I just can't get enough."

"I just want more of this writer's books."

"Only a great author could weave all of the genres together the way she did. There is a great balance between what happened in the past and why and how it affects the present." Nicely Done! (J Hall)

"This is one journey through time you won't want to miss. Just be

sure to bring a box of tissue with you as this may well be the most emotional journey yet!"

(Tiffany A Harkleroad, Vine Voice) "I am completely enchanted with this series. I think that this third book may be my favorite yet, because it truly elicited emotional responses from me."

"Love, love, love this series. Sad to finish, but happy there are more books to read by this author. Next up, Once Again!" (Melissa S)

After the Trilogy comes...

THE REWINDING TIME SERIES

Inspirational novels of history, mystery & romance
www.deborahheal.com

Fast-forward fifteen years and Merrideth Randall, the troubled pre-teen of the trilogy, is now a history professor at McKendree College. At least, that's her day job. But after hours she turns to her first love, historical research. And she has a tool other historians can only dreams of—a computer program that rewinds time for a first-hand look at the past!

An Excerpt from

Every Hill and Mountain

Chapter 1

"Did Doug say how long this is going to take?" Abby said, blowing her bangs out of her eyes. "And remind me. Why exactly are we using this antique instead of an electric one?"

"He said using an electric ice cream maker meant it didn't count as homemade," John said, wiping his forehead with first his left T-shirt sleeve and then his right.

"Really?"

"Really. And I'm supposed to crank until I can't turn it anymore."

The day was typical for southern Illinois in late August: hot and humid. At least she was sitting on an icy, albeit uncomfortable, seat in the shady pavilion. Doug Buchanan had to be sweltering out in the sun where he manned the deep-fat fryer along with three of his cousins. Wearing a Cardinals cap to keep the sun off his balding head and an apron that said, "Kiss the Cook," Doug looked so friendly and benign that Abby wondered again how she had ever thought of him as The Hulk.

One of Doug's cousins gestured their way and said something that she couldn't make out. Whatever it was made the other men laugh.

A short distance away, under the shade of a maple tree, Jason and Jackson, Doug's twin teenage sons were practicing their washer-throwing skills in preparation for the tournament to be held tomorrow. The washers clinked and clacked, depending upon how, or whether, they hit the sand-filled wooden boxes. Those sounds along with the rhythm of the turning crank and the hot afternoon made Abby drowsy, and she surveyed the activities going on around her through a sleepy haze.

Next to them, Doug's wife Dora and a dozen other Buchanan women began unpacking coolers and setting out dish after dish onto the groaning picnic tables under Alton City Park Pavilion #1. Abby turned and smiled at the look on John's face as cakes, pies, bowls of watermelon chunks, and dozens of other goodies made their appearance.

"Hey, Dora, is that potato salad?" he asked.

"Yep," she said with a wide smile. "And I brought macaroni salad and deviled eggs."

John sighed blissfully.

"This is nothing. Wait'll tomorrow," Doug called to them. "That's when the ladies go all out. I heard Aunt Hil's making her chocolate chip cake."

Under the second pavilion reserved for the event, Eulah and Beulah played dominoes with several of the other elderly relatives. Fanning themselves with paper plates, they chattered happily while they waited their turns.

Abby smiled and a wave of contentment washed over her, knowing that she had been instrumental in getting the Old Dears in touch with their Buchanan relatives. And now the 85-year-old twins were at their first-ever family reunion.

Eleven-year-old Merri came over, panting and red-faced, but smiling. On each arm clung—as they had from the first half hour there—an adoring little girl. One little blonde looked about four, the other about six.

"What are you doing?" Abby asked.

"We're taking a break from the kiddie games," Merri

said. "I'm hot."

Merri was a different girl from the one Abby had met when she had arrived at the beginning of summer to be her tutor. Naturally, she still had her moments of sadness and snarky attitude. After all, her mother was hardly ever around and her father was serving time in Joliet Prison. But Eulah and Beulah had made her their pretend granddaughter and invited her to come along to the Buchanan reunion.

Abby pushed Merri's hair away from her sweaty face and grinned. "It's hard work being an honorary cousin, isn't it?"

Merri frowned, but it was easy to see she loved the little girls' attention. "Yeah, tell me about it," she said. "Is the ice cream about done?"

"Not quite," John said. "I can still turn the crank. Slowly, but still."

"Come on, Mewwi," the smaller girl lisped. "Let's go swing on the swings."

"Okay," Merri said good-naturedly. She turned to look back as she was being dragged away. "But don't forget, John. You're on my team in the water balloon war."

"I won't forget, squirt."

Abby lifted her hair and waited for a breeze to cool her own sweaty neck.

John blew gently and then leaned down to kiss it. "Watch out, girlie. That's what led to the ice incident before."

Earlier John had put a piece of ice down the back of her T-shirt, which had made her leap up from the ice cream churn with a squeal. He had chased her around the pavilion threatening her with more ice until she told him to behave or he'd have to get someone else to help.

John's breath on her neck did anything but cool her

off. Abby leaned back and kissed his cheek. "Just stick to your job, ice cream boy."

Doug Buchanan brought a huge platter of fried fish over and handed it to his wife. "Is the ice cream about done, John?"

"I'm still cranking."

Doug laughed and glanced back at his grinning cousins. "You can stop now. Anyone else would have quit a half hour ago. Anyone with normal-sized muscles, anyway."

"Dang it, Doug!" John said. "I think my arm may fall off."

Abby rose from her bumpy perch and rubbed her sore rear. "Yes, and a certain part of my anatomy."

Doug packed the ice cream maker with more ice and covered it with thick blankets. Then, after conferring with the women about the readiness of the food, he put his fingers to his mouth and whistled for everyone to come and eat.

After Reverend Goodson, the Old Dears' pastor, prayed an uncharacteristically short prayer, Merri and a gaggle of other kids converged on the food table. Dora shooed them back and invited the oldest members of the family, including Eulah and Beulah, to fill their plates first. John held Eulah's plate while she made her selections, and Abby held Beulah's, and then they helped the ladies onto the awkward picnic benches near their friends.

Then she and John filled their plates and went to sit by Merri.

"What's that pinky fluffy stuff?" John said, pointing to Merri's plate.

"Dora said it's a salad, but it tastes good enough to be dessert."

"Sounds good to me," he said after he had swallowed

what looked to Abby like a mountain-sized bite of potato salad. "I'm going to get some on my next trip."

"This is going to take a while, isn't it?" Abby said.

"Yep," John said.

"Could you try to hurry?" Merri said. "Me and Abby have to—"

"Abby and I," Abby said.

"Whatever," Merri said. "Anyway, we have to get home and get ready for our girls' night with Kate. We're going to make snickerdoodles and—"

"You are?" he said. "Bless you, my child. You know how I love snickerdoodles."

"Well, you're not a girl, John," Merri explained earnestly. "So you know you can't come to our girls' night, right?"

"Yeah, John," Abby said, patting his bicep. "You're definitely not a girl."

"That's okay, Merri," he said. "I'll survive."

"Merri, you're going to love Kate," Abby said. "She's a riot."

"That doesn't sound good."

Abby laughed. "I mean, she's a lot of fun. She always thinks of something crazy to do."

After Abby's disastrous roommate her freshman year at Ambassador College, Kate had been a Godsend. After only a few weeks as sophomores, they had become best friends. They didn't share any classes together since Kate was majoring in art and Abby in elementary education. But together they had explored Chicago's art museums to Kate's delight, and bookstores and coffee shops to Abby's.

While it was true that Kate's personality was so different from her own, Abby knew they each brought balance to the friendship. As for herself, she needed to stop being so serious all the time, to lighten up and go with the flow once in a while. When Kate had decided to wear outdated and mismatched polyester clothes from the thrift store to the dining hall just to see people's faces, Abby had gone along with the joke. Seeing the reactions had been educational, like one of the experiments in her sociology class. And it had been amazingly freeing to do something spontaneous and random.

But sometimes Kate needed Abby to be the voice of reason. When Kate got the idea to paint their dorm room purple suddenly after chapel one day, Abby had reminded her that she had a test to study for and that they'd have to pay a small fortune in primer and paint to convert the walls back to boring white for the next students to occupy 205b Whitaker Hall.

Kate's visit today was another example of her spontaneity. Abby had been trying to get Kate to come visit for weeks, but she had been caught up in a project with her mother and unable to get away. Then, just two hours ago, she'd texted to say she was coming. Now. But instead of spending their time together at Merri's house as they had planned all along, Kate had proposed a "friend-fest weekend in Equality," which according to John was a tiny, Podunk town three hours southeast of Alton.

She would have to talk Kate down from that hare-brained idea when she got there.

"Look at the idiot," John said, gesturing with a thumb.

An electric blue PT Cruiser roared down the gravel road toward them, slowing only minimally before skidding to a stop alongside the pavilions.

White dust coated the windshield, and Abby couldn't see the car's occupants. But she recognized the ARTCRZY license plate and began to disentangle herself from the picnic table. "That idiot would be Kate," she said with a laugh.

"Oh. Sorry." John wiped his hands and rose from the picnic table.

"Come on, both of you," Abby said. "I want to introduce you."

Merri wiggled out of her space at the picnic table and went to stand expectantly at Abby's side. "I thought she wasn't supposed to be here until tonight."

"She wasn't," Abby said. "But that's Kate for you."

The car door opened, and Kate stepped out and rushed toward Abby. She was wearing a pristine white sundress and heeled sandals. Her hair was a shining mahogany mane that fell half way down her back.

Abby threw her arms around her friend. "You look fabulous. How did you find us?"

"We went to the house first, and Merri's mom told us where you were."

"It seems like ages since the beginning of summer break. Wait a minute," Abby said, pulling back to look into Kate's face. "We? We who?" Then, over her shoulder she saw Kate's boyfriend unfolding his tall, lanky frame from the passenger seat. His polo shirt was the same brilliant white of Kate's dress, and he wore charcoal gray tailored slacks.

Abby felt a quick burst of disappointment and shot a look at Kate, but she was looking at Ryan as if he were the best thing since the invention of air conditioning. She must have gone spontaneous again and decided to bring him along. So much for their girls-only weekend.

Abby pasted on a smile and said, "Ryan. You came too. Good. I want you to meet Merri and John. Guys, this is my infamous roommate Kate Greenfield and her boyfriend Ryan Turner."

Ryan and John shook hands, but Kate thrust hers in Abby's face. "Not boyfriend anymore—fiancé! I told you he was going to ask. Isn't it gorgeous?"

The sun glinted off a huge diamond ring on Kate's left hand. "You're engaged? You didn't tell me." Abby shook her head to clear it. "I mean, yes, it's gorgeous."

"I wanted to surprise you. I've been dying to tell you ever since Ryan popped the question last weekend."

Abby hugged her again. "Have you set a date?"

Ryan smiled contentedly. "Next June after Kathryn graduates," he said with an indulgent smile. "One and a half carets of sparkle to hold her until then." He put an arm around Kate's neck and kissed her temple. "But don't worry, Kathryn. I promise to upsize it as soon as I get my law practice."

"Ryan just graduated from the pre-law program at the University of Illinois," Abby explained to John.

"Really? I've never seen you around."

"Chicago campus," Ryan said. "I think Kate said you're at Urbana?"

"That's right. Where will you go to law school?"

"Loyola," Ryan said. "It's really the only choice."

"Do you really think so?" John said. "I have my eye on Kent."

Ryan pushed a strand of silky dark brown hair back from his face. It was similar in color and texture to John's, only freakishly perfect in cut and style.

Kate pulled her to the side and said in what passed for her version of a whisper, "Why didn't you tell me how hot John is? Wow! No wonder you've been going crazy for him. We could have a double wedding, Abby."

Abby blinked in panic, but sneaking a look at the guys, she saw that they were still talking about law schools. Hopefully, John hadn't heard Kate's outrageous comment. "Kate! We've only known each other for a few weeks."

Kate just smiled knowingly and then turned and held

out a hand to Merri. "You must be Merri," she said. "Abby's told me so much about you."

Merri shook her hand, her expression changing to uncertainty. "Uh, really?"

"Really," Kate said. "About how smart you are, and nice."

Merri's face brightened. "Abby told me about you, too. We're going to my house after this."

"I'm looking forward to it."

"Come on, let's get you guys some food first," Abby said. "Wait until you see the selection."

"How about if John and I go get food so you two can get started gabbing?" Ryan said.

"You're so thoughtful." Kate patted his arm.

When the guys were lost in the crowd, Abby said, "Another imaginary star on Ryan's imaginary chart?"

Kate grinned. "He just keeps on racking them up."

"John, too," Abby said. "I've lost track of how many stars he's collected this week. But, hey, you're the one with stars—in your eyes." She put her arms around Kate and squeezed again. "I'm so glad you're here."

"Do you think I should tell Ryan about his chart—you know, since we're engaged now?"

"No way! Well, at least not here with John around." As far as Abby was concerned, the fact that they had been rating them as possible marriage material was something they never needed to know about.

Merri smiled slyly. "Hmmm. You'd better be nice to me."

"Come on, brat," Abby said, edging her way past a man carrying two heaping plates. "Let's show Kate where we're sitting."

Abby was glad that she'd worn shorts. Hiking first one leg and then the other over the picnic table bench, she managed to sit down halfway gracefully and then glanced doubtfully at Kate's skinny white dress.

Seeing her look, Kate said, "Don't worry. I'm the queen of picnic table sitting. I did a lot of contortions wearing fancy dresses when I ran for Miss Sangamon County. I didn't win the crown, but I did pick up this skill. Watch and learn."

Kate pulled it off gracefully, quickly, and without once flashing her underwear.

"Amazing," Abby said. "I can't imagine why they didn't pick you for queen. So quick, tell me all about it before the guys get back. Did Ryan get down on one knee when he proposed?"

"Yes, he did. Of course, he asked the waiter to bring an extra napkin to kneel on so he wouldn't mess up his pants. He took me to Sixteen in the Trump Tower. It looks out over the lights of downtown Chicago. It was so romantic. I wish you could have been there. Well, not really. But you know what I mean."

"Did they have waiters in tuxedos," Merri asked. "I always thought that'd be cool."

"They did," Kate said, grinning at Merri. "And it was cool."

"Did he hide the ring in your dessert," Merri asked.

"No, I don't think that's Ryan's style," Kate said, laughing. "But it was wrapped in beautiful paper and ribbons. I nearly fainted when I opened the box and saw the size of the diamond." She held her ring out for them to admire again.

"Kathryn, you're going to ruin your Manuela sitting on that picnic bench." Ryan was back with two plates. A small frown marred his handsome face for a moment and then was gone.

"It'll be fine," Kate said.

"Hey, Merri Christmas, move over," John said.

When she had scooted over, Merri looked up at Ryan. "What's a Manuela?"

John and Ryan set the plates they carried on the table and then squeezed in at the picnic table.

Kate smiled her thanks and answered the question for Ryan. "Manuela is a designer from New York," she explained. "I'm wearing one of her dresses."

"I bought that dress for Kathryn last weekend in Chicago. It set me back three hundred dollars." He smiled down at Kate. "But she's worth every penny."

Abby concentrated on keeping a pleasant expression on her face. People who dropped price tags into a conversation never impressed her. It was a pretty dress but not Kate's usual casual style. And she wasn't wearing the bright, funky jewelry she usually did—jewelry she had designed, created, and made a small business of selling on campus.

Kate looked from John's plate heaped high with fried fish and various side dishes to the plate of raw broccoli and carrot sticks Ryan had put in front of her. "Where's the food, Ryan?"

"Oh, drat. Is all the good stuff gone?" Abby asked.

"I assumed you wouldn't want any of it, Kathryn. It's all loaded with carbs and fat."

"Well, I do," Merri declared and headed back to the food table with her plate.

Ryan watched Merri leave and muttered something that Abby didn't quite catch. It sounded like, "I rest my case."

Abby blinked. She waited for her roomie to say she loved carbs and fat. That she lived for carbs and fat. That her favorite entertainment was carbs and fat.

But Kate merely smoothed the front of her dress and

smiled. "You're right, Ryan."

"We'll get something later in the city." Ryan took a meager bite of fruit salad from his plate. "I was reading online about St. Charles and the downtown St. Louis scene. Sounds like there are a few decent restaurants around."

"Yeah," John said drily, "they have a few."

"We want you to come celebrate with us," Kate said.

Ryan patted his lips with a napkin and took out his phone. "You, too, Roberts, of course. I'll make reservations. Is seven o'clock all right?"

"And then, after dinner," Kate said, "we can zip on down to Equality so that tomorrow we'll have all day to—"

"About that. What made you choose Equality for our little friend-fest weekend," Abby said, using air quotes. "John says it's just a tiny town."

"Tiny town, but a big help with my project. At least I hope so."

"Kate says you have some kind of weird genealogy program." Ryan's voice rose at the end and Abby wasn't sure if he was making a statement or asking a question.

"That's not what *Beautiful Houses* is… not exactly."

"It's all your fault, Abby," Kate said. "I made the mistake of telling Mom about your adventures with the Old Dears' genealogy. Now she is obsessed with tracing our family tree. But we came to a dead end with the Greenfield side of the family. Since you got us hooked, it's only fair you lend us your expertise."

"Genealogy is kind of addictive," Abby said. "And Eulah and Beulah are so happy we found their Buchanan relatives for them."

"Mom wants me to paint a wall mural of our family tree in Dad's den as a surprise. Here, let me show you what I had in mind." Kate took a pen from her purse and began sketching a whimsical tree on a paper napkin. "I thought I'd draw faces on the leaves. And each person will have some sort of item symbolizing them. Like for me, I'll put a paint brush to show my love for art."

In mere seconds, Kate had drawn an amazingly detailed sketch, and as always Abby was astounded by her talent.

"That is so cool," Merri said, returning with a plate of mostly potato chips and pink fluffy salad.

Kate smiled. "Thanks, sweetie. But it won't look very cool if it's all lopsided. And I'm running out of time. The only opportunity I'll have to paint it is next month while Mom and Dad are gone to Colorado on vacation. So that's why I thought if you went with us and we used the program…"

Abby shot a meaningful look at Kate, willing her to stop talking. Fortunately, she seemed to get the message.

"Let's talk about it later," Abby said, tipping her head toward Merri. Whether or not she agreed to go along with them to Equality, it sounded like the girls-only night was off the agenda, and she needed time to figure out how to tell Merri.

Abby glanced at John for his take. He didn't look happy. It was flattering to think he was disappointed that she'd be gone for the weekend. But then he was probably only worried about losing control of the program.

Abby had been telling Kate about *Beautiful House*s and all they'd uncovered with it for the past two and a half months. And for those two and a half months, Kate had steadfastly insisted Abby was joking about the program's abilities. Eventually, she had decided it was just as well Kate didn't believe her because they had begun to realize how dangerous it would be if the program fell into the wrong hands.

But now that Kate had finally come, she couldn't resist setting her straight. "Listen to me," she said, putting her face up to Kate's. "Look at my face. Read my lips. Notice that I'm not kidding around. This is not ordinary genealogy software. It—"

"It no longer works," John said, staring at Abby behind Kate's back. "Not right anyway, not since the Fourth of July."

"But it does still work a little?" Kate said hopefully.

"Yes, but—" John said.

"Great," Ryan said. "Let's go have a look at it."

"Okay," Abby said, shrugging her shoulders at the look John gave her. "But first I want you to meet the Old Dears. There they are at the far end of the pavilion."

The twins, in their identical lavender pants and sequined tops, stood one on either side of Doug Buchanan, as he struggled with a karaoke microphone.

"Aren't they cute," Kate said, laughing. "How do you ever tell them apart?"

"Beaulah's always cheerful and Eulah's…not so much."

The microphone squealed. "Test, test, test," Doug said into it. "Can you hear me in the back?"

A woman behind them called out, "Louder, Dougie."

A man two tables over called out, "Hey, if you're taking requests, I want *Proud Mary*."

The crowd laughed, and Ryan rolled his eyes. "If they're going to start singing, I'm leaving."

"No, wait," Abby said. "Doug's up to something."

"By now," Doug said, "you've all met these two sweet ladies. Now, it's time to welcome them officially into the Buchanan clan." One of Doug's sons handed each beaming lady a yellow T-shirt.

Grinning happily, the Old Dears held up the shirts so

the audience could see that printed on the fronts were the words, I Survived My First Buchanan Reunion. The crowd erupted in applause and whistles.

"And we put their names on the back so you can tell them apart," Doug continued.

The cheers turned to laughter when the audience realized the twins had been handed the wrong shirts. After trading, Eulah and Beulah held the shirts up again for everyone to see their names in blue script. Doug went on to remind everyone to be back tomorrow for more great food, the water balloon war, the quilt auction, and the washer tournament.

"Can we leave now?" Kate asked. "I can't wait to try out your program."

"You sure you don't want to stick around?" Ryan said in a fake southern accent. "I have a hankerin' to play worshers. I bet you five dollars I can whup you, too."

"Okay. I guess we can leave now," Abby said. She had looked forward to Kate meeting the ladies, but Eulah and Beulah would have lots of questions that were bound to take more time than Kate—and especially Ryan—would want to spend.

On the way to their cars, John waited until Kate and Ryan were out of earshot. "I thought we agreed not to let anyone else in on this until we could figure out what to do with the program. You know how dangerous it could be if this gets out."

"Yeah," Merri said. "That's the first rule. Besides, we're the three musketeers. Whoever heard of the five musketeers?"

"I know, I know," Abby said. "I don't know what came over me. Kate's always been so...so...annoying about it, an agnostic, you might say. I don't know what made her change her mind, and I had no idea she had told

Ryan about it."

"Speaking of which, how well do you know Turner?"

"I've only met him a few times when he came to campus to visit Kate. He seemed nice enough. Then."

"I think he's a jackass," Merri declared.

John snorted a laugh. "Yeah, you're right about that, squirt. But don't say that word, okay?"

"We just have to give it time," Abby said. "Maybe he'll grow on us."

"Well, until he does," John said, "I think we should stall on showing them the program."

"Why?" Merri said. "Now that it's not working right, all they'll see is a bunch of houses from around the world."

"It won't hurt for them to see that," Abby said, "We just won't mention that the way we helped Eulah and Beulah fill out their family tree was by time-surfing back to meet their ancestors.

82699687R00171

Made in the USA
Columbia, SC
05 December 2017